# THE GREAT IMPERSONATION

### E. PHILLIPS OPPENHEIM

With an Introduction by Tim Crook

THE BRITISH LIBRARY

This edition published in 2014 by

The British Library
96 Euston Road
London NW1 2DB

Originally published in London in 1935 by Hodder & Stoughton

Cataloguing in Publication Data
A catalogue record for this book is available from The British Library

ISBN 978 0 7123 5721 0

Typeset by IDSUK (DataConnection) Ltd
Printed and bound in England by TJ International

# CONTENTS

# INTRODUCTION

Edward Phillips Oppenheim was rightly crowned 'the Prince of Storytellers', which was also the title of his 1957 biography by Robert Standish. 'Oppy' or 'Mr Op', as he was known to his friends, is among the most significant writers of popular English fiction of the late nineteenth and early to mid-twentieth centuries. Superlatives abound. Will Cuppy in 1934 said 'When in doubt, grab an Oppenheim'. Barrie Hayne in 1985 said that Oppenheim's output of well over 150 novels and collections of short stories was the product of 'one of the most fertile imaginations ever to apply itself to the thriller'.

Born in London in 1866, Oppenheim had to leave grammar school in Leicester early to work in his father's leather business. For twenty years he carried on the merchant trade by day and wrote by night. In 1905, his book sales made him so wealthy he could sell the family firm and move to live the life of a country squire in Norfolk. He soon migrated to the French Riviera, where he mixed with the global super-rich from whom he drew inspiration for characterization and plots.

Oppenheim was interviewed for the Secret Intelligence Service in 1914. He was not fluent enough in German or French and was turned down. He took solace in the knowledge that the person taken on instead of him disappeared in his first mission in enemy territory. He volunteered his services to waging war through propaganda, but despaired of intoning patriotic bombast at recruitment rallies. He was happier escorting journalists to the Western Front. By being spared the exhaustion and peril of real espionage, he was able to write the fictional version.

Oppenheim lived a sultanic existence on the Côte d'Azur through the 1920s and 30s. As Standish wrote, 'he loved soft living and basked in the smiles of suave maîtres d'hôtels'. He loved too 'the excitement of roulette, the popping of champagne corks and the rustle of scented petticoats'. Happily married to Elsie from 1892 until his death in Guernsey in 1946, he discreetly carried on affairs with the indigent countesses and princesses also enjoying life in Cagnes Sur Mer, Nice and Monte Carlo, usually on Mediterranean cruises in his huge yacht *Echo*.

The fall of France in 1940 and his failure to take the last British ship to leave the Riviera meant that the seventy-four-year-old Prince of Storytellers and his wife could have been interned by the Nazis. Reports in the British press feared for their safety, particularly when it emerged that his daughter and son-in-law had fled on the last boat to leave Saint Malo on 6 June, crammed with 1500 refugees in a terrible voyage. Oppy and Elsie were fortunate to find a way home via Spain and Portugal before German military occupation of the Vichy Zone in 1942.

Oppenheim's storytelling had a huge impact on the cultural imagination. Few writers have been as rich and successful. He was a global literary superstar and even made the cover of *Time* magazine on 12 September 1927. Between 1930 and 1937 he received well over $500,000 in royalties from book sales and serialization rights in America. More than thirty of his books were made into films. His fame owed much to the insatiable demand for popular fiction fuelled by an exponential growth in literacy, leisure-time reading, and distribution of cheap editions and private lending library copies at railway station kiosks and high street retailers. The episodic serialization of his novels was also a mainstay of popular newspapers. Oppenheim first broke into this market in the late 1880s with publications in the London *Pictorial World*, *Whitehall Review* and the British regional paper the *Sheffield Weekly Independent*.

In time he became the metaphor by which professional spies would define their trade. The British Security Service's director of counter-espionage during the Second World War, Guy Liddell, wrote in his diary in 1939 that a plot to use newspaper and radio bulletins to make contact with Nazi dissidents 'all sounds rather Phillips Oppenheim, but there may perhaps be something in it'.

Only Edgar Wallace and Somerset Maugham rivalled him in popularity and earnings. Standish described Oppenheim's novels as an 'unending battle between the hedonist and the Puritan, the playboy libertine and the hard-headed man of affairs'. The romance was always intense and passionate, but unlike Ian Fleming's James Bond books, bedroom scenes were not explicit. Hayne observes that an Oppy novel addressed, perhaps by exaggerating, the anxieties of his times: 'Typically there are killings, often by villains of exotic race; the hero is often outwardly one who lives idly for pleasure, but is in fact working to save his country; there is usually a love interest; and Oppenheim has as much sense as Alfred Hitchcock of how terror may impinge upon the commonplace.'

It is somewhat fashionable in academic and espionage circles to dismiss his achievements and importance. That would be a mistake. *The Great Impersonation* – published in Britain by Hodder and Stoughton and in the USA by Little, Brown in 1920 – sold millions of copies. It was made into three films and as recently as 1985 was dramatized as a classic radio serial by the BBC. Its republication in the year commemorating the beginning of the Great War is highly resonant. For as the *Times Literary Supplement* observed on its publication, 'The Kaiser, a noisy spectre, an intrusive spy, an earnest Duke, an amorous Hungarian Princess all help to make the running hot up to the final dénouement, which, as may be expected, takes place on or about August 4, 1914.'

*The Scotsman*'s reviewer in 1921 said that the author had scored again with high-quality light entertainment and lively incident. The novel became a classic in popular spy fiction. In 1984 David Lehman would say in *Newsweek* that it was Oppenheim's best thriller and 'escapism on a grand scale'. In 2009 the *Guardian* included it in its list of 1000 novels everyone must read.

One clue to the novel's extraordinary appeal can be located in the way Oppenheim was able to combine the high-octane blend of spy thriller genre with a growing sense of Britain's military and diplomatic fragility and imperialist anxiety. He delivered fantastic entertainment marked with the angst of a world power struggling to address the challenge of modernist war and catastrophic changes in moral values and technology.

*The Great Impersonation* was included in the famous collected edition of 'five full-length novels of international intrigue' marketed as *The Secret Service Omnibus* (Hodder and Stoughton, 1932). Alongside *Miss Brown of X.Y.O.*, *The Wrath To Come*, *Matorni's Vineyard*, and *Gabriel Samara*, *The Great Impersonation* cemented Oppenheim as the pre-eminent spy thriller writer of his time.

He begins the novel with English aristocrat Sir Everard Dominey being rescued by the Baron von Ragastein in German East Africa. They had studied together in Oxford. They have a remarkable resemblance. Dominey has fled England under suspicion of murder. Ragastein is to be deployed by the German Secret Service to infiltrate London. Ragastein contrives to have his look-alike drink himself to death in the African bush while he steals his identity and inveigles himself into the British establishment pretending to be Sir Everard. The artifice of coincidences, double identities and masked intrigue is Shakespearean in parts.

Oppenheim would rarely pre-plan and structure his novels. He would dictate to secretaries and not rewrite. Yet *The Great Impersonation* is sophisticated prose crafted with an interest in the exquisite dramatic interplay of multiple ironies. Its flawed protagonists are morally ambiguous and toy with the reader's sympathy and disapproval.

Hayne says that the device of introducing 'a Trojan horse into the very citadel of the British ruling class' makes *The Great Impersonation* 'one of the few novels of Oppenheim's which depends upon surprise, and the secret is well kept to the end'.

William A. S. Sarjeant accorded this remarkable author a decent epitaph in his Oxford National Dictionary entry as being somebody who created 'an escape for readers from their own drab lives into a dream world of adventure, wealth, and luxury'. 'Mr Op' and *The Great Impersonation* more than merit rediscovery and a greater degree of literary and cultural appreciation.

*Professor Tim Crook, Goldsmiths, University of London and Birmingham City University.*

# CHAPTER I

THE trouble from which great events were to come began when Everard Dominey, who had been fighting his way through the scrub for the last three quarters of an hour towards those thin, spiral wisps of smoke, urged his pony to a last despairing effort and came crashing through the great oleander shrub to pitch forward on his head in the little clearing. It developed the next morning, when he found himself for the first time for many months on a truckle bed, between linen sheets, with a cool, bamboo-twisted roof between him and the relentless sun. He raised himself a little in the bed.

"Where the mischief am I?" he demanded.

A black boy, seated cross-legged in the entrance of the banda, rose to his feet, mumbled something and disappeared. In a few moments the tall, slim figure of a European, in spotless white riding clothes, stooped down and came over to Dominey's side.

"You are better?" he enquired politely.

"Yes, I am," was the somewhat brusque rejoinder. "Where the mischief am I, and who are you?"

The newcomer's manner stiffened. He was a person of digni-fied carriage, and his tone conveyed some measure of rebuke.

"You are within half a mile of the Iriwarri River, if you know where that is," he replied,—"about seventy-two miles southeast of the Darawaga Settlement."

"The devil! Then I am in German East Africa?"

"Without a doubt."

"And you are German?"

"I have that honour."

Dominey whistled softly.

"Awfully sorry to have intruded," he said. "I left Marlinstein two and a half months ago, with twenty boys and plenty of stores. We were doing a big trek after lions. I took some new Askaris in and they made trouble,—looted the stores one night and there was the devil to pay. I was obliged to shoot one or two, and the rest deserted. They took my compass, damn them, and I'm nearly a hundred miles out of my bearings. You couldn't give me a drink, could you?"

"With pleasure, if the doctor approves," was the courteous answer. "Here, Jan!"

The boy sprang up, listened to a word or two of brief command in his own language, and disappeared through the hanging grass which led into another hut. The two men exchanged glances of rather more than ordinary interest. Then Dominey laughed.

"I know what you're thinking," he said. "It gave me quite a start when you came in. We're devilishly alike, aren't we?"

"There is a very strong likeness between us," the other admitted.

Dominey leaned his head upon his hand and studied his host. The likeness was clear enough, although the advantage was all in favour of the man who stood by the side of the camp bedstead with folded arms. Everard Dominey, for the first twenty-six years of his life, had lived as an ordinary young Englishman of his position,—Eton, Oxford, a few years in the Army, a few years about town, during which he had succeeded in making a still more hopeless muddle of his already encumbered estates: a few months of tragedy, and then a blank. Afterwards ten years—at first in the cities, then in the dark places of Africa— years of which no man knew anything. The Everard Dominey of ten years ago had been, without a doubt, good-looking. The finely shaped features remained, but the eyes had lost their lustre, his figure its elasticity, his mouth its firmness. He had the look of a man run prematurely to seed, wasted by fevers and dissipation. Not so his present companion. His features were as finely shaped, cast in an even stronger though similar mould. His eyes were bright and full of fire, his mouth and chin firm, bespeaking a man of deeds, his tall figure lithe and supple. He had the air of being in perfect health, in perfect mental and physical condition, a man who lived with dignity and some measure of content, notwithstanding the slight gravity of his expression.

"Yes," the Englishman muttered, "there's no doubt about the likeness, though I suppose I should look more like you than I do if I'd taken care of myself. But I haven't. That's the devil of it. I've gone the other way; tried to chuck my life away and pretty nearly succeeded, too."

The dried grasses were thrust on one side, and the doctor entered,—a little round man, also clad in immaculate white, with yellow-gold hair and thick spectacles. His countryman pointed towards the bed.

"Will you examine our patient, Herr Doctor, and prescribe for him what is necessary? He has asked for drink. Let him have wine, or whatever is good for him. If he is well enough, he will join our evening meal. I present my excuses. I have a despatch to write."

The man on the couch turned his head and watched the departing figure with a shade of envy in his eyes.

"What is my preserver's name?" he asked the doctor.

The latter looked as though the question were irreverent.

"It is His Excellency the Major-General Baron Leopold von Ragastein."

"All that!" Dominey muttered. "Is he the Governor, or something of that sort?"

"He is Military Commandant of the Colony," the doctor replied. "He has also a special mission here."

"Damned fine-looking fellow for a German," Dominey remarked, with unthinking insolence.

The doctor was unmoved. He was feeling his patient's pulse. He concluded his examination a few minutes later.

"You have drunk much whisky lately, so?" he asked.

"I don't know what the devil it's got to do with you," was the curt reply, "but I drink whisky whenever I can get it. Who wouldn't in this pestilential climate!"

The doctor shook his head.

"The climate is good as he is treated," he declared. "His Excellency drinks nothing but light wine and seltzer water. He has been here for five years, not only here but in the swamps, and he has not been ill one day."

"Well, I have been at death's door a dozen times," the Englishman rejoined a little recklessly, "and I don't much mind when I hand in my checks, but until that time comes I shall drink whisky whenever I can get it."

"The cook is preparing you some luncheon," the doctor announced, "which it will do you good to eat. I cannot give you whisky at this moment, but you can have some hock and seltzer with bay leaves."

"Send it along," was the enthusiastic reply. "What a constitution I must have, doctor! The smell of that cooking outside is making me ravenous."

"Your constitution is still sound if you would only respect it," was the comforting assurance.

"Anything been heard of the rest of my party?" Dominey inquired.

"Some bodies of Askaris have been washed up from the river," the doctor informed him, "and two of your ponies have been eaten by lions. You will excuse. I have the wounds of a native to dress, who was bitten last night by a jaguar."

The traveller, left alone, lay still in the hut, and his thoughts wandered backwards. He looked out over the bare, scrubby stretch of land which had been cleared for this encampment to the mass of bush and flowering shrubs beyond, mysterious and impenetrable save for that rough elephant track along which he had travelled; to the broad-bosomed river, blue as the sky above, and to the mountains fading into mist beyond. The face of his host had carried him back into the past. Puzzled reminiscence tugged at the strings of memory. It came to him later on at dinner time, when they three, the Commandant, the doctor and himself, sat at a little table arranged just outside the hut, that they might catch the faint breeze from the mountains, herald of the swift-falling darkness. Native servants beat the air around them with bamboo fans to keep off the insects, and the air was heavy almost to noxiousness with perfume of some sickly, exotic shrub.

"Why, you're Devinter!" he exclaimed suddenly,—"Sigismund Devinter! You were at Eton with me—Horrock's House—semifinal in the racquets."

"And Magdalen afterwards, number five in the boat."

"And why the devil did the doctor here tell me that your name was Von Ragastein?"

"Because it happens to be the truth," was the somewhat measured reply. "Devinter is my family name, and the one by which I was known when in England. When I succeeded to the barony and estates at my uncle's death, however, I was compelled to also take the title."

"Well, it's a small world!" Dominey exclaimed. "What brought you out here really—lions or elephants?"

"Neither."

"You mean to say that you've taken up this sort of political business just for its own sake, not for sport?"

"Entirely so. I do not use a sporting rifle once month, except for necessity. I came to Africa for different reasons."

Dominey drank deep of his hock and seltzer and leaned back, watching the fireflies rise above the tall-bladed grass, above the stumpy clumps of shrub, and hang miniature stars in the clear, violet air.

"What a world!" he soliloquised. "Siggy Devinter, Baron von Ragastein, out here, slaving for God knows what, drilling niggers to fight God knows whom, a political machine, I suppose, future Governor-General of German Africa, eh? You were always proud of your country, Devinter."

"My country is a country to be proud of," was the solemn reply.

"Well, you're in earnest, anyhow," Dominey continued, "in earnest about something. And I—well, it's finished with me. It would have been finished last night if I hadn't seen the smoke from your fires, and I don't much care—that's the trouble. I go blundering on. I suppose the end will come somehow, sometime.—Can I have some rum or whisky, Devinter—I mean Von Ragastein—Your Excellency—or whatever I ought to say? You see those wreaths of mist down by the river? They'll mean malaria for me unless I have spirits."

"I have something better than either," Von Ragastein replied. "You shall give me your opinion of this."

The orderly who stood behind his master's chair, received a whispered order, disappeared into the commissariat hut and came back presently with a bottle at the sight of which the Englishman gasped.

"Napoleon!" he exclaimed.

"Just a few bottles I had sent to me," his host explained. "I am delighted to offer it to some one who will appreciate it."

"By Jove, there's no mistake about that!" Dominey declared, rolling it around in his glass. "What a world! I hadn't eaten for thirty hours when I rolled up here last night, and drunk nothing but filthy water for days. Tonight, fricassee of chicken, white bread, cabinet hock and Napoleon brandy. And tomorrow again—well, who knows? When do you move on, Von Ragastein?"

"Not for several days."

"What the mischief do you find to do so far from headquarters, if you don't shoot lions or elephants?" his guest asked curiously.

"If you really wish to know," Von Ragastein replied, "I am annoying your political agents immensely by moving from place to place, collecting natives for drill."

"But what do you want to drill them for?" Dominey persisted. "I heard some time ago that you have four times as many natives under arms as we have. You don't want an army here. You're not likely to quarrel with us or the Portuguese."

"It is our custom," Von Ragastein declared a little didactically, "in Germany and wherever we Germans go, to be prepared not only for what is likely to happen but for what might possibly happen."

"A war in my younger days, when I was in the Army," Dominey mused, "might have made a man of me."

"Surely you had your chance out here?"

Dominey shook his head.

"My battalion never left the country," he said. "We were shut up in Ireland all the time. That was the reason I chucked the army when I was really only a boy."

Later on they dragged their chairs a little farther out into the darkness, smoking cigars and drinking some rather wonderful coffee. The doctor had gone off to see a patient, and Von Ragastein was thoughtful. Their guest, on the other hand, continued to be reminiscently discursive.

"Our meeting," he observed, lazily stretching out his hand for his glass, "should be full of interest to the psychologist. Here we are, brought together by some miraculous chance to spend one night of our lives in an African jungle, two human beings of the same age, brought up together thousands of miles away, jogging on towards the eternal blackness along lines as far apart as the mind can conceive."

"Your eyes are fixed," Von Ragastein murmured, "upon that very blackness behind which the sun will rise at dawn. You will see it come up from behind the mountains in that precise spot, like a new and blazing world."

"Don't put me off with allegories," his companion objected petulantly. "The eternal blackness exists surely enough, even if my metaphor is faulty. I am disposed to be philosophical. Let me ramble on. Here am I, an idler in my boyhood, a harmless pleasure-seeker in my youth till I ran up against tragedy, and since then a drifter, a drifter with a slowly growing vice, lolling through life with no definite purpose, with no definite hope or wish, except," he went on a little drowsily, "that I think I'd like to be buried somewhere near the base of those mountains, on the other side of the river, from behind which you say the sun comes up every morning like a world on fire."

"You talk foolishly," Von Ragastein protested. "If there has been tragedy in your life, you have time to get over it. You are not yet forty years old."

"Then I turn and consider you," Dominey continued, ignoring altogether his friend's remark. "You are only my age, and you look ten years younger. Your muscles are hard, your eyes are as bright as they were in your school days. You carry yourself like a man with a purpose. You rise at five every morning, the doctor tells me, and you return here, worn out, at dusk. You spend every moment of your time drilling those filthy blacks. When you are not doing that, you are prospecting, supervising reports home, trying to make the best of your few millions of acres of fever swamps. The doctor worships you but who else knows? What do you do it for, my friend?"

"Because it is my duty," was the calm reply.

"Duty! But why can't you do your duty in your own country, and live a man's life, and hold the hands of white men, and look into the eyes of white women?"

"I go where I am needed most," Von Ragastein answered. "I do not enjoy drilling natives, I do not enjoy passing the years as an outcast from the ordinary joys of human life. But I follow my star."

"And I my will-o'-the-wisp," Dominey laughed mockingly. "The whole thing's as plain as a pike-staff. You may be a dull dog—you always were on the serious side—but you're a man of principle. I'm a slacker."

"The difference between us," Von Ragastein pronounced, "is something which is inculcated into the youth of our country and which is not inculcated into yours. In England, with a little money, a little birth, your young men expect to find the world a playground for sport, a garden for loves. The mightiest German noble who ever lived has his work to do. It is work which makes fibre, which gives balance to life."

Dominey sighed. His cigar, dearly prized though it had been, was cold between his fingers. In that perfumed darkness, illuminated only by the faint gleam of the shaded lamp behind, his face seemed suddenly white and old. His host leaned towards him and spoke for the first time in the kindlier tones of their youth.

"You hinted at tragedy, my friend. You are not alone. Tragedy also has entered my life. Perhaps if things had been otherwise, I should have found work in more joyous places, but sorrow came to me, and I am here."

A quick flash of sympathy lit up Dominey's face.

"We met trouble in a different fashion," he groaned.

# CHAPTER II

DOMINEY slept till late the following morning, and when he woke at last from a long, dreamless slumber, he was conscious of a curious quietness in the camp. The doctor, who came in to see him, explained it immediately after his morning greeting.

"His Excellency," he announced, "has received important despatches from home. He has gone to meet an envoy from Dar-es-Salaam. He will be away for three days. He desired that you would remain his guest until his return."

"Very good of him," Dominey murmured. "Is there any European news?"

"I do not know," was the stolid reply. "His Excellency desired me to inform you that if you cared for a short trip along the banks of the river, southward, there are a dozen boys left and some ponies. There are plenty of lion, and rhino may be met with at one or two places which the natives know of."

Dominey bathed and dressed, sipped his excellent coffee, and lounged about the place in uncertain mood. He unburdened himself to the doctor as they drank tea together late in the afternoon.

"I am not in the least keen on hunting," he confessed, "and I feel like a horrible sponge, but all the same I have a queer sort of feeling that I'd like to see Von Ragastein again. Your silent chief rather fascinates me, Herr Doctor. He is a man. He has something which I have lost."

"He is a great man," the doctor declared enthusiastically. "What he sets his mind to do, he does."

"I suppose I might have been like that," Dominey sighed, "if I had had an incentive. Have you noticed the likeness between us, Herr Doctor?"

The latter nodded.

"I noticed it from the first moment of your arrival," he assented. "You are very much alike yet very different. The resemblance must have been still more remarkable in your youth. Time has dealt with your features according to your deserts."

"Well, you needn't rub it in," Dominey protested irritably.

"I am rubbing nothing in," the doctor replied with unruffled calm. "I speak the truth. If you had been possessed of the same moral stamina as His Excellency, you might have preserved your health and the things that count. You might have been as useful to your country as he is to his."

"I suppose I am pretty rocky, eh?"

"Your constitution has been abused. You still, however, have much vitality. If you cared to exercise self-control for a few months, you would be a different man.—You must excuse. I have work."

Dominey spent three restless days. Even the sight of a herd of elephants in the river and that strange, fierce chorus of night sounds, as beasts of prey crept noiselessly around the camp, failed to move him. For the moment his love of sport, his last hold upon the world of real things, seemed dead. What did it matter, the killing of an animal more or less? His mind was fixed uneasily upon the past, searching always for something which he failed to discover. At dawn he watched for that strangely wonderful, transforming birth of the day, and at night he sat outside the banda, waiting till the mountains on the other side of the river had lost shape and faded into the violet darkness. His conversation with Von Ragastein had unsettled him. Without knowing definitely why, he wanted him back again. Memories that had long since ceased to torture were finding their way once more into his brain. On the first day he had striven to rid himself of them in the usual fashion.

"Doctor, you've got some whisky, haven't you?" he asked.

The doctor nodded.

"There is a case somewhere to be found," he admitted. "His Excellency told me that I was to refuse you nothing, but he advises you to drink only the white wine until his return."

"He really left that message?"

"Precisely as I have delivered it."

The desire for whisky passed, came again but was beaten back, returned in the night so that he sat up with the sweat pouring down his face and his tongue parched. He drank lithia water instead. Late in the afternoon of the third day, Von Ragastein rode into the camp. His clothes were torn and drenched with the black mud of the swamps, dust and dirt were thick upon his face. His pony almost collapsed as he swung himself off. Nevertheless, he paused to greet his guest with punctilious courtesy, and there was a gleam of real satisfaction in his eyes as the two men shook hands.

"I am glad that you are still here," he said heartily. "Excuse me while I bathe and change. We will dine a little earlier. So far I have not eaten today."

"A long trek?" Dominey asked curiously.

"I have trekked far," was the quiet reply.

At dinner time, Von Ragastein was once more himself, immaculate in white duck, with clean linen, shaved, and with little left of his fatigue. There was something different in his manner, however, some change which puzzled Dominey. He was at once more attentive to his guest, yet further removed from him in spirit and sympathy. He kept the conversation with curious insistence upon incidents of their school and college days, upon the subject of Dominey's friends and relations, and the later episodes of his life. Dominey felt himself all the time encouraged to talk about his earlier life, and all the time he was conscious that for some reason or other his host's closest and most minute attention was being given to his slightest word. Champagne had been served and served freely, and Dominey, up to the very gates of that one secret chamber, talked volubly and without reserve. After the meal was over, their chairs were dragged as before into the open. The silent orderly produced even larger cigars, and Dominey found his glass filled once more with the wonderful brandy. The doctor had left them to visit the native camp nearly a quarter of a mile away, and the orderly was busy inside, clearing the table. Only the black shapes of the servants were dimly visible as they twirled their fans,—and overhead the leaning stars. They were alone.

"I've been talking an awful lot of rot about myself," Dominey said. "Tell me a little about your career now and your life in Germany before you came out here."

Von Ragastein made no immediate reply, and a curious silence ebbed and flowed between the two men. Every now and then a star shot across the sky. The red rim of the moon rose a little higher from behind the mountains. The bush stillness, always the most mysterious of silences, seemed gradually to become charged with unvoiced passion. Soon the animals began to call around them, creeping nearer and nearer to the fire which burned at the end of the open space.

"My friend," Von Ragastein said at last, speaking with the air of a man who has spent much time in deliberation, "you speak to me of Germany, of my homeland. Perhaps you have guessed that it is not duty alone which has brought me here to these wild places. I, too, left behind me a tragedy."

Dominey's quick impulse of sympathy was smothered by the stern, almost harsh repression of the other's manner. The words seemed to have been torn from his throat. There was no spark of tenderness or regret in his set face.

"Since the day of my banishment," he went on, "no word of this matter has passed my lips. Tonight it is not weakness which assails me, but a desire to yield to the strange arm of coincidence. You and I, schoolmates and college friends, though sons of a different country, meet here in the wilderness, each with the iron in our souls. I shall tell you the thing which happened to me, and you shall speak to me of your own curse."

"I cannot!" Dominey groaned.

"But you will," was the stern reply. "Listen."

An hour passed, and the voices of the two men had ceased. The howling of the animals had lessened with the paling of the fires, and a slow, melancholy ripple of breeze was passing through the bush and lapping the surface of the river. It was Von Ragastein who broke through what might almost have seemed a trance. He rose to his feet, vanished inside the banda, and reappeared a moment or two later with two tumblers. One he set down in the space provided for it in the arm of his guest's chair.

"Tonight I break what has become a rule with me," he announced. "I shall drink a whisky and soda. I shall drink to the new things that may yet come to both of us."

"You are giving up your work here?" Dominey asked curiously.

"I am part of a great machine," was the somewhat evasive reply. "I have nothing to do but obey."

A flicker of passion distorted Dominey's face, flamed for a moment in his tone.

"Are you content to live and die like this?" he demanded. "Don't you want to get back to where a different sort of sun will warm your heart and fill your pulses? This primitive world is in its way colossal, but it isn't human, it isn't a life for humans. We want the streets, Von Ragastein, you and I. We want the tide of people flowing around us, the roar of wheels and the hum of human voices. Curse these animals! If I live in this country much longer, I shall go on all fours."

"You yield too much to environment," his companion observed. "In the life of the cities you would be a sentimentalist."

"No city nor any civilised country will ever claim me again," Dominey sighed. "I should never have the courage to face what might come."

Von Ragastein rose to his feet. The dim outline of his erect form was in a way majestic. He seemed to tower over the man who lounged in the chair below him.

"Finish your whisky and soda to our next meeting, friend of my school days," he begged. "Tomorrow, before you awake, I shall be gone."

"So soon?"

"By tomorrow night," Von Ragastein replied, "I must be on the other side of those mountains. This must be our farewell."

Dominey was querulous, almost pathetic. He had a sudden hatred of solitude.

"I must trek westward myself directly," he protested, "or eastward, or northward—it doesn't so much matter. Can't we travel together?"

Von Ragastein shook his head.

"I travel officially, and I must travel alone," he replied. "As for yourself, they will be breaking up here tomorrow, but they will lend you an escort and put you in the direction you wish to take. This, alas, is as much as I can do for you. For us it must be farewell."

"Well, I can't force myself upon you," Dominey said a little wistfully. "It seems strange, though, to meet right out here, far away even from the by-ways of life, just to shake hands and pass on. I am sick to death of niggers and animals."

"It is Fate," Von Ragastein decided. "Where I go, I must go alone. Farewell, dear friend! We will drink the toast we drank our last night in your rooms at Magdalen. That Sanscrit man translated it for us: 'May each find what he seeks!' We must follow our star."

Dominey laughed a little bitterly. He pointed to a light glowing fitfully in the bush.

"My will-o'-the-wisp," he muttered recklessly, "leading where I shall follow—into the swamps!"

A few minutes later Dominey threw himself upon his couch, curiously and unaccountably drowsy. Von Ragastein, who had come in to wish him good night, stood looking down at him for several moments with significant intentness. Then, satisfied that his guest really slept, he turned and passed through the hanging curtain of dried grasses into the next banda, where the doctor, still fully dressed, was awaiting him. They spoke together in German and with lowered voices. Von Ragastein had lost something of his imperturbability.

"Everything progresses according to my orders?" he demanded.

"Everything, Excellency! The boys are being loaded, and a runner has gone on to Wadihuan for ponies to be prepared."

"They know that I wish to start at dawn?"

"All will be prepared, Excellency."

Von Ragastein laid his hand upon the doctor's shoulder.

"Come outside, Schmidt," he said. "I have something to tell you of my plans."

The two men seated themselves in the long, wicker chairs, the doctor in an attitude of strict attention. Von Ragastein turned his head and listened. From Dominey's quarters came the sound of deep and regular breathing.

"I have formed a great plan, Schmidt," Von Ragastein proceeded. "You know what news has come to me from Berlin?"

"Your Excellency has told me little," the doctor reminded him.

"The Day arrives," Von Ragastein pronounced, his voice shaking with deep emotion. He paused a moment in thought and continued, "The time, even the month, is fixed. I am recalled from here to take the place for which I was destined. You know what that place is? You know why I was sent to an English public school and college?"

"I can guess."

"I am to take up my residence in England. I am to have a special mission. I am to find a place for myself there as an Englishman. The means are left to my ingenuity. Listen, Schmidt. A great idea has come to me."

The doctor lit a cigar.

"I listen, Excellency."

Von Ragastein rose to his feet. Not content with the sound of that regular breathing, he made his way to the opening of the banda and gazed in at Dominey's slumbering form. Then he returned.

"It is something which you do not wish the Englishman to hear?" the doctor asked.

"It is."

"We speak in German."

"Languages," was the cautious reply, "happen to be that man's only accomplishment. He can speak German as fluently as you or I. That, however, is of no consequence. He sleeps and he will continue to sleep. I mixed him a sleeping draught with his whisky and soda."

"Ah!" the doctor grunted.

"My principal need in England is an identity," Von Ragastein pointed out. "I have made up my mind. I shall take this Englishman's. I shall return to England as Sir Everard Dominey."

"So!"

"There is a remarkable likeness between us, and Dominey has not seen an Englishman who knows him for eight or ten years. Any school or college friends whom I may encounter I shall be able to satisfy. I have stayed at Dominey. I know Dominey's relatives. Tonight he has babbled for hours, telling me many things that it is well for me to know."

"What about his near relatives?"

"He has none nearer than cousins."

"No wife?"

Von Ragastein paused and turned his head. The deep breathing inside the banda had certainly ceased. He rose to his feet and, stealing uneasily to the opening, gazed down upon his guest's outstretched form. To all appearance, Dominey still slept deeply. After a moment or two's watch, Von Ragastein returned to his place.

"Therein lies his tragedy," he confided, dropping his voice a little lower. "She is insane—insane, it seems, through a shock for which he is responsible. She might have been the only stumbling block, and she is as though she did not exist."

"It is a great scheme," the doctor murmured enthusiastically.

"It is a wonderful one! That great and unrevealed Power, Schmidt, which watches over our country and which will make her mistress of the world, must have guided this man to us. My position in England will be unique. As Sir Everard Dominey I shall be able to penetrate into the inner circles of Society—perhaps, even, of political life. I shall be able, if necessary, to remain in England even after the storm bursts."

"Supposing," the doctor suggested, "this man Dominey should return to England?"

Von Ragastein turned his head and looked towards his questioner.

"He must not," he pronounced.

"So!" the doctor murmured.

Late in the afternoon of the following day, Dominey, with a couple of boys for escort and his rifle slung across his shoulder, rode into the bush along the way he had come. The little fat doctor stood and watched him, waving his hat until he was out of sight. Then he called to the orderly.

"Heinrich," he said, "you are sure that the Herr Englishman has the whisky?"

"The water bottles are filled with nothing else, Herr Doctor," the man replied.

"There is no water or soda water in the pack?"

"Not one drop, Herr Doctor."

"How much food?"

"One day's rations."

"The beef is salt?"

"It is very salt, Herr Doctor."

"And the compass?"

"It is ten degrees wrong."

"The boys have their orders?"

"They understand perfectly, Herr Doctor. If the Englishman does not drink, they will take him at midnight to where

## CHAPTER III

MR. JOHN LAMBERT MANGAN of Lincoln's Inn gazed at the card which a junior clerk had just presented in blank astonishment, an astonishment which became speedily blended with dismay.

"Good God, do you see this, Harrison?" he exclaimed, passing it over to his manager, with whom he had been in consultation. "Dominey—Sir Everard Dominey—back here in England!"

The head clerk glanced at the narrow piece of pasteboard and sighed.

"I'm afraid you will find him rather a troublesome client, sir," he remarked.

His employer frowned. "Of course I shall," he answered testily. "There isn't an extra penny to be had out of the estates—you know that, Harrison. The last two quarters' allowance which we sent to Africa came out of the timber. Why the mischief didn't he stay where he was!"

"What shall I tell the gentleman, sir?" the boy enquired.

"Oh, show him in!" Mr. Mangan directed ill-temperedly. "I suppose I shall have to see him sooner or later. I'll finish these affidavits after lunch, Harrison."

The solicitor composed his features to welcome a client who, however troublesome his affairs had become, still represented a family who had been valued patrons of the firm for several generations. He was prepared to greet a seedy-looking and degenerate individual, looking older than his years. Instead, he found himself extending his hand to one of the best turned out and handsomest men who had ever crossed the threshold of his not very inviting office. For a moment he stared at his visitor, speechless. Then certain points of familiarity—the well-shaped nose, the rather deep-set grey eyes—presented themselves. The

His Excellency will be encamped at the bend of the Blue River."

The doctor sighed. He was not at heart an unkindly man.

"I think," he murmured, "it will be better for the Englishman that he drinks."

surprise enabled him to infuse a little real heartiness into his welcome.

"My dear Sir Everard!" he exclaimed. "This is a most unexpected pleasure—most unexpected! Such a pity, too, that we only posted a draft for your allowance a few days ago. Dear me—you'll forgive my saying so—how well you look!"

Dominey smiled as he accepted an easy chair.

"Africa's a wonderful country, Mangan," he remarked, with just that faint note of patronage in his tone which took his listener back to the days of his present client's father.

"It—pardon my remarking it—has done wonderful things for you, Sir Everard. Let me see, it must be eleven years since we met."

Sir Everard tapped the toes of his carefully polished brown shoes with the end of his walking stick.

"I left London," he murmured reminiscently, "in April, nineteen hundred and two. Yes, eleven years, Mr. Mangan. It seems queer to find myself in London again, as I dare say you can understand."

"Precisely," the lawyer murmured. "I was just wondering—I think that last remittance we sent to you could be stopped. I have no doubt you will be glad of a little ready money," he added, with a confident smile.

"Thanks, I don't think I need any just at present," was the amazing answer. "We'll talk about financial affairs a little later on."

Mr. Mangan metaphorically pinched himself. He had known his present client even during his school days, had received a great many visits from him at different times, and could not remember one in which the question of finance had been dismissed in so casual a manner.

"I trust," he observed, chiefly for the sake of saying something, "that you are thinking of settling down here for a time now?"

"I have finished with Africa, if that is what you mean," was the somewhat grave reply. "As to settling down here, well, that depends a little upon what you have to tell me."

The lawyer nodded.

"I think," he said, "that you may make yourself quite easy as regards the matter of Roger Unthank. Nothing has ever been heard of him since the day you left England."

"His—body has not been found?"

"Nor any trace of it."

There was a brief silence. The lawyer looked hard at Dominey, and Dominey searchingly back again at the lawyer.

"And Lady Dominey?" the former asked at length.

"Her ladyship's condition is, I believe, unchanged," was the somewhat guarded reply.

"If the circumstances are favourable," Dominey continued, after another moment's pause, "I think it very likely that I may decide to settle down at Dominey Hall."

The lawyer appeared doubtful.

"I am afraid," he said, "you will be very disappointed with the condition of the estate, Sir Everard. As I have repeatedly told you in our correspondence, the rent roll, after deducting your settlement upon Lady Dominey, has at no time reached the interest on the mortgages, and we have had to make up the difference and send you your allowance out of the proceeds of the outlying timber."

"That is a pity," Dominey replied, with a frown. "I ought, perhaps, to have taken you more into my confidence. By the by," he added, "when—er—about when did you receive my last letter?"

"Your last letter?" Mr. Mangan repeated. "We have not had the privilege of hearing from you, Sir Everard, for over four years. The only intimation we had that our payments had reached you was the exceedingly prompt debit of the South African bank."

"I have certainly been to blame," this unexpected visitor confessed. "On the other hand, I have been very much absorbed. If you haven't happened to hear any South African gossip lately, Mangan, I suppose it will be a surprise to you to hear that I have been making a good deal of money."

"Making money?" the lawyer gasped. "You making money, Sir Everard?"

"I thought you'd be surprised," Dominey observed coolly. "However, that's neither here nor there. The business object of my visit to you this morning is to ask you to make arrangements as quickly as possible for paying off the mortgages on the Dominey estates."

Mr. Mangan was a lawyer of the new-fashioned school,— Harrow and Cambridge, the Bath Club, racquets and fives, rather than gold and lawn tennis. Instead of saying "God bless my soul!" he exclaimed "Great Scott!" dropped a very modern-looking eyeglass from his left eye, and leaned back in his chair with his hands in his pockets.

"I have had three or four years of good luck," his client continued. "I have made money in gold mines, in diamond mines and in land. I am afraid that if I had stayed out another year, I should have descended altogether to the commonplace and come back a millionaire."

"My heartiest congratulations!" Mr. Mangan found breath to murmur. "You'll forgive my being so astonished, but you are the first Dominey I ever knew who has ever made a penny of money in any sort of way, and from what I remember of you in England—I'm sure you'll forgive my being so frank—I should never have expected you to have even attempted such a thing."

Dominey smiled good-humouredly.

"Well," he said, "if you enquire at the United Bank of Africa, you will find that I have a credit balance there of something over a hundred thousand pounds. Then I have also—well, let us say a trifle more, invested in first-class mines. Do me the favour of lunching with me, Mr. Mangan, and although Africa will never be a favourite topic of conversation with me, I will tell you about some of my speculations."

The solicitor groped around for his hat.

"I will send the boy for a taxi," he faltered.

"I have a car outside," this astonishing client told him. "Before we leave, could you instruct your clerk to have a list of the Dominey mortgages made out, with the terminable dates and redemption values?"

"I will leave instructions," Mr. Mangan promised. "I think that the total amount is under eighty thousand pounds."

Dominey sauntered through the office, an object of much interest to the little staff of clerks. The lawyer joined him on the pavement in a few minutes.

"Where shall we lunch?" Dominey asked. "I'm afraid my clubs are a little out of date. I am staying at the Carlton."

"The Carlton grill room is quite excellent," Mr. Mangan suggested.

"They are keeping me a table until half-past one," Dominey replied. "We will lunch there, by all means."

They drove off together, the returned traveller gazing all the time out of the window into the crowded streets, the lawyer a little thoughtful.

"While I think of it, Sir Everard," the latter said, as they drew near their destination, "I should be glad of a short conversation with you before you go down to Dominey."

"With regard to anything in particular?"

"With regard to Lady Dominey," the lawyer told him a little gravely.

A shadow rested on his companion's face.

"Is her ladyship very much changed?"

"Physically, she is in excellent health, I believe. Mentally I believe that there is no change. She has unfortunately the same rather violent prejudice which I am afraid influenced your departure from England."

"In plain words," Dominey said bitterly, "she has sworn to take my life if ever I sleep under the same roof."

"She will need, I am afraid, to be strictly watched," the lawyer answered evasively. "Still, I think you ought to be told that time does not seem to have lessened her tragical antipathy."

"She regards me still as the murderer of Roger Unthank?" Dominey asked, in a measured tone.

"I am afraid she does."

"And I suppose that every one else has the same idea?"

"The mystery," Mr. Mangan admitted, "has never been cleared up. It is well known, you see, that you fought in the park and that you staggered home almost senseless. Roger Unthank has never been seen from that day to this."

"If I had killed him," Dominey pointed out, "why was his body not found?"

The lawyer shook his head.

"There are all sorts of theories, of course," he said, "but for one superstition you may as well be prepared. There is scarcely a man or a woman for miles around Dominey who doesn't believe that the ghost of Roger Unthank still haunts the Black Wood near where you fought."

"Let us be quite clear about this," Dominey insisted. "If the body should ever be found, am I liable, after all these years, to be indicted for manslaughter?"

"I think you may make your mind quite at ease," the lawyer assured him. "In the first place, I don't think you would ever be indicted."

"And in the second?"

"There isn't a human being in that part of Norfolk would ever believe that the body of man or beast, left within the shadow of the Black Wood, would ever be seen or heard of again!"

# CHAPTER IV

Mr. Mangan, on their way into the grill room, loitered for a few minutes in the small reception room, chatting with some acquaintances, whilst his host, having spoken to the *maître d'hôtel* and ordered a cocktail from a passing waiter, stood with his hands behind his back, watching the inflow of men and women with all that interest which one might be supposed to feel in one's fellows after a prolonged absence. He had moved a little on one side to allow a party of young people to make their way through the crowded chamber, when he was conscious of a woman standing alone on the topmost of the three thickly carpeted stairs. Their eyes met, and hers, which had been wandering around the room as though in search of some acquaintance, seemed instantly and fervently held. To the few loungers about the room, ignorant of any special significance in that studied contemplation of the man on the part of the woman, their two personalities presented an agreeable, almost a fascinating study. Dominey was six feet two in height and had to its fullest extent the natural distinction of his class, together with the half military, half athletic bearing which seemed to have been so marvellously restored to him. His complexion was no more than becomingly tanned; his slight moustache, trimmed very close to the upper lip, was of the same ruddy brown shade as his sleekly brushed hair. The woman, who had commenced now to move slowly towards him, save that her cheeks, at that moment, at any rate, were almost unnaturally pale, was of the same colouring. Her red-gold hair gleamed beneath her black hat. She was tall, a Grecian type of figure, large without being coarse, majestic though still young. She carried a little dog under one arm and a plain black silk bag, on which was a coronet in platinum and diamonds, in the other hand. The major-domo who presided over the room, watching her approach, bowed with more than his usual urbanity. Her eyes, however, were still fixed upon the person who had engaged so large a share of her attention. She came towards him, her lips a little parted.

"Leopold!" she faltered. "The Holy Saints, why did you not let me know!"

Dominey bowed very slightly. His words seemed to have a cut and dried flavour.

"I am so sorry," he replied, "but I fear that you make a mistake. My name is not Leopold."

She stood quite still, looking at him with the air of not having heard a word of his polite disclaimer.

"In London, of all places," she murmured. "Tell me, what does it mean?"

"I can only repeat, madam," he said, "that to my very great regret I have not the honour of your acquaintance."

She was puzzled, but absolutely unconvinced.

"You mean to deny that you are Leopold von Ragastein?" she asked incredulously. "You do not know me?"

"Madame," he answered, "it is not my great pleasure. My name is Dominey—Everard Dominey."

She seemed for a moment to be struggling with some embarrassment which approached emotion. Then she laid her fingers upon his sleeve and drew him to a more retired corner of the little apartment.

"Leopold," she whispered, "nothing can make it wrong or indiscreet for you to visit me. My address is 17, Belgrave Square. I desire to see you tonight at seven o'clock."

"But, my dear lady," Dominey began—

Her eyes suddenly glowed with a new light.

"I will not be trifled with," she insisted. "If you wish to succeed in whatever scheme you have on hand, you must not make an enemy of me. I shall expect you at seven o'clock."

She passed away from him into the restaurant. Mr. Mangan, now freed from his friends, rejoined his host, and the two men took their places at the side table to which they were ushered with many signs of attention.

"Wasn't that the Princess Eiderstrom with whom you were talking?" the solicitor asked curiously.

"A lady addressed me by mistake," Dominey explained. "She mistook me, curiously enough, for a man who used to be called my double at Oxford. Sigismund Devinter he was then, although I think he came into a title later on."

"The Princess is quite a famous personage," Mr. Mangan remarked, "one of the richest widows in Europe. Her husband was killed in a duel some six or seven years ago."

Dominey ordered the luncheon with care, slipping into a word or two of German once to assist the waiter, who spoke English with difficulty. His companion smiled.

"I see that you have not forgotten your languages out there in the wilds."

"I had no chance to," Dominey answered. "I spent five years on the borders of German East Africa, and I traded with some of the fellows there regularly."

"By the by," Mr. Mangan enquired, "what sort of terms are we on with the Germans out there?"

"Excellent, I should think," was the careless reply. "I never had any trouble."

"Of course," the lawyer continued, "this will all be new to you, but during the last few years Englishmen have become divided into two classes—the people who believe that the Germans wish to go to war and crush us, and those who don't."

"Then since my return the number of the 'don'ts' has been increased by one."

"I am amongst the doubtfuls myself," Mr. Mangan remarked. "All the same, I can't quite see what Germany wants with such an immense army, and why she is continually adding to her fleet."

Dominey paused for a moment to discuss the matter of a sauce with the head waiter. He returned to the subject a few minutes later on, however.

"Of course," he pointed out, "my opinions can only come from a study of the newspapers and from conversations with such Germans as I have met out in Africa, but so far as her army is concerned, I should have said that Russia and France were responsible for that, and the more powerful it is, the less chance of any European conflagration. Russia might at any time come to the conclusion that a war is her only salvation against a revolution, and you know the feeling in France about Alsace-Lorraine as well as I do. The Germans themselves say that there is more interest in military matters and more progress being made in Russia today than ever before."

"I have no doubt that you are right," agreed Mr. Mangan. "It is a matter which is being a great deal discussed just now, however. Let us speak of your personal plans. What do you intend to do for the next few weeks, say? Have you been to see any of your relatives yet?"

"Not one," Dominey replied. "I am afraid that I am not altogether keen about making advances."

Mr. Mangan coughed. "You must remember that during the period of your last residence in London," he said, "you were in a state of chronic impecuniosity. No doubt that rather affected the attitude of some of those who would otherwise have been more friendly."

"I should be perfectly content never to see one of them again," declared Dominey, with perfect truth.

"That of course, is impossible," the lawyer protested. "You must go and see the Duchess, at any rate. She was always your champion."

"The Duchess was always very kind to me," Dominey admitted doubtfully, "but I am afraid she was rather fed up before I left England."

Mr. Mangan smiled. He was enjoying a very excellent lunch, which it seemed hard to believe was ordered by a man just home from the wilds of Africa, and he thoroughly enjoyed talking about duchesses.

"Her Grace," he began—

"Well?"

The lawyer had paused, with his eyes glued upon the couple at a neighbouring table. He leaned across towards his companion.

"The Duchess herself, Sir Everard, just behind you, with Lord St. Omar."

"This place must certainly be the rendezvous of all the world," Dominey declared, as he held out his hand to a man who had approached their table. "Seaman, my friend, welcome! Let me introduce you to my friend and legal adviser, Mr. Mangan—Mr. Seaman."

Mr. Seaman was a short, fat man, immaculately dressed in the most conventional morning attire. He was almost bald, except for a little tuft on either side, and a few long, fair hairs carefully brushed back over a shining scalp. His face was extraordinarily round except towards his chin, where it came to a point; his eyes bright and keen, his mouth the mouth of a professional humourist. He shook hands with the lawyer with an *empressment* which was scarcely English.

"Within the space of half an hour," Dominey continued, "I find a princess who desires to claim my acquaintance; a cousin," he dropped his voice a little, "who lunches only a few tables away, and the man of whom I have seen most during the last ten years amidst scenes a little different from these, eh, Seaman?"

Seaman accepted the chair which the waiter had brought and sat down. The lawyer was immediately interested.

"Do I understand, then," he asked, addressing the newcomer, "that you knew Sir Everard in Africa?"

Seaman beamed. "Knew him?" he repeated, and with the first words of his speech the fact of his foreign nationality was established. "There was no one of whom I knew so much. We did business together—a great deal of business—and when we were not partners, Sir Everard generally got the best of it."

Dominey laughed. "Luck generally comes to a man either early or late in life. My luck came late. I think, Seaman, that you must have been my mascot. Nothing went wrong with me during the years that we did business together."

Seaman was a little excited. He brushed upright with the palm of his hand one of those little tufts of hair left on the side of his head, and he laid his plump fingers upon the lawyer's shoulder.

"Mr. Mangan," he said, "you listen to me. I sell this man the controlling interests in a mine, shares which I have held for four and a half years and never drew a penny dividend. I sell them to him, I say, at par. Well, I need the money and it seems to me that I had given the shares a fair chance.

Within five weeks—five weeks, sir," he repeated, struggling to attune his voice to his civilised surroundings, "those shares had gone from par to fourteen and a half. Today they stand at twenty. He gave me five thousand pounds for those shares. Today he could walk into your stock market and sell them for one hundred thousand. That is the way money is made in Africa, Mr. Mangan, where innocents like me are to be found every day."

Dominey poured out a glass of wine and passed it to their visitor.

"Come," he said, "we all have our ups and downs. Africa owes you nothing, Seaman."

"I have done well in my small way," Seaman admitted, fingering the stem of his wineglass, "but where I have had to plod, Sir Everard here has stood and commanded fate to pour her treasures into his lap."

The lawyer was listening with a curious interest and pleasure to this half bantering conversation. He found an opportunity now to intervene.

"So you two were really friends in Africa?" he remarked, with a queer and almost inexplicable sense of relief.

"If Sir Everard permits our association to be so called," Seaman replied. "We have done business together in the great cities—in Johannesburg and Pretoria, in Kimberley and Cape Town—and we have prospected together in the wild places. We have trekked the veldt and been lost to the world for many months at a time. We have seen the real wonders of Africa together, as well as her tawdry civilisation."

"And you, too," Mr. Mangan asked, "have you retired?"

Seaman's smile was almost beatific.

"The same deal," he said, "which brought Sir Everard's fortune to wonderful figures brought me that modest sum which

I had sworn to reach before I returned to England. It is true. I have retired from money-making. It is now that I take up again my real life's work."

"If you are going to talk about your hobby," Dominey observed, "you had better order them to serve your lunch here."

"I had finished my lunch before you came in," his friend replied. "I drink another glass of wine with you, perhaps. Afterwards a liqueur—who can say? In this climate one is favoured, one can drink freely. Sir Everard and I, Mr. Mangan, have been in places where thirst is a thing to be struggled against, where for months a little weak brandy and water was our chief dissipation."

"Tell us about this hobby?" the lawyer enquired.

Dominey intervened promptly. "I protest. If he begins to talk of that, he'll be here all the afternoon."

Seaman held out his hands and rolled his head from side to side.

"But I am not so unreasonable," he objected. "Just one word—so? Very well, then," he proceeded quickly, with the air of one fearing interruption. "This must be clear to you, Mr. Mangan. I am a German by birth, naturalised in England for the sake of my business, loving Germany, grateful to England. One third of my life I have lived in Berlin, one third at Forest Hill here in London, and in the city, one third in Africa. I have watched the growth of commercial rivalries and jealousies between the two nations. There is no need for them. They might lead to worse things. I would brush them all away. My aim is to encourage a league for the promotion of more cordial social and business relations between the people of Great Britain and the people of the German Empire. There! Have

I wasted much of your time? Can I not speak of my hobby without a flood of words?"

"Conciseness itself," Mangan admitted, "and I compliment you most heartily upon your scheme. If you can get the right people into it, it should prove a most valuable society."

"In Germany I have the right people. All Germans who live for their country and feel for their country loathe the thought of war. We want peace, we want friends, and, to speak as man to man," he concluded, tapping the lawyer upon the coat sleeve, "England is our best customer."

"I wish one could believe," the latter remarked, "that yours was the popular voice in your country."

Seaman rose reluctantly to his feet.

"At half-past two," he announced, glancing at his watch, "I have an appointment with a woollen manufacturer from Bradford. I hope to get him to join my council."

He bowed ceremoniously to the lawyer, nodded to Dominey with the familiarity of an old friend, and made his bustling, good-humoured way out of the room.

"A sound business man, I should think," was the former's comment. "I wish him luck with his League. You yourself, Sir Everard, will need to develop some new interests. Why not politics?"

"I really expect to find life a little difficult at first," admitted Dominey, with a shrug of his shoulders. "I have lost many of the tastes of my youth, and I am very much afraid that my friends over here will call me colonial. I can't fancy myself doing nothing down in Norfolk all the rest of my days. Perhaps I shall go into Parliament."

"You must forgive my saying," his companion declared impulsively, "that I never knew ten years make such a difference in a man in my life."

"The colonies," Dominey pronounced, "are a kill or cure sort of business. You either take your drubbing and come out a stronger man, or you go under. I had the very narrowest escape from going under myself, but I just pulled together in time. Today I wouldn't have been without my hard times for anything in the world."

"If you will permit me," Mr. Mangan said, with an inherited pomposity, "on this our first meeting under the new conditions, I should like to offer you my hearty congratulations, not only upon what you have accomplished but upon what you have become."

"And also, I hope," Dominey rejoined, smiling a little seriously and with a curious glint in his eyes, "upon what I may yet accomplish."

The Duchess and her companion had risen to their feet, and the former, on her way out, recognising her solicitor, paused graciously.

"How do you do, Mr. Mangan?" she said. "I hope you are looking after those troublesome tenants of mine in Leicestershire?"

"We shall make our report in due course, Duchess," Mangan assured her. "Will you permit me," he added, "to bring back to your memory a relative who has just returned from abroad—Sir Everard Dominey?"

Dominey had risen to his feet a moment previously and now extended his hand. The Duchess, who was a tall, graceful woman, with masses of fair hair only faintly interspersed with grey, very fine brown eyes, the complexion of a girl, and, to quote her own confession, the manners of a kitchen maid, stared at him for a moment without any response.

"Sir Everard Dominey?" she repeated. "Everard? Ridiculous!"

Dominey's extended hand was at once withdrawn, and the tentative smile faded from his lips. The lawyer plunged into the breach.

"I can assure your Grace," he insisted earnestly, "that there is no doubt whatever about Sir Everard's identity. He only returned from Africa during the last few days."

The Duchess's incredulity remained, wholly good-natured but ministered to by her natural obstinacy.

"I simply cannot bring myself to believe it," she declared. "Come, I'll challenge you. When did we meet last?"

"At Worcester House," was the prompt reply. "I came to say good-bye to you."

The Duchess was a little staggered. Her eyes softened, a faint smile played at the corners of her lips. She was suddenly a very attractive-looking woman.

"You came to say good-bye," she repeated, "and?"

"I am to take that as a challenge?" Dominey asked, standing very upright and looking her in the eyes.

"As you will."

"You were a little kinder to me," he continued, "than you are today. You gave me—this," he added, drawing a small picture from his pocketbook, "and you permitted—"

"For heaven's sake, put that thing away," she cried, "and don't say another word! There's my grown-up nephew, St. Omar, paying his bill almost within earshot. Come and see me at half-past three this afternoon, and don't be a minute late. And, St. Omar," she went on, turning to the young man who stood now by her side, "this is a connection of yours—Sir Everard Dominey. He is a terrible person, but do shake hands with him and come along. I am half an hour late for my dressmaker already."

Lord St. Omar chuckled vaguely, then shook hands with his new-found relative, nodded affably to the lawyer and followed his aunt out of the room. Mangan's expression was beatific.

"Sir Everard," he exclaimed, "God bless you! If ever a woman got what she deserved! I've seen a duchess blush—first time in my life!"

# CHAPTER V

WORCESTER HOUSE was one of those semi-palatial residences set down apparently for no reason whatever in the middle of Regent's Park. It had been acquired by a former duke at the instigation of the Regent, who was his intimate friend, and retained by later generations in mute protest against the disfiguring edifices which had made a millionaire's highway of Park Lane. Dominey, who was first scrutinised by an individual in buff waistcoat and silk hat at the porter's lodge, was interviewed by a major-domo in the great stone hall, conducted through an extraordinarily Victorian drawing-room by another myrmidon in a buff waistcoat, and finally ushered into a tiny little boudoir leading out of a larger apartment and terminating in a conservatory filled with sweet-smelling exotics. The Duchess, who was reclining in an easy-chair, held out her hand, which her visitor raised to his lips. She motioned him to a seat by her side and once more scrutinised him with unabashed intentness.

"There's something wrong about you, you know," she declared.

"That seems very unfortunate," he rejoined, "when I return to find you wholly unchanged."

"Not bad," she remarked critically. "All the same, I have changed. I am not in the least in love with you any longer."

"It was the fear of that change in you," he sighed, "which kept me for so long in the furthest corners of the world."

She looked at him with a severity which was obviously assumed.

"Look here," she said, "it is better for us to have a perfectly clear understanding upon one point. I know the exact position of your affairs, and I know, too, that the two hundred a year which your lawyer has been sending out to you came partly out of a few old trees and partly out of his own pocket. How you are going to live over here I cannot imagine, but it isn't the least use expecting Henry to do a thing for you. The poor man has scarcely enough pocket money to pay his travelling expenses when he goes lecturing."

"Lecturing?" Dominey repeated. "What's happened to poor Henry?"

"My husband is an exceedingly conscientious man," was the dignified reply. "He goes from town to town with Lord Roberts and a secretary, lecturing on national defence."

"Dear Henry was always a little cranky, wasn't he?" Dominey observed. "Let me put your mind at rest on that other matter, though, Caroline. I can assure you that I have come back to England not to borrow money but to spend it."

His cousin shook her head mournfully. "And a few minutes ago I was nearly observing that you had lost your sense of humour!"

"I am in earnest," he persisted. "Africa has turned out to be my Eldorado. Quite unexpectedly, I must admit, I came in for a considerable sum of money towards the end of my stay there. I am paying off the mortgages at Dominey at once, and I want Henry to jot down on paper at once those few amounts he was good enough to lend me in the old days."

Caroline, Duchess of Worcester, sat perfectly still for a moment with her mouth open, a condition which was entirely natural but unbecoming.

"And you mean to tell me that you really are Everard Dominey?" she exclaimed.

"The weight of evidence is rather that way," he murmured.

He moved his chair deliberately a little nearer, took her hand and raised it to his lips. Her face was perilously near to his. She drew a little back—not too abruptly.

"My dear Everard," she whispered, "Henry is in the house! Besides—Yes, I suppose you must be Everard. Just now there was something in your eyes exactly like his. But you are so stiff. Have you been drilling out there or anything?"

He shook his head.

"One spends half one's time in the saddle."

"And you are really well off?" she asked again wonderingly.

"If I had stayed there another year," he replied, "and been able to marry a Dutch Jewess, I should have qualified for Park Lane."

She sighed.

"It's too wonderful. Henry will love having his money back."

"And you?"

She looked positively distressed.

"You've lost all your manners," she complained. "You make love like a garden rake. You should have leaned towards me with a quiver in your voice when you said those last two words, and instead of that you look as though you were sitting at attention, with a positive glint of steel in your eyes."

"One sees a woman once in a blue moon out there," he pleaded.

She shook her head. "You've changed. It was a sixth sense with you to make love in exactly the right tone, to say exactly the right thing in the right manner."

"I shall pick it up," he declared hopefully, "with a little assistance."

She made a little grimace.

"You won't want an old woman like me to assist you, Everard. You'll have the town at your feet. You'll be able to frivol with musical comedy, flirt with our married beauties, or—I'm sorry, Everard. I forgot."

"You forgot what?" he asked steadfastly.

"I forgot the tragedy which finally drove you abroad. I forgot your marriage. Is there any change in your wife?"

"Not much, I am afraid."

"And Mr. Mangan—he thinks that you are safe over here?"

"Perfectly."

She looked at him earnestly. Perhaps she had never admitted, even to herself, how fond she had been of this scapegrace cousin.

"You'll find that no one will have a word to say against you," she told him, "now that you are wealthy and regenerate. They'll forget everything you want them to. When will you come and dine here and meet all your relatives?"

"Whenever you are kind enough to ask me," he answered. "I thought of going down to Dominey tomorrow."

She looked at him with a new thing in her eyes—something of fear, something, too, of admiration.

"But—your wife?"

"She is there, I believe," he said. "I cannot help it. I have been an exile from my home long enough."

"Don't go," she begged suddenly. "Why not be brave and have her removed. I know how tender-hearted you are, but you have your future and your career to consider. For her sake, too, you ought not to give her the opportunity—"

Dominey could never make up his mind whether the interruption which came at that moment was welcome or otherwise. Caroline suddenly broke off in her speech and glanced warningly towards the larger room. A tall, grey-haired man, dressed in old-fashioned clothes and wearing a pince-nez, had lifted the curtains. He addressed the Duchess in a thin, reedy voice.

"My dear Caroline," he began,—"ah, you must forgive me. I did not know that you were engaged. We will not stay, but

I should like to present to you a young friend of mine who is going to help me at the meeting this evening."

"Do bring him in," his wife replied, her voice once more attuned to its usual drawl. "And I have a surprise for you too, Henry—a very great surprise, I think you will find it!"

Dominey rose to his feet—a tall, commanding figure—and stood waiting the approach of the newcomer. The Duke advanced, looking at him enquiringly. A young man, very obviously a soldier in mufti, was hovering in the background.

"I must plead guilty to the surprise," the Duke confessed courteously. "There is something exceedingly familiar about your face, sir, but I cannot remember having had the privilege of meeting you."

"You see," Caroline observed, "I am not the only one, Everard, who did not accept you upon a glance. This is Everard Dominey, Henry, returned from foreign exile and regenerated in every sense of the word."

"How do you do?" Dominey said, holding out his hand. "I seem to be rather a surprise to every one, but I hope you haven't quite forgotten me."

"God bless my soul!" the Duke exclaimed. "You don't mean to say that you're really Everard Dominey?"

"I am he, beyond a doubt," was the calm assurance.

"Most amazing!" the Duke declared, as he shook hands. "Most amazing! I never saw such a change in my life. Yes, yes, I see—same complexion, of course—nose and eyes—yes, yes! But you seem taller, and you carry yourself like a soldier. Dear, dear me! Africa has done wonderfully by you. Delighted, my dear Everard! Delighted!"

"You'll be more delighted still when you hear the rest of the news," his wife remarked drily. "In the meantime, do present your friend."

"Precisely so," the Duke acquiesced, turning to the young man in the background. "Most sorry, my dear Captain Bartram. The unexpected return of a connection of my wife must be my apology for this lapse of manners. Let me present you to the Duchess. Captain Bartram is just back from Germany, my dear, and is an enthusiastic supporter of our cause.—Sir Everard Dominey."

Caroline shook hands kindly with her husband's protégé, and Dominey exchanged a solemn handshake with him.

"You, too, are one of those, then, Captain Bartram, who are convinced that Germany has evil designs upon us?" the former said, smiling.

"I have just returned from Germany after twelve months' stay there," the young soldier replied. "I went with an open mind. I have come back convinced that we shall be at war with Germany within a couple of years."

The Duke nodded vigorously.

"Our young friend is right," he declared. "Three times a week for many months I have been drumming the fact into the handful of wooden-headed Englishmen who have deigned to come to our meetings. I have made myself a nuisance to the House of Lords and the Press. It is a terrible thing to realise how hard it is to make an Englishman reflect, so long as he is making money and having a good time.—You are just back from Africa, Everard?"

"Within a week, sir."

"Did you see anything of the Germans out there? Were you anywhere near their Colony?"

"I have been in touch with them for some years," Dominey replied.

"Most interesting!" his questioner exclaimed. "You may be of service to us, Everard. You may, indeed! Now tell me, isn't it true that they have secret agents out there, trying to provoke unsettlement and disquiet amongst the Boers? Isn't it true that they apprehend a war with England before very long and are determined to stir up the Colony against us?"

"I am very sorry," Dominey replied, "but I am not a politician in any shape or form. All the Germans whom I have met out there seem a most peaceable race of men, and there doesn't seem to be the slightest discontent amongst the Boers or any one else."

The Duke's face fell. "This is very surprising."

"The only people who seem to have any cause for discontent," Dominey continued, "are the English settlers. I didn't commence to do any good myself there till a few years ago, but I have heard some queer stories about the way our own people were treated after the war."

"What you say about South Africa, Sir Everard," the young soldier remarked, "is naturally interesting, but I am bound to say that it is in direct opposition to all I have heard."

"And I," the Duke echoed fervently.

"I have lived there for the last eleven years," Dominey continued, "and although I spent the earlier part of that time trekking after big game, lately I am bound to confess that every thought and energy I possess have been centered upon money-making. For that reason, perhaps, my observations may have been at fault. I shall claim the privilege of coming to one of your first meetings, Duke, and of trying to understand this question."

His august connection blinked at him a little curiously for a moment behind his glasses.

"My dear Everard," he said, "forgive my remarking it, but I find you more changed than I could have believed possible."

"Everard is changed in more ways than one," his wife observed, with faint irony.

Dominey, who had risen to leave, bent over her hand.

"What about my dinner party, sir?" she added.

"As soon as I return from Norfolk," he replied.

"Dominey Hall will really find you?" she asked a little curiously.

"Most certainly!"

There was again that little flutter of fear in her eyes, followed by a momentary flash of admiration. Dominey shook hands gravely with his host and nodded to Bartram. The servant whom the Duchess had summoned stood holding the curtains on one side.

"I shall hope to see you again shortly, Duke," Dominey said, as he completed his leave-taking. "There is a little matter of business to be adjusted between us. You will probably hear from Mr. Mangan in a day or two."

The Duke gazed after the retreating figure of this very amazing visitor. When the curtains had fallen he turned to his wife.

"A little matter of business," he repeated. "I hope you have explained to Everard, my dear, that although, of course, we are very glad to see him back again, it is absolutely hopeless for him to look to me for any financial assistance at the present moment."

Caroline smiled.

"Everard was alluding to the money he already owes you," she explained. "He intends to repay it at once. He is also paying off the Dominey mortgages. He has apparently made a fortune in Africa."

The Duke collapsed into an easy-chair.

"Everard pay his debts?" he exclaimed. "Everard Dominey pay off the mortgages?"

"That is what I understand," his wife acquiesced.

The Duke clutched at the last refuge of a weak but obstinate man. His mouth came together like a rattrap.

"There's something wrong about it somewhere," he declared.

# CHAPTER VI

DOMINEY spent a very impatient hour that evening in his sitting-room at the Carlton, waiting for Seaman. It was not until nearly seven that the latter appeared.

"Are you aware," Dominey asked him, "that I am expected to call upon the Princess Eiderstrom at seven o'clock?"

"I have your word for it," Seaman replied, "but I see no tragedy in the situation. The Princess is a woman of sense and a woman of political insight. While I cannot recommend you to take her entirely into your confidence, I still think that a middle course can be judiciously pursued."

"Rubbish!" Dominey exclaimed. "As Leopold von Ragastein, the Princess has indisputable claims upon me and my liberty, claims which would altogether interfere with the career of Everard Dominey."

With methodical neatness, Seaman laid his hat, gloves and walking stick upon the sideboard. He then looked into the connecting bedroom, closed and fastened the door and extended himself in an easy-chair.

"Sit opposite to me, my friend," he said. "We will talk together."

Dominey obeyed a little sullenly. His companion, however, ignored his demeanour.

"Now, my friend," he said, beating upon the palm of one hand with the forefinger of his other, "I am a man of commerce and I do things in a business way. Let us take stock of our position. Three months ago last week, we met by appointment at a certain hotel in Cape Town."

"Only three months," Dominey muttered.

"We were unknown to one another," Seaman continued. "I had only heard of the Baron von Ragastein as a devoted

German citizen and patriot, engaged in an important enterprise in East Africa by special intercession of the Kaiser, on account of a certain unfortunate happening in Hungary."

"I killed a man in a duel," Dominey said slowly, with his eyes fixed upon his companion's. "It was not an unforgivable act."

"There are duels and duels. A fight between two young men, in defence of the honour of or to gain the favour of a young lady in their own station of life, has never been against the conventions of the Court. On the other hand, to become the lover of the wife of one of the greatest nobles in Hungary, and to secure possession by killing the husband in the duel which his honour makes a necessity is looked upon very differently."

"I had no wish to kill the Prince," Dominey protested, "nor was it at my desire that we met at all. The prince fought like a madman and slipped, after a wild lunge, onto the point of my stationary sword."

"Let that pass," Seaman said. "I am not of your order and I probably do not understand the etiquette of these matters. I simply look upon you as a culprit in the eyes of our master, and I feel that he has a right to demand from you much in the way of personal sacrifice."

"Perhaps you will tell me," Dominey demanded, "what more he would have? I have spent weary years in a godless and fever-ridden country, raising up for our arms a great troop of natives. I have undertaken other political commissions in the Colony which may bear fruit. I am to take up the work for which I was originally intended, for which I was given an English education. I am to repair to England, and, under such identity as I might assume after consultation with you at Cape Town, I am to render myself so far as possible a *persona grata* in that country. I do not wait for our meeting. I see a great chance and

I make use of it. I transform myself into an English country gentleman, and I think you will admit that I have done so with great success."

"All that you say is granted," Seaman agreed. "You met me at Cape Town in your new identity, and you certainly seemed to wear it wonderfully. You have made it uncommonly expensive, but we do not grudge money."

"I could not return home to a poverty-stricken domain," Dominey pointed out. "I should have held no place what-ever in English social life, and I should have received no welcome from those with whom I imagine you desire me to stand well."

"Again I make no complaints," Seaman declared. "There is no bottom to our purse, nor any stint. Neither must there be any stint to our loyalty," he added gravely.

"In this instance," Dominey protested, "it is not a matter of loyalty. Everard Dominey cannot throw himself at the feet of the Princess Eiderstrom, well-known to be one of the most passion-ate women in Europe, whilst her love affair with Leopold von Ragastein is still remembered. Remember that the question of our identities might crop up any day. We were friends over here in England, at school and at college, and there are many who will still remember the likeness between us. Perfectly though I may play my part, here and there there may be doubts. These will be doubts no longer if I am to be dragged at the chariot wheels of the Princess."

Seaman was silent for a moment.

"There is reason in what you say," he admitted presently. "It is for a few months only. What is your proposition?"

"That you see the Princess in my place at once," Dominey suggested eagerly. "Point out to her that for the present, for political reasons, I am and must remain Everard Dominey, to her as to the rest of the world. Let her be content with such measure of friendship and admiration as Sir Everard Dominey might reasonably offer to a beautiful woman whom he met today for the first time, and I am entirely and with all my heart at her service. But let her remember that even between us two, in the solitude of her room as in the drawing-rooms where we might meet, it can be Everard Dominey only until my mission is ended. You think, perhaps, that I lay unnecessary stress upon this. I do not. I know the Princess and I know myself."

Seaman glanced at the clock. "At what hour was your appointment?"

"It was not an appointment, it was a command," Dominey replied. "I was told to be at Belgrave Square at seven o'clock."

"I will have an understanding with the Princess," promised Seaman, as he took up his hat. "Dine with me downstairs at eight o'clock on my return."

Dominey, descending about an hour later, found his friend Seaman already established at a small, far-away table set in one of the recesses of the grill room. He was welcomed with a little wave of the hand, and cocktails were at once ordered.

"I have done your errand," Seaman announced. "Since my visit I am bound to admit that I realise a little more fully your anxiety."

"You probably had not met the Princess before?"

"I had not. I must confess that I found her a lady of some-what overpowering temperament. I fancy, my young friend," Seaman continued, with a twitch at the corner of his lips, "that somewhere about August next year you will find your hands full."

"August next year can take care of itself," was the cool reply.

"In the meantime," Seaman continued, "the Princess understands the situation and is, I think, impressed. She will at any rate do nothing rash. You and she will meet within the course of the next few hours, but on reasonable terms. To proceed! As I drove back here after my interview with the Princess, I decided that it was time you made the acquaintance of the person who is chiefly responsible for your presence here."

"Terniloff?"

"Precisely! You have maintained, my young friend," Seaman went on after a brief pause, during which one waiter had brought their cocktails and another received their order for dinner, "a very discreet and laudable silence with regard to those further instructions which were promised to you immediately you should arrive in London. Those instructions will never be committed to writing. They are here."

Seaman touched his forehead and drained the remaining contents of his glass.

"My instructions are to trust you absolutely," Dominey observed, "and, until the greater events stir, to concentrate the greater part of my energies in leading the natural life of the man whose name and place I have taken."

"Quite so," Seaman acquiesced.

He glanced around the room for a moment or two, as though interested in the people. Satisfied at last that there was no chance of being overheard, he continued:

"The first idea you have to get out of your head, my dear friend, if it is there, is that you are a spy. You are nothing of the sort. You are not connected with our remarkably perfect system of espionage in the slightest degree. You are a free agent in all that you may choose to say or do. You can believe in Germany or fear her—whichever you like. You can join your cousin's husband in his crusade for National Service, or you can join me in my efforts to cement the bonds of friendship and affection between the citizens of the two countries. We really do not care in the least. Choose your own part. Live yourself thoroughly into the life of Sir Everard Dominey, Baronet, of Dominey Hall, Norfolk, and pursue exactly the course which you think Sir Everard himself would be likely to take."

"This," Dominey admitted, "is very broadminded."

"It is common sense," was the prompt reply. "With all your ability, you could not in six months' time appreciably affect the position either way. Therefore, we choose to have you concentrate the whole of your energies upon one task and one task only. If there is anything of the spy about your mission here, it is not England or the English which are to engage your attention. We require you to concentrate wholly and entirely upon Terniloff."

Dominey was startled.

"Terniloff?" he repeated. "I expected to work with him, but—"

"Empty your mind of all preconceived ideas," Seaman enjoined. "What your duties are with regard to Terniloff will grow upon you gradually as the situation develops."

"As yet," Dominey remarked, "I have not even made his acquaintance."

"I was on the point of telling you, earlier in our conversation, that I have made an appointment for you to see him at eleven o'clock tonight at the Embassy. You will go to him at that hour. Remember, you know nothing, you are waiting for instructions. Let speech remain with him alone. Be particularly careful not to drop him a hint of your knowledge of what is coming. You will find him absolutely satisfied with the situation, absolutely content. Take care not to disturb him. He is a missioner of peace. So are you."

"I begin to understand," Dominey said thoughtfully.

"You shall understand everything when the time comes for you to take a hand," Seaman promised, "and do not in your zeal forget, my friend, that your utility to our great cause will depend largely upon your being able to establish and maintain your position as an English gentleman. So far all has gone well?"

"Perfectly, so far as I am concerned," Dominey replied. "You must remember, though, that there is your end to keep up. Berlin will be receiving frantic messages from East Africa as to my disappearance. Not even my immediate associates were in the secret."

"That is all understood," Seaman assured his companion. "A little doctor named Schmidt has spent many marks of the Government money in frantic cables. You must have endeared yourself to him."

"He was a very faithful associate."

"He has been a very troublesome friend. It seems that the natives got their stories rather mixed up concerning your namesake, who apparently died in the bush, and Schmidt continually emphasised your promise to let him hear from Cape Town. However, all this has been dealt with satisfactorily. The only real dangers are over here, and so far you seem to have encountered the principal ones."

"I have at any rate been accepted," Dominey declared, "by my nearest living relative, and incidentally I have discovered the one farseeing person in England who knows what is in store for us."

Seaman was momentarily anxious.

"Whom do you mean?"

"The Duke of Worcester, my cousin's husband, of whom you were speaking just now."

The little man's face relaxed.

"He reminds me of the geese who saved the Capitol," he said, "a brainless man obsessed with one idea. It is queer how often these fanatics discover the truth. That reminds me," he added, taking a small memorandum book from his waistcoat pocket and glancing it through. "His Grace has a meeting tonight at the Holborn Town Hall. I shall make one of my usual interruptions."

"If he has so small a following, why don't you leave him alone?" Dominey enquired.

"There are others associated with him," was the placid reply, "who are not so insignificant. Besides, when I interrupt I advertise my own little hobby."

"These—we English are strange people," Dominey remarked, glancing around the room after a brief but thoughtful pause. "We advertise and boast about our colossal wealth, and yet we are incapable of the slightest self-sacrifice in order to preserve it. One would have imagined that our philosophers, our historians, would warn us in irresistible terms, by unanswerable scientific deduction, of what was coming."

"My compliments to your pronouns," Seaman murmured, with a little bow. "*A propos* of what you were saying, you will never make an Englishman—I beg your pardon, one of your countrymen—realise anything unpleasant. He prefers to keep his head comfortably down in the sand. But to leave generalities, when do you think of going to Norfolk?"

"Within the next few days," Dominey replied.

"I shall breathe more freely when you are securely established there," his companion declared. "Great things wait upon your complete acceptance, in the country as well as in town, as Sir Everard Dominey. You are sure that you perfectly understand your position there as regards your—er—domestic affairs?"

"I understand all that is necessary," was the somewhat stiff reply.

"All that is necessary is not enough," Seaman rejoined irritably. "I thought that you had wormed the whole story out of that drunken Englishman?"

"He told me most of it. There were just one or two points which lay beyond the limits where questioning was possible."

Seaman frowned angrily.

"In other words," he complained, "you remembered that you were a gentleman and not that you were a German."

"The Englishman of a certain order," Dominey pronounced, "even though he be degenerate, has a certain obstinacy, generally connected with one particular thing, which nothing can break. We talked together on that last night until morning; we drank wine and brandy. I tore the story of my own exile from my breast and laid it bare before him. Yet I knew all the time, as I know now, that he kept something back."

There was a brief pause. During the last few minutes a certain tension had crept in between the two men. With it, their personal characteristics seemed to have become intensified. Dominey was more than ever the aristocrat; Seaman the plebian schemer, unabashed and desperately in earnest. He leaned presently a little way across the table. His eyes had narrowed but they were as bright as steel. His teeth were more prominent than usual.

"You should have dragged it from his throat," he insisted. "It is not your duty to nurse fine personal feelings. Heart and soul you stand pledged to great things. I cannot at this moment give you any idea what you may not mean to us after the trouble has come, if you are able to play your part still in this country as Everard Dominey of Dominey Hall. I know well enough that the sense of personal honour amongst the

Prussian aristocracy is the finest in the world, and yet there is not a single man of your order who should not be prepared to lie or cheat for his country's sake. You must fall into line with your fellows. Once more, it is not only your task with regard to Terniloff which makes your recognition as Everard Dominey so important to us. It is the things which are to come later.—Come, enough of this subject. I know that you understand. We grow too serious. How shall you spend your evening until eleven o'clock? Remember you did not leave England an anchorite, Sir Everard. You must have your amusements. Why not try a music hall?"

"My mind is too full of other things," Dominey objected.

"Then come with me to Holborn," the little man suggested. "It will amuse you. We will part at the door, and you shall sit at the back of the hall, out of sight. You shall hear the haunting eloquence of your cousin-in-law. You shall hear him trying to warn the men and women of England of the danger awaiting them from the great and rapacious German nation. What do you say?"

"I will come," Dominey replied in spiritless fashion. "It will be better than a music hall, at any rate. I am not at all sure, Seaman, that the hardest part of my task over here will not be this necessity for self-imposed amusements."

His companion struck the table gently but impatiently with his clenched fist.

"Man, you are young!" he exclaimed. "You are like the rest of us. You carry your life in your hands. Don't nourish past griefs. Cast the memory of them away. There's nothing which narrows a man more than morbidness. You have a past which may sometimes bring the ghosts around you, but remember the sin was not wholly yours, and there is an atonement which in measured fashion you may commence whenever you please. I have said enough about that. Greatness and gaiety go hand in hand. There! You see, I was a philosopher before I became a professor of propaganda. Good! You smile. That is something gained, at any rate. Now we will take a taxicab to Holborn and I will show you something really humorous."

At the entrance to the town hall, the two men, at Seaman's instigation, parted, making their way inside by different doors. Dominey found a retired seat under a balcony, where he was unlikely to be recognised from the platform. Seaman, on the other hand, took up a more prominent position at the end of one of the front rows of benches. The meeting was by no means overcrowded, overenthusiastic, overanything. There were rows of empty benches, a good many young couples who seemed to have come in for shelter from the inclement night, a few sturdy, respectable-looking tradesmen who had come because it seemed to be the respectable thing to do, a few genuinely interested, and here and there, although they were decidedly in the minority, a sprinkling of enthusiasts. On the platform was the Duke, with civic dignitaries on either side of him; a distinguished soldier, a Member of Parliament, a half dozen or so of nondescript residents from the neighbourhood, and Captain Bartram. The meeting was on the point of commencement as Dominey settled down in his corner.

First of all the Duke rose, and in a few hackneyed but earnest sentences introduced his young friend Captain Bartram. The latter, who sprang at once into the middle of his subject, was nervous and more than a little bitter. He explained that he had resigned his commission and was therefore free to speak his mind. He spoke of enormous military preparations in Germany and a general air of tense expectation. Against whom were these preparations? Without an earthly doubt against Germany's greatest rival, whose millions of young men, even in this hour of danger, preferred playing or watching football or cricket on Saturday afternoons to realising their duty. The conclusion of an ill-pointed but earnest speech was punctuated by the furtive entrance into the hall of a small boy selling evening newspapers, and there was a temporary diversion from any interest in the proceedings on the part of the younger portion of the audience, whilst they satisfied themselves as to the result of various Cup Ties. The Member of Parliament then descended upon them in a whirlwind of oratory and in his best House of Commons style. He spoke of black clouds and of the cold breeze that went before the coming thunderstorm. He pointed to the collapse of every great nation throughout history who had neglected the arts of self-defence. He appealed to the youth of the nation to prepare themselves to guard their womenkind, their homes, the sacred soil of their country, and at that point was interrupted by a drowsy member of the audience with stentorian lungs, who seemed just at that moment to have waked up.

"What about the Navy, guv'nor?"

The orator swept upon the interrupter in his famous platform manner. The Navy, he declared, could be trusted at all times to do its duty, but it could not fight on sea and land. Would the young man who had just interrupted do his, and enrol his name for drill and national service that evening?—and so on. The distinguished soldier, who was suffering from a cold, fired off a few husky sentences only, to the tune of rounds of applause. The proceedings were wound up by the Duke, who was obviously, with the exception of the distinguished soldier, much more in earnest than any of them, and secured upon the whole a respectful attention. He brought in a few historical allusions, pleaded for a greater spirit of earnestness and citizenship amongst the men of the country, appealed even to the women to develop their sense of responsibility, and sat down amidst a little burst of quite enthusiastic applause.—The vote of thanks to the chairman was on the point of being proposed when Mr. Seaman, standing up in his place, appealed to the chairman for permission to say a few words. The Duke, who had had some experience with Mr. Seaman before, looked at him severely, but the smile with which Mr. Seaman looked around upon the audience was so good-natured and attractive that he had no alternative but to assent. Seaman scrambled up the steps on to the platform, coughed apologetically, bowed to the Duke, and took possession of the meeting. After a word or two of compliment to the chairman, he made his confession. He was a German citizen—he was indeed one of that bloodthirsty race. (Some laughter.) He was also, and it was his excuse for standing there, the founder and secretary of a league, doubtless well known to them, a league for promoting more friendly relations between the business men of Germany and England. Some of the remarks which he had heard that evening had pained him deeply. Business often took him to Germany, and as a German he would be doing less than his duty if he did not stand up there and tell them that the average German loved the Englishman like a brother, that the object of his life was to come into greater kinship with him, that Germany, even at that moment, was standing with hand outstretched to her relatives across the North Sea, begging for a deeper sympathy, begging for a larger understanding. (Applause from the audience, murmurs of dissent from the platform.) And as to those military preparations of which they had heard so much (with a severe glance at Captain Bartram), let them glance for one moment at the frontiers of Germany, let them realise that eastwards Germany was being continually pressed by an ancient and historic foe of enormous strength. He would not waste their time telling them of the political difficulties which Germany had had to face during the last generation. He would simply tell them this great truth,—the foe for whom Germany was obliged to make these great military preparations was Russia. If ever they were used it would be against Russia, and at Russia's instigation.—In his humble way he was striving for the betterment of relations between the dearly beloved country of his birth and the equally beloved country of his adoption. Such meetings as these, instituted, as it seemed to him, for the propagation of unfair and unjustified suspicions, were one of the greatest difficulties in his way. He could not for a moment doubt that these gentlemen upon the platform were patriots. They would prove it more profitably, both to themselves and their country, if they abandoned their present prejudiced and harmful campaign and became patriots of his Society.

Seaman's little bow to the chairman was good-humoured, tolerant, a little wistful. The Duke's few words, prefaced by an indignant protest against the intrusion of a German propagandist into an English patriotic meeting, did nothing to undo the effect produced by this undesired stranger. When the meeting broke up, it was doubtful whether a single adherent had been gained to the cause of National Service. The Duke went home full of wrath, and Seaman chuckled with genuine merriment as he stepped into the taxi which Dominey had secured, at the corner of the street.

"I promised you entertainment," he observed. "Confess that I have kept my word."

Dominey smiled enigmatically. "You certainly succeeded in making fools of a number of respectable and well-meaning men."

"The miracle of it extends further," Seaman agreed. "Tonight, in its small way, is a supreme example of the transcendental follies of democracy. England is being slowly choked and strangled with too much liberty. She is like a child being over-fed with jam. Imagine, in our dear country, an Englishman being allowed to mount the platform and spout, undisturbed, English propaganda in deadly opposition to German interests. The so-called liberty of the Englishman is like the cuckoo in his political nest. Countries must be governed. They cannot govern themselves. The time of war will prove all that."

"Yet in any great crisis of a nation's history," Dominey queried, "surely there is safety in a multitude of counsellors?"

"There would be always a multitude of counsellors," Seaman replied, "in Germany as in England. The trouble for this country is that they would be all expressed publicly and in the press, each view would have its adherents, and the Government be split up into factions. In Germany, the real destinies of the country are decided in secret. There are counsellors there, too, earnest and wise counsellors, but no one knows their varying views. All that one learns is the result, spoken through the lips of the Kaiser, spoken once and for all."

Dominey was showing signs of a rare interest in his companion's conversation. His eyes were bright, his usually impassive features seemed to have become more mobile and strained. He laid his hand on Seaman's arm.

"Listen," he said, "we are in London, alone in a taxicab, secure against any possible eavesdropping. You preach the advantage of our Kaiser-led country. Do you really believe that the Kaiser is the man for the task which is coming?"

Seaman's narrow eyes glittered. He looked at his companion in satisfaction. His forehead was puckered, his eternal smile gone. He was the man of intellect.

"So you are waking up from the lethargy of Africa, my friend!" he exclaimed. "You are beginning to think. As you ask me, so shall I answer. The Kaiser is a vain, bombastic dreamer, the greatest egotist who ever lived, with a diseased personality, a ceaseless craving for the limelight. But he has also the genius for government. I mean this: he is a splendid medium for the expression of the brain power of his counsellors. Their words will pass through his personality, and he will believe them his. What is more, they will sound like his. He will see himself the knight in shining armour. All Europe will bow down before this self-imagined Cæsar, and no one except we who are behind will realise the ass's-head. There is no one else in this world whom I have ever met so well fitted to lead our great nation on to the destiny she deserves.—And now, my friend, tomorrow, if you like, we will speak of these matters again. Tonight, you have other things to think about. You are going into the great places where I never penetrate. You have an hour to change and prepare. At eleven o'clock the Prince von Terniloff will expect you."

# CHAPTER VII

THERE HAD BEEN a dinner party and a very small reception afterwards at the great Embassy in Carlton House Terrace. The Ambassador, Prince Terniloff, was bidding farewell to his wife's cousin, the Princess Eiderstrom, the last of his guests. She drew him on one side for a moment.

"Your Excellency," she said, "I have been hoping for a word with you all the evening."

"And I with you, dear Stephanie," he answered. "It is very early. Let us sit down for a moment."

He led her towards a settee but she shook her head.

"You have an appointment at half-past eleven," she said. "I wish you to keep it."

"You know, then?"

"I lunched today at the Carlton grill room. In the reception-room I came face to face with Leopold von Ragastein."

The Ambassador made no remark. It seemed to be his wish to hear first all that his companion had to say. After a moment's pause she continued:

"I spoke to him, and he denied himself. To me! I think that those were the most terrible seconds of my life. I have never suffered more. I shall never suffer so much again."

"It was most unfortunate," the Prince murmured sympathetically.

"This evening," she went on, "I received a visit from a man whom I took at first to be an insignificant member of the German bourgeoisie. I learnt something of his true position later. He came to me to explain that Leopold was engaged in this country on secret service, that he was passing under the name which he gave me,—Sir Everard Dominey, an English baronet, long lost in Africa. You know of this?"

"I know that tonight I am receiving a visit from Sir Everard Dominey."

"He is to work under your auspices?"

"By no means," the Prince rejoined warmly. "I am not favourably inclined towards this network of espionage. The school of diplomacy in which I have been brought up tries to work without such ignoble means."

"One realises that," she said. "Leopold is coming, however, tonight, to pay his respects to you."

"He is waiting for me now in my study," the Ambassador asserted.

"You will do me the service of conveying to him a message from me," she continued. "This man Seaman pointed out to me the unwisdom of any association between myself and Leopold, under present conditions. I listened to all that he had to say. I reserved my decision. I have now considered the matter. I will compromise with necessity. I will be content with the acquaintance of Sir Everard Dominey, but that I will have."

"For myself," the Ambassador reflected, "I do not even know what Von Ragastein's mission over here is, but if in Berlin they decide that, for the more complete preservation of his incognito, association between you and him is undesirable—"

She laid her fingers upon his arm.

"Stop!" she ordered. "I am not of Berlin. I am not a German. I am not even an Austrian. I am Hungarian, and though I am willing to study your interests, I am not willing to place them before my own life. I make terms, but I do not surrender. Those terms I will discuss with Leopold. Ah, be kind to me!" she went on, with a sudden change of voice. "Since those few minutes at midday I have lived in a dream. Only one thing can quiet me. I must speak to him, I must decide with him what I will do. You will help?"

"An acquaintance between you and Sir Everard Dominey," he admitted, "is certainly a perfectly natural thing."

"Look at me," she begged.

He turned and looked into her face. Underneath her beautiful eyes were dark lines; there was something pitiful about the curve of her mouth. He remembered that although she had carried herself throughout the evening with all the dignity which was second nature to her, he had overheard more than one sympathetic comment upon her appearance.

"I can see that you are suffering," he remarked kindly.

"My eyes are hot, and inside I am on fire," she continued. "I must speak to Leopold. Freda has asked me to stay and talk to her for an hour. My car waits. Arrange that he drives me home. Oh! believe me, dear friend, I am a very human woman, and there is nothing in the world to be gained by treating me as though I were of wood or stone. Tonight I can see him without observation. If you refuse, I shall take other means. I will make no promises. I will not even promise that I will not call out before him in the streets that he is a liar, that his life is a lie. I will call him Leopold von Ragastein—"

"Hush!" he begged her. "Stephanie, you are nervous. I have not yet answered your entreaty."

"You consent?"

"I consent," he promised. "After our interview, I shall bring the young man to Freda's room and present him. You will be there. He can offer you his escort."

She suddenly stooped and kissed his hand. An immense relief was in her face.

"Now I will keep you no longer. Freda is waiting for me."

The Ambassador strolled thoughtfully away into his own den at the back of the house, where Dominey was waiting for him.

"I am glad to see you," the former said, holding out his hand. "For five minutes I desire to talk to your real self. After that, for the rest of your time in England, I will respect your new identity."

Dominey bowed in silence. His host pointed to the sideboard.

"Come," he continued, "there are cigars and cigarettes at your elbow, whisky and soda on the sideboard. Make yourself at home in that chair there. Africa has really changed you very little. Do you remember our previous meeting, in Saxony?"

"I remember it perfectly, your Excellency."

"His Majesty knew how to keep Court in those days," the Ambassador went on. "One was tempted to believe oneself at an English country party. However, that much of the past. You know, of course, that I entirely disapprove of your present position here?"

"I gathered as much, your Excellency."

"We will have no reserves with one another," the Prince declared, lighting a cigar. "I know quite well that you form part of a network of espionage in this country which I consider wholly unnecessary. That is simply a question of method. I have no doubt that you are here with the same object as I am, the object which the Kaiser has declared to me with his own lips is nearest to his heart—to cement the bonds of friendship between Germany and England."

"You believe, sir, that that is possible?"

"I am convinced of it," was the earnest reply. "I do not know what the exact nature of your work over here is to be, but I am glad to have an opportunity of putting before you my convictions. I believe that in Berlin the character of some of the leading statesmen here has been misunderstood and misrepresented. I find on all sides of me an earnest and sincere desire for peace.

I have convinced myself that there is not a single statesman in this country who is desirous of war with Germany."

Dominey was listening intently, with the air of one who hears unexpected things.

"But, your Excellency," he ventured, "what about the matter from our point of view? There are a great many in our country, whom you and I know of, who look forward to a war with England as inevitable. Germany must become, we all believe, the greatest empire in the world. She must climb there, as one of our friends once said, with her foot upon the neck of the British lion."

"You are out of date," the Ambassador declared earnestly. "I see now why they sent you to me. Those days have passed. There is room in the world for Great Britain and for Germany. The disintegration of Russia in the near future is a certainty. It is eastward that we must look for any great extension of territory."

"These things have been decided?"

"Absolutely! They form the soul of my mission here. My mandate is one of peace, and the more I see of English statesmen and the more I understand the British outlook, the more sanguine I am as to the success of my efforts. This is why all this outside espionage with which Seaman is so largely concerned seems to me at times unwise and unnecessary."

"And my own mission?" Dominey enquired.

"Its nature," the Prince replied, "is not as yet divulged, but if, as I have been given to understand, it is to become closely connected with my own, then I am very sure you will presently find that its text also is Peace."

Dominey rose to his feet, prepared to take his leave.

"These matters will be solved for us," he murmured.

"There is just one word more, on a somewhat more private matter," Terniloff said in an altered tone. "The Princess Eiderstrom is upstairs."

"In this house?"

"Waiting for a word with you. Our friend Seaman has been with her this evening. I understand that she is content to subscribe to the present situation. She makes one condition, however."

"And that?"

"She insists upon it that I present Sir Everard Dominey."

The latter did not attempt to conceal his perturbation.

"I need scarcely point out to you, sir," he protested, "that any association between the Princess and myself is likely to largely increase the difficulties of my position here."

The Ambassador sighed.

"I quite appreciate that," he admitted. "Both Seaman and I have endeavoured to reason with her, but, as you are doubtless aware, the Princess is a woman of very strong will. She is also very powerfully placed here, and it is the urgent desire of the Court at Berlin to placate in every way the Hungarian nobility. You will understand, of course, that I speak from a political point of view only. I cannot ignore the fact of your unfortunate relations with the late Prince, but in considering the present position you will, I am sure, remember the greater interests."

His visitor was silent for a moment.

"You say that the Princess is waiting here?"

"She is with my wife and asks for your escort home. My wife also looks forward to the pleasure of renewing her acquaintance with you."

"I shall accept your Excellency's guidance in the matter," Dominey decided.

The Princess Terniloff was a woman of world culture, an artist, and still an extremely attractive woman. She received the visitor whom her husband brought to her in a very charming little room furnished after the style of the simplest French period, and she did her best to relieve the strain of what she understood must be a somewhat trying moment.

"We are delighted to welcome you to London, Sir Everard Dominey," she said, taking his hand, "and I hope that we shall often see you here. I want to present you to my cousin, who is interested in you, I must tell you frankly, because of your likeness to a very dear friend of hers. Stephanie, this is Sir Everard Dominey—the Princess Eiderstrom."

Stephanie, who was seated upon the couch from which her cousin had just risen, held out her hand to Dominey, who made her a very low and formal bow. Her gown was of unrelieved black. Wonderful diamonds flashed around her neck, and she wore also a tiara fashioned after the Hungarian style, a little low on her forehead. Her manner and tone still indicated some measure of rebellion against the situation.

"You have forgiven me for my insistence this morning?" she asked. "It was hard for me to believe that you were not indeed the person for whom I mistook you."

"Other people have spoken to me of the likeness," Dominey replied. "It is a matter of regret to me that I can claim to be no more than a simple Norfolk baronet."

"Without any previous experience of European Courts?"

"Without any at all."

"Your German is wonderfully pure for an untravelled man."

"Languages were the sole accomplishment I brought away from my misspent school days."

"You are not going to bury yourself in Norfolk, Sir Everard?" the Princess Terniloff enquired.

"Norfolk is very near London these days," Dominey replied, "and I have experienced more than my share of solitude during the last few years. I hope to spend a portion of my time here."

"You must dine with us one night," the Princess insisted, "and tell us about Africa. My husband would be so interested."

"You are very kind."

Stephanie rose slowly to her feet, leaned gracefully over and kissed her hostess on both cheeks, and submitted her hand to the Prince, who raised it to his lips. Then she turned to Dominey.

"Will you be so kind as to see me home?" she asked. "Afterwards, my car can take you on wherever you choose to go."

"I shall be very happy," Dominey assented.

He, too, made his farewells. A servant in the hall handed him his hat and coat, and he took his place in the car by Stephanie's side. She touched the electric switch as they glided off. The car was in darkness.

"I think," she murmured, "that I could not have borne another moment of this juggling with words. Leopold—we are alone!"

He caught the flash of her jewels, the soft brilliance of her eyes as she leaned towards him. His voice sounded, even to himself, harsh and strident.

"You mistake, Princess. My name is not Leopold. I am Everard Dominey."

"Oh, I know that you are very obstinate," she said softly, "very obstinate and very devoted to your marvellous country, but you have a soul, Leopold; you know that there are human duties as great as any your country ever imposed upon you. You know what I look for from you, what I must find from you or go down into hell, ashamed and miserable."

He felt his throat suddenly dry.

"Listen," he muttered, "until the hour strikes, I must remain to you as to the world, alone or in a crowd—Everard Dominey. There is one way and one way only of carrying through my appointed task."

She gave a little hysterical sob.

"Wait," she begged. "I will answer you in a moment. Give me your hand."

He opened the fingers which he had kept clenched together, and he felt the hot grip of her hand, holding his passionately, drawing it towards her until the fingers of her other hand, too, fell upon it. So she sat for several moments.

"Leopold," she continued presently, "I understand. You are afraid that I shall betray our love. You have reason. I am full of impulses and passion, as you know, but I have restraint. What we are to one another when we are alone, no soul in this world need know. I will be careful. I swear it. I will never even look at you as though my heart ached for your notice, when we are in the presence of other people. You shall come and see me as seldom as you wish. I will receive you alone only as often as you say. But don't treat me like this. Tell me you have come back. Throw off this hideous mask, if it be only for a moment."

He sat quite still, although her hands were tearing at his, her lips and eyes beseeching him.

"Whatever may come afterwards," he pronounced inexorably, "until the time arrives I am Everard Dominey. I cannot take advantage of your feelings for Leopold von Ragastein. He is not here. He is in Africa. Perhaps some day he will come back to you and be all that you wish."

She flung his hands away. He felt her eyes burning into his, this time with something more like furious curiosity.

"Let me look at you," she cried. "Let me be sure. Is this just some ghastly change, or are you an impostor? My heart is growing chilled. Are you the man I have waited for all these years? Are you the man to whom I have given my lips, for whose sake I offered up my reputation as a sacrifice, the man who slew my husband and left me?"

"I was exiled," he reminded her, his own voice shaking with emotion. "You know that. So far as other things are concerned, I am exiled now. I am working out my expiation."

She leaned back in her seat with an air of exhaustion. Her eyes closed. Then the car drove in through some iron gates and stopped in front of her door, which was immediately opened. A footman hurried out. She turned to Dominey.

"You will not enter," she pleaded, "for a short time?"

"If you will permit me to pay you a visit, it will give me great pleasure," he answered formally. "I will call, if I may, on my return from Norfolk."

She gave him her hand with a set smile.

"Let my people take you wherever you want to go," she invited, "and remember," she added, dropping her voice, "I do not admit defeat. This is not the last word between us."

She disappeared in some state, escorted through the great front door of one of London's few palaces by an attractive major-domo and footman in the livery of her House. Dominey drove back to the Carlton, where in the lounge he found the band playing, crowds still sitting around, amongst whom Seaman was conspicuous, in his neat dinner clothes and with his cherubic air of inviting attention from prospective new acquaintances. He greeted Dominey enthusiastically.

"Come," he exclaimed, "I am weary of solitude! I have seen scarcely a face that I recognise. My tongue is parched with inaction. I like to talk, and there has been no one to talk to. I might as well have opened up my little house in Forest Hill."

"I'll talk to you if you like," Dominey promised a little grimly, glancing at the clock and hastily ordering a whisky and soda. "I will begin by telling you this," he added, lowering his tone. "I have discovered the greatest danger I shall have to face during my enterprise."

"What is that?"

"A woman—the Princess Eiderstrom."

Seaman lit one of his inevitable cigars and threw one of his short, fat legs over the other. He gazed for a moment with an air of satisfaction at his small foot, neatly encased in court shoes.

"You surprise me," he confessed. "I have considered the matter. I cannot see any great difficulty."

"Then you must be closing your eyes to it wilfully," Dominey retorted, "or else you are wholly ignorant of the Princess's temperament and disposition."

"I believe I appreciate both," Seaman replied, "but I still do not see any peculiar difficulty in the situation. As an English nobleman you have a perfect right to enjoy the friendship of the Princess Eiderstrom."

"And I thought you were a man of sentiment!" Dominey scoffed. "I thought you understood a little of human nature. Stephanie Eiderstrom is Hungarian born and bred. Even race has never taught her self-restraint. You don't seriously suppose that after all these years, after all she has suffered—and she has suffered—she is going to be content with an emasculated form of friendship? I talk to you without reserve, Seaman. She has made it very plain tonight that she is going to be content with nothing of the sort."

"What takes place between you in private," Seaman began—

"Rubbish!" his companion interrupted. "The Princess is an impulsive, a passionate, a distinctly primitive woman, with a good deal of the wild animal in her still. Plots or political necessities are not likely to count a snap of the fingers with her."

"But surely," Seaman protested, "she must understand that your country has claimed you for a great work?"

Dominey shook his head.

"She is not a German," he pointed out. "On the contrary, like a great many other Hungarians, I think she rather dislikes Germany and Germans. Her only concern is that personal question between us. She considers that every moment of the rest of my life should be devoted to her."

"Perhaps it is as well," Seaman remarked, "that you have arranged to go down tomorrow to Dominey. I will think out a scheme. Something must be done to pacify her."

The lights were being put out. The two men rose a little unwillingly. Dominey felt singularly indisposed for sleep, but anxious at the same time to get rid of his companion. They strolled into the darkened hall of the hotel together.

"I will deal with this matter for you as well as I can," Seaman promised. "To my mind, your greatest difficulty will be encountered tomorrow. You know what you have to deal with down at Dominey."

Dominey's face was very set and grave.

"I am prepared," he said.

Seaman still hesitated.

"Do you remember," he asked, "that when we talked over your plans at Cape Town, you showed me a picture of—of Lady Dominey?"

"I remember."

"May I have one more look at it?"

Dominey, with fingers that trembled a little, drew from the breast pocket of his coat a leather case, and from that a worn picture. The two men looked at it side by side beneath one of the electric standards which had been left burning. The face was the face of a girl, almost a child, and the great eyes seemed filled with a queer, appealing light. There was something of the same suggestion to be found in the lips, a certain helplessness, an appeal for love and protection to some stronger being.

Seaman turned away with a little grunt, and commented:

"Permitting myself to reassume for a moment or two the ordinary sentiments of an ordinary human being, I would sooner have a dozen of your Princesses to deal with than the original of that picture."

# CHAPTER VIII

"Your ancestral home," Mr. Mangan observed, as the car turned the first bend in the grass-grown avenue and Dominey Hall came into sight. "Damned fine house, too!"

His companion made no reply. A storm had come up during the last few minutes, and, as though he felt the cold, he had dragged his hat over his eyes and turned his coat collar up to his ears. The house, with its great double front, was now clearly visible—the time-worn, Elizabethan, red brick outline that faced the park southwards, and the stone-supported, grim and weather-stained back which confronted the marshes and the sea. Mr. Mangan continued to make amiable conversation.

"We have kept the old place weathertight, somehow or other," he said, "and I don't think you'll miss the timber much. We've taken it as far as possible from the outlying woods."

"Any from the Black Wood?" Dominey asked, without turning his head.

Mr. Mangan shook his head.

"Not a stump," he replied, "and for a very excellent reason. Not one of the woodmen would ever go near the place."

"The superstition remains, then?"

"The villagers are absolutely rabid about it. There are at least a dozen who declare that they have seen the ghost of Roger Unthank, and a score or more who will swear by all that is holy that they have heard his call at night."

"Does he still select the park and the terrace outside the house for his midnight perambulations?" Dominey enquired.

The lawyer hesitated.

"The idea is, I believe," he said, "that the ghost makes his way out from the wood and sits on the terrace underneath Lady Dominey's window. All bunkum, of course, but I can assure you that every servant and caretaker we've had there has given notice within a month. That is the sole reason why I haven't ventured to recommend long ago that you should get rid of Mrs. Unthank."

"She is still in attendance upon Lady Dominey, then?"

"Simply because we couldn't get any one else to stay there," the lawyer explained, "and her ladyship positively declines to leave the Hall. Between ourselves, I think it's time a change was made. We'll have a chat after dinner, if you've no objection.—You see, we've left all the trees in the park," he went on, with an air of satisfaction. "Beautiful place, this, in the springtime. I was down last May for a night, and I never saw such buttercups in my life. The cows here were almost up to their knees in pasture, and the bluebells in the home woods were wonderful. The whole of the little paint-ing colony down at Flankney turned themselves loose upon the place last spring."

"Some of the old wall is down, I see," Dominey remarked with a frown, as he gazed towards the enclosed kitchen garden.

Mr. Mangan was momentarily surprised.

"That wall has been down, to my knowledge, for twenty years," he reminded his companion.

Dominey nodded. "I had forgotten," he muttered.

"We wrote you, by the by," the lawyer continued, "suggesting the sale of one or two of the pictures, to form a fund for repairs, but thank goodness you didn't reply! We'll have some work-people here as soon as you've decided what you'd like done. I'm afraid," he added, as they turned in through some iron gates and entered the last sweep in front of the house, "you won't find many familiar faces to welcome you. There's Lovey-bond, the gardener, whom you would scarcely remember, and Middleton, the head keeper, who has really been a godsend so far as the game is concerned. No one at all indoors, except—Mrs. Unthank."

The car drew up at that moment in front of the great porch. There was nothing in the shape of a reception. They had even to ring the bell before the door was opened by a manservant sent down a few days previously from town. In the background, wearing a brown velveteen coat, with breeches and leggings of corduroy, stood an elderly man with white side whiskers and skin as brown as a piece of parchment, leaning heavily upon a long ash stick. Half a dozen maidservants, new importations, were visible in the background, and a second man was taking possession of the luggage. Mr. Mangan took charge of the proceedings.

"Middleton," he said, resting his hand upon the old man's shoulder, "here's your master come back again. Sir Everard was very pleased to hear that you were still here; and you, Loveybond."

The old man grasped the hand which Dominey stretched out with both of his.

"I'm right glad you're back again, Squire," he said, looking at him with curious intentness, "and yet the words of welcome stick in my throat."

"Sorry you feel like that about it, Middleton," Dominey said pleasantly. "What is the trouble about my coming back, eh?"

"That's no trouble, Squire," the old man replied. "That's a joy—leastways to us. It's what it may turn out to be for you which makes one hold back like."

Dominey drew himself more than ever erect—a commanding figure in the little group.

"You will feel better about it when we have had a day or two with the pheasants, Middleton," he said reassuringly. "You have not changed much, Loveybond," he added, turning to the man who had fallen a little into the background, very stiff and uncomfortable in his Sunday clothes.

"I thankee, Squire," the latter replied a little awkwardly, with a motion of his hand towards his forehead. "I can't say the same for you, sir. Them furrin parts has filled you out and hardened you. I'll take the liberty of saying that I should never have recognised you, sir, and that's sure."

"This is Parkins," Mr. Mangan went on, pushing his way once more into the foreground, "the butler whom I engaged in London. And—"

There was a queer and instantaneous silence. The little group of maidservants, who had been exchanging whispered confidences as to their new master's appearance, were suddenly dumb. All eyes were turned in one direction. A woman whose advent had been unperceived, but who had evidently issued from one of the recesses of the hall, stood suddenly before them all. She was as thin as a lath, dressed in severe black, with grey hair brushed back from her head and not even a white collar at her neck. Her face was long and narrow, her features curiously large, her eyes filled with anger. She spoke very slowly, but with some trace in her intonation of a north-country dialect.

"There's no place in this house for you, Everard Dominey," she said, standing in front of him as though to bar his progress. "I wrote last night to stop you, but you've shown indecent haste in coming. There's no place here for a murderer. Get back where you came from, back to your hiding."

"My good woman!" Mangan gasped. "This is really too much!"

"I've not come to bandy words with lawyers," the woman retorted. "I've come to speak to him. Can you face me, Everard Dominey, you who murdered my son and made a madwoman of your wife?"

The lawyer would have answered her, but Dominey waved him on one side.

"Mrs. Unthank," he said sternly, "return to your duties at once, and understand that this house is mine, to enter or leave when I choose."

She was speechless for a moment, amazed at the firmness of his words.

"The house may be yours, Sir Everard Dominey," she said threateningly, "but there's one part of it at least in which you won't dare to show yourself."

"You forget yourself, woman," he replied coldly. "Be so good as to return to your mistress at once, announce my coming, and say that I wait only for her permission before presenting myself in her apartments."

The woman laughed, unpleasantly, horribly. Her eyes were fixed upon Dominey curiously.

"Those are brave words," she said. "You've come back a harder man. Let me look at you."

She moved a foot or two to where the light was better. Very slowly a frown developed upon her forehead. The longer she looked, the less assured she became.

"There are things in your face I miss," she muttered.

Mr. Mangan was glad of an opportunity of asserting himself.

"The fact is scarcely important, Mrs. Unthank," he said angrily. "If you will allow me to give you a word of advice, you will treat your master with the respect to which his position here entitles him."

Once more the woman blazed up.

"Respect! What respect have I for the murderer of my son? Respect! Well, if he stays here against my bidding, perhaps her ladyship will show him what respect means."

She turned around and disappeared. Every one began bustling about the luggage and talking at once. Mr. Mangan took his patron's arm and led him across the hall.

"My dear Sir Everard," he said anxiously, "I am most distressed that this should have occurred. I thought that the woman would probably be sullen, but I had no idea that she would dare to attempt such an outrageous proceeding."

"She is still, I presume, the only companion whom Lady Domi006ney will tolerate?" Dominey enquired with a sigh.

"I fear so," the lawyer admitted. "Nevertheless we must see Doctor Harrison in the morning. It must be understood distinctly that if she is suffered to remain, she adopts an entirely different attitude. I never heard anything so preposterous in all my life. I shall pay her a visit myself after dinner.—You will feel quite at home here in the library, Sir Everard," Mr. Mangan went on, throwing open the door of a very fine apartment on the seaward side of the house. "Grand view from these windows, especially since we've had a few of the trees cut down. I see that Parkins has set out the sherry. Cocktails, I'm afraid, are an institution you will have to inaugurate down here. You'll be grateful to me when I tell you one thing, Sir Everard. We've been hard pressed more than once, but we haven't sold a single bottle of wine out of the cellars."

Dominey accepted the glass of sherry which the lawyer had poured out but made no movement towards drinking it. He seemed during the last few minutes to have been wrapped in a brown study.

"Mangan," he asked a little abruptly, "is it the popular belief down here that I killed Roger Unthank?"

The lawyer set down the decanter and coughed.

"A plain answer," Dominey insisted.

Mr. Mangan adapted himself to the situation. He was beginning to understand his client.

"I am perfectly certain, Sir Everard," he confessed, "that there isn't a soul in these parts who isn't convinced of it. They believe that there was a fight and that you had the best of it."

"Forgive me," Dominey continued, "if I seem to ask unnecessary questions. Remember that I spent the first portion of my exile in Africa in a very determined effort to blot out the memory of everything that had happened to me earlier in life. So that is the popular belief?"

"The popular belief seems to match fairly well with the facts," Mr. Mangan declared, wielding the decanter again in view of his client's more reasonable manner. "At the time of your unfortunate visit to the Hall Miss Felbrigg was living practically alone at the Vicarage after her uncle's sudden death there, with Mrs. Unthank as housekeeper. Roger Unthank's infatuation for her was patent to the whole neighbourhood and a source of great annoyance to Miss Felbrigg. I am convinced that at no time did Lady Dominey give the young man the slightest encouragement."

"Has any one ever believed the contrary?" Dominey demanded.

"Not a soul," was the emphatic reply. "Nevertheless, when you came down, fell in love with Miss Felbrigg and carried her off, every one felt that there would be trouble."

"Roger Unthank was a lunatic," Dominey pronounced deliberately. "His behaviour from the first was the behaviour of a madman."

"The Eugene Aram type of village schoolmaster gradually drifting into positive insanity," Mangan acquiesced. "So far, every one is agreed. The mystery began when he came back from his holidays and heard the news."

"The sequel was perfectly simple," Dominey observed. "We met at the north end of the Black Wood one evening, and he attacked me like a madman. I suppose I had to some extent the best of it, but when I got back to the Hall my arm was broken, I was covered with blood, and half unconscious. By some cruel stroke of fortune, almost the first person I saw was Lady Dominey. The shock was too much for her—she fainted and—"

"And has never been quite herself since," the lawyer concluded. "Most tragic!"

"The cruel part of it was," Dominey went on, standing before the window, his hands clasped behind his back, "that my wife from that moment developed a homicidal mania against me—I, who had fought in the most absolute self-defence. That was what drove me out of the country, Mangan—not the fear of being arrested for having caused the death of Roger Unthank. I'd have stood my trial for that at any moment. It was the other thing that broke me up."

"Quite so," Mangan murmured sympathetically. "As a matter of fact, you were perfectly safe from arrest, as it happened. The body of Roger Unthank has never been found from that day to this."

"If it had—"

"You must have been charged with either murder or manslaughter."

Dominey abandoned his post at the window and raised his glass of sherry to his lips. The tragical side of these reminiscences seemed, so far as he was concerned, to have passed.

"I suppose," he remarked, "it was the disappearance of the body which has given rise to all this talk as to his spirit still inhabiting the Black Wood."

"Without a doubt," the lawyer acquiesced. "The place had a bad name already, as you know. As it is, I don't suppose there's a villager here would cross the park in that direction after dark."

Dominey glanced at his watch and led the way from the room.

"After dinner," he promised, "I'll tell you a few West African superstitions which will make our local one seem anæmic."

# CHAPTER IX

"I CERTAINLY OFFER you my heartiest congratulations upon your cellars, Sir Everard," his guest said, as he sipped his third glass of port that evening. "This is the finest glass of seventy I've drunk for a long time, and this new fellow I've sent you down—Parkins—tells me there's any quantity of it."

"It has had a pretty long rest," Dominey observed.

"I was looking through the cellar-book before dinner," the lawyer went on, "and I see that you still have forty-seven and forty-eight, and a small quantity of two older vintages. Something ought to be done about those."

"We will try one of them tomorrow night," Dominey suggested. "We might spend half an hour or so in the cellars, if we have any time to spare."

"And another half an hour," Mr. Mangan said gravely, "I should like to spend in interviewing Mrs. Unthank. Apart from any other question, I do not for one moment believe that she is the proper person to be entrusted with the care of Lady Dominey. I made up my mind to speak to you on this subject, Sir Everard, as soon as we had arrived here."

"Mrs. Unthank was old Mr. Felbrigg's housekeeper and my wife's nurse when she was a child," Dominey reminded his companion. "Whatever her faults may be, I believe she is devoted to Lady Dominey."

"She may be devoted to your wife," the lawyer admitted, "but I am convinced that she is your enemy. The situation doesn't seem to me to be consistent. Mrs. Unthank is firmly convinced that, whether in fair fight or not, you killed her son. Lady Dominey believes that, too, and it was the sight of you after the fight that sent her insane. I cannot but believe that it would be far better for Lady Dominey to have some one with her unconnected with this unfortunate chapter of your past."

"We will consult Doctor Harrison tomorrow," Dominey said. "I am very glad you came down with me, Mangan," he went on, after a minute's hesitation. "I find it very difficult to get back into the atmosphere of those days. I even find it hard sometimes," he added, with a curious little glance across the table, "to believe that I am the same man."

"Not so hard as I have done more than once," Mr. Mangan confessed.

"Tell me exactly in what respects you consider me changed?" Dominey insisted.

The lawyer hesitated.

"You seem to have lost a certain pliability, or perhaps I ought to call it looseness of disposition," he admitted. "There are many things connected with the past which I find it almost impossible to associate with you. For a trifling instance," he went on, with a slight smile, inclining his head towards his host's untasted glass. "You don't drink port like any Dominey I ever knew."

"I'm afraid that I never acquired the taste for port," Dominey observed.

The lawyer gazed at him with raised eyebrows.

"Not acquired the taste for port?" he repeated blankly.

"I should have said reacquired," Dominey hastened to explain. "You see, in the bush we drank a simply frightful amount of spirits, and that vitiates the taste for all wine."

The lawyer glanced enviously at his host's fine bronzed complexion and clear eyes.

"You haven't the appearance of ever having drunk anything, Sir Everard," he observed frankly. "One finds it hard to believe the stories that were going about ten or fifteen years ago."

"The Dominey constitution, I suppose!"

The new butler entered the room noiselessly and came to his master's chair.

"I have served coffee in the library, sir," he announced. "Mr. Middleton, the gamekeeper, has just called, and asks if he could have a word with you before he goes to bed tonight, sir. He seems in a very nervous and uneasy state."

"He can come to the library at once," Dominey directed; "that is, if you are ready for your coffee, Mangan."

"Indeed I am," the lawyer assented, rising. "A great treat, that wine. One thing the London restaurants can't give us. Port should never be drunk away from the place where it was laid down."

The two men made their way across the very fine hall, the walls of which had suffered a little through lack of heating, into the library, and seated themselves in easy-chairs before the blazing log fire. Parkins silently served them with coffee and brandy. He had scarcely left the room before there was a timid knock and Middleton made his somewhat hesitating entrance.

"Come in and close the door," Dominey directed. "What is it, Middleton? Parkins says you wish to speak to me."

The man came hesitatingly forward. He was obviously distressed and uneasy, and found speech difficult. His face glistened with the rain which had found its way, too, in long streaks down his velveteen coat. His white hair was wind-tossed and disarranged.

"Bad night," Dominey remarked.

"It's to save its being a worse one that I'm here, Squire," the old man replied hoarsely. "I've come to ask you a favour and to beg you to grant it for your own sake. You'll not sleep in the oak room tonight?"

"And why not?" Dominey asked.

"It's next to her ladyship's."

"Well?"

The old man was obviously perturbed, but his master, as though of a purpose, refused to help him. He glanced at Mangan and mumbled to himself.

"Say exactly what you wish to, Middleton," Dominey invited. "Mr. Mangan and his father and grandfather have been solicitors to the estate for a great many years. They know all our family history."

"I can't get rightly into touch with you, Squire, and that's a fact," Middleton went on despairingly. "The shape of you seems larger and your voice harder. I don't seem to be so near to you as I'd wished, to say what's in my heart."

"I have had a rough time, Middleton," Dominey reminded him. "No wonder I have changed! Never mind, speak to me just as man to man."

"It was I who first met you, Squire," the old man went on, "when you tottered home that night across the park, with your arm hanging helplessly by your side, and the blood streaming down your face and clothes, and the red light in your eyes— murderous fire, they called it. I heard her ladyship go into hysterics. I saw her laugh and sob like a maniac, and, God help us! that's what she's been ever since."

The two men were silent. Middleton had raised his voice, speaking with fierce excitement. It was obvious that he had only paused for breath. He had more to say.

"I was by your side, Squire," he went on, "when her ladyship caught up the knife and ran at you, and, as you well know, it was I, seizing her from behind, that saved a double tragedy that night, and it was I who went for the doctor the next morning, when she'd stolen into your room in the night and missed your throat by a bare inch. I heard her call to you, heard her threat. It was a madwoman's threat, Squire, but her ladyship is a madwoman at this moment, and with a knife in her hand you'll never be safe in this house."

"We must see," Dominey said quietly, "that she is not allowed to get possession of any weapon."

"Aye! Make sure of that," Middleton scoffed, "with Mother Unthank by her side! Her ladyship's mad because of the horror of that night, but Mother Unthank is mad with hate, and there isn't a week passes," the old man went on, his voice dropping lower and his eyes burning, "that Roger Unthank's spirit doesn't come and howl for your blood beneath their window. If you stay here this night, Squire, come over and sleep in the little room they've got ready for you on the other side of the house."

Mr. Mangan had lost his smooth, after-dinner appearance. His face was distinctly pale, his smoothly brushed hair was rumpled, and his coffee was growing cold. This was a very different thing from the vague letters and rumours which had reached him from time to time and which he had put out of his mind with all the contempt of the materialist.

"It is very good of you to warn me, Middleton," Dominey said, "but I can lock my door, can I not?"

"Lock the door of the oak room!" was the scornful reply. "And what good would that do? You know well enough that the wall's double on three sides, and there are more secret entrances than even I know of. The oak room's not for you this night, Squire. It's hoping to get you there that's keeping them quiet."

"Tell us what you meant, Middleton," the lawyer asked, with ill-assumed indifference, "when you spoke of the howling of Roger Unthank's spirit?"

The old man turned patiently around.

"Just that, sir," he replied. "It's round the house most weeks. Except for me odd nights, and Mrs. Unthank, there's been scarcely a servant would sleep in the Hall for years. Some of the maids they do come up from the village, but back they go before nightfall, and until morning there isn't a living soul would cross the park—no, not for a hundred pounds."

"A howl, you call it?" Mr. Mangan observed.

"That's mostly like a dog what's hurt itself," Middleton explained equably, "like a dog, that is, with a touch of the human in its throat, as we've all heard in our time, sir. You'll hear it yourself, sir, maybe tonight or tomorrow night."

"You've heard it then, Middleton?" his master asked.

"Why, surely, sir," the old man replied in surprise. "Most weeks for the last ten years."

"Haven't you ever got up and gone out to see what it was?"

The old man shook his head.

"But I knew right well what that was, sir," he said, "and I'm not one for looking on spirits. Spirits there are that walk this world, as we well know, and the spirit of Roger Unthank walks from between the Black Wood and these windows, come every week of the year. But I'm not for looking at him. There's evil comes of that. I turn over in my bed, and I stop my ears, but I've never yet raised a blind."

"Tell me, Middleton," Dominey asked, "is Lady Dominey terrified at these—er—visitations?"

"That I can't rightly say, sir. Her ladyship's always sweet and gentle, with kind words on her lips for every one, but there's the terror there in her eyes that was lit that night when you staggered into the hall, Squire, and I've never seen it properly quenched yet, so to speak. She carries fear with her, but whether it's the fear of seeing you again, or the fear of Roger Unthank's spirit, I could not tell."

Dominey seemed suddenly to become possessed of a strange desire to thrust the whole subject away. He dismissed the old man kindly but a little abruptly, accompanying him to the corridor which led to the servants' quarters and talking all the time about the pheasants. When he returned, he found that his guest had emptied his second glass of brandy and was surreptitiously mopping his forehead.

"That," the latter remarked, "is the class of old retainer who lives too long. If I were a Dominey of the Middle Ages, I think a stone around his neck and the deepest well would be the sensible way of dealing with him. He made me feel positively uncomfortable."

"I noticed it," Dominey remarked, with a faint smile. "I'm not going to pretend that it was a pleasant conversation myself."

"I've heard some ghost stories," Mangan went on, "but a spook that comes and howls once a week for ten years takes some beating."

Dominey poured himself out a glass of brandy with a steady hand.

"You've been neglecting things here, Mangan," he complained. "You ought to have come down and exorcised that ghost. We shall have those smart maidservants of yours off tomorrow, I suppose, unless you and I can get a little ghost-laying in first."

Mr. Mangan began to feel more comfortable. The brandy and the warmth of the burning logs were creeping into his system.

"By the by, Sir Everard," he enquired, a little later on, "where are you going to sleep tonight?"

Dominey stretched himself out composedly.

"There is obviously only one place for me," he replied. "I can't disappoint any one. I shall sleep in the oak room."

## CHAPTER X

FOR the first few tangled moments of nightmare, slowly developing into a live horror, Dominey fancied himself back in Africa, with the hand of an enemy upon his throat. Then a rush of awakened memories—the silence of the great house, the mysterious rustling of the heavy hangings around the black oak four-poster on which he lay, the faint pricking of something deadly at his throat—these things rolled back the curtain of unreality, brought him acute and painful consciousness of a situation almost appalling. He opened his eyes, and although a brave and callous man he lay still, paralysed with the fear which forbids motion. The dim light of a candle, recently lit, flashed upon the bodkin-like dagger held at his throat. He gazed at the thin line of gleaming steel, fascinated. Already his skin had been broken, a few drops of blood were upon the collar of his pyjamas. The hand which held that deadly, assailing weapon—small, slim, very feminine, curving from somewhere behind the bed curtain—belonged to some unseen person. He tried to shrink farther back upon the pillow. The hand followed him, displaying glimpses now of a soft, white-sleeved arm. He lay quite still, the muscles of his right arm growing tenser as he prepared for a snatch at those cruel fingers. Then a voice came,—a slow, feminine and rather wonderful voice.

"If you move," it said, "you will die. Remain quite still."

Dominey was fully conscious now, his brain at work, calculating his chances with all the cunning of the trained hunter who seeks to avoid death. Reluctantly he was compelled to realise that no movement of his could be quick enough to prevent the driving of that thin stiletto into his throat, if his hidden assailant should keep her word. So he lay still.

"Why do you want to kill me?" he asked, a little tensely.

There was no reply, yet somehow he knew that he was being watched. Ever so slightly those curtains around which the arm had come were being parted. Through the chink some one was looking at him. The thought came that he might call out for help, and once more his unseen enemy read his thought.

"You must be very quiet," the voice said,—that voice which it was difficult for him to believe was not the voice of a child. "If you even speak above a whisper, it will be the end. I wish to look at you."

A little wider the crack opened, and then he began to feel hope. The hand which held the stiletto was shaking, he heard something which sounded like quick breathing from behind the curtains—the breathing of a woman astonished or terrified—and then, so suddenly that for several seconds he could not move or take advantage of the circumstance, the hand with its cruel weapon was withdrawn around the curtain and a woman began to laugh, softly at first, and then with a little hysterical sob thrusting its way through that incongruous note of mirth.

He lay upon the bed as though mesmerised, finding at his first effort that his limbs refused their office, as might the limbs of one lying under the thrall of a nightmare. The laugh died away, there was a sound like a scraping upon the wall, the candle was suddenly blown out. Then his nerve began to return and with it his control over his limbs. He crawled to the side of the bed remote from the curtains, stole to the little table on which he had left his revolver and an electric torch, snatched at them, and, with the former in his right hand, flashed a little orb of light into the shadows of the great apartment. Once more something like terror seized him. The figure which had been standing by the side of his bed had vanished. There was no hiding place in view. Every inch of the room was lit up by the powerful torch he carried, and, save for himself, the room was empty. The first moment of realisation was chill and unnerving. Then the slight smarting of the wound at his throat became convincing proof to him that there was nothing supernatural about this visit. He lit up a half dozen of the candles distributed about the place and laid down his torch. He was ashamed to find that his forehead was dripping with perspiration.

"One of the secret-passages, of course," he muttered to himself, stooping for a moment to examine the locked, folding doors which separated his room from the adjoining one. "Perhaps, when one reflects, I have run unnecessary risks."

Dominey was standing at the window, looking out at the tumbled grey waters of the North Sea, when Parkins brought him hot water and tea in the morning. He thrust his feet into slippers and held out his arms for a dressing-gown.

"Find out where the nearest bathroom is, Parkins," he ordered, "and prepare it. I have quite forgotten my way about here."

"Very good, sir."

The man was motionless for a moment, staring at the blood on his master's pyjamas. Dominey glanced down at it and turned the dressing-gown up to his throat.

"I had a slight accident this morning," he remarked carelessly. "Any ghost alarms last night?"

"None that I heard of, sir," the man replied. "I am afraid we should have difficulty in keeping the young women from London, if they heard what I heard the night of my arrival."

"Very terrible, was it?" Dominey asked with a smile.

Parkins' expression remained immovable. There was in his tone, however, a mute protest against his master's levity.

"The cries were the most terrible I have ever heard, sir," he said. "I am not a nervous person, but I found them most disturbing."

"Human or animal?"

"A mixture of both, I should say, sir."

"You should camp out for the night on the skirts of an African forest," Dominey remarked. "There you get a whole orchestra of wild animals, every one of them trying to freeze your blood up."

"I was out in South Africa during the Boer War, sir," Parkins replied, "and I went big-game hunting with my master afterwards. I do not think that any animal was ever born in Africa with so terrifying a cry as we heard the night before last."

"We must look into the matter," Dominey muttered.

"I have already prepared a bath, sir, at the end of the corridor," the man announced. "If you will allow me, I will show you the way."

Dominey, when he descended about an hour later, found his guest awaiting him in a smaller dining-room, which looked out eastwards towards the sea, a lofty apartment with great windows and with an air of faded splendour which came from the ill-cared-for tapestries, hanging in places from the wall. Mr. Mangan had, contrary to his expectations, slept well and was in excellent spirits. The row of silver dishes upon the sideboard inspired him with an added cheerfulness.

"So there were no ghosts walking last night, eh?" he remarked, as he took his place at the table. "Wonderful thing this absolute quiet is after London. Give you my word, I never heard a sound from the moment my head touched the pillow until I woke a short while ago."

Dominey returned from the sideboard, carrying also a well-filled plate.

"I had a pretty useful night's rest myself," he observed.

Mangan raised his eyeglass and gazed at his host's throat.

"Cut yourself, eh?" he queried.

"Razor slipped," Dominey told him. "You get out of the use of those things in Africa."

"You've managed to give yourself a nasty gash," Mr. Mangan observed curiously.

"Parkins is going to send up for a new set of safety razors for me," Dominey announced. "About our plans for the day,—I've ordered the car for two-thirty this afternoon, if that suits you. We can look around the place quietly this morning. Mr. Johnson is sleeping over at a farmhouse near here. We shall pick him up en route. And I have told Lees, the bailiff, to come with us too."

Mr. Mangan nodded his approval.

"Upon my word," he confessed, "it will be a joy to me to go and see some of these fellows without having to put 'em off about repairs and that sort of thing. Johnson has had the worst of it, poor chap, but there are one or two of them took it into their heads to come up to London and worry me at the office."

"I intend that there shall be no more dissatisfaction amongst my tenants."

Mr. Mangan set off for another prowl towards the sideboard.

"Satisfied tenants you never will get in Norfolk," he declared. "I must admit, though, that some of them have had cause to grumble lately. There's a fellow round by Wells who farms nearly eight hundred acres—"

He broke off in his speech. There was a knock at the door, not an ordinary knock at all, but a measured, deliberate tapping, three times repeated.

"Come in," Dominey called out.

Mrs. Unthank entered, severer, more unattractive than ever in the hard morning light. She came to the end of the table, facing the place where Dominey was seated.

"Good morning, Mrs. Unthank," he said.

She ignored his greeting.

"I am the bearer of a message," she announced.

"Pray deliver it," Dominey replied.

"Her ladyship would be glad for you to visit her in her apartment at once."

Dominey leaned back in his chair. His eyes were fixed upon the face of the woman whose antagonism to himself was so apparent. She stood in the path of a long gleam of morning sunlight. The wrinkles in her face, her hard mouth, her cold, steely eyes were all clearly revealed.

"I am not at all sure," he said, with a purpose in his words, "that any further meeting between Lady Dominey and myself is at present desirable."

If he had thought to disturb this messenger by his suggestion, he was disappointed.

"Her ladyship desires me to assure you," she added, with a note of contempt in her tone, "that you need be under no apprehension."

Dominey admitted defeat and poured himself out some more coffee. Neither of the two noticed that his fingers were trembling.

"Her ladyship is very considerate," he said. "Kindly say that I shall follow you in a few minutes."

Dominey, following within a very few minutes of his summons, was ushered into an apartment large and sombrely elegant, an apartment of faded white and gold walls, of chandeliers glittering with lustres, of Louis Quinze furniture, shabby but priceless. To his surprise, although he scarcely noticed it at the time, Mrs. Unthank promptly disappeared. He was from the first left alone with the woman whom he had come to visit.

She was sitting up on her couch and watching his approach. A woman? Surely only a child, with pale cheeks, large, anxious eyes, and masses of brown hair brushed back from her forehead. After all, was he indeed a strong man, vowed to great things? There was a queer feeling in his throat, almost a mist before his eyes. She seemed so fragile, so utterly, sweetly pathetic. And all the time there was the strange light, or was it want of light, in those haunting eyes. His speech of greeting was never spoken.

"So you have come to see me, Everard," she said, in a broken tone. "You are very brave."

He possessed himself of her hand, the hand which a few hours ago had held a dagger to his throat, and kissed the wax-enlike fingers. It fell to her side like a lifeless thing. Then she raised it and began rubbing softly at the place where his lips had fallen.

"I have come to see you at your bidding," he replied, "and for my pleasure."

"Pleasure!" she murmured, with a ghastly little smile. "You have learned to control your words, Everard. You have slept here and you live. I have broken my word. I wonder why?"

"Because," he pleaded, "I have not deserved that you should seek my life."

"That sounds strangely," she reflected. "Doesn't it say somewhere in the Bible—'A life for a life'? You killed Roger Unthank."

"I have killed other men since in self-defence," Dominey told her. "Sometimes it comes to a man that he must slay or be slain. It was Roger Unthank—"

"I shall not talk about him any longer," she decided quite calmly. "The night before last, his spirit was calling to me below my window. He wants me to go down into Hell and live with him. The very thought is horrible."

"Come," Dominey said, "we will speak of other things. You must tell me what presents I can buy you. I have come back from Africa rich."

"Presents?"

For a single wonderful moment, hers was the face of a child who has been offered toys. Her smile of anticipation was delightful, her eyes had lost that strange vacancy. Then, before he could say another word, it all came back again.

"Listen to me," she said. "This is important. I have sent for you because I do not understand why, quite suddenly last night, after I had made up my mind, I lost the desire to kill you. It is gone now. I am not sure about myself any longer. Draw your chair nearer to mine. Or no, come to my side, here at the other end of the sofa."

She moved her skirts to make room for him. When he sat down, he felt a strange trembling through all his limbs.

"Perhaps," she went on, "I shall break my oath. Indeed, I have already broken it. Let me look at you, my husband. It is a strange thing to own after all these years—a husband."

Dominey felt as though he were breathing an atmosphere of turgid and poisoned sweetness. There was a flavour of unreality about the whole situation,—the room, this child woman, her beauty, her deliberate, halting speech and the strange things she said.

"You find me changed?" he asked.

"You are very wonderfully changed. You look stronger, you are perhaps better-looking, yet there is something gone from your face which I thought one never lost."

"You," he said cautiously, "are more beautiful than ever, Rosamund."

She laughed a little drearily.

"Of what use has my beauty been to me, Everard, since you came to my little cottage and loved me and made me love you, and took me away from Dour Roger? Do you remember the school children used to call him Dour Roger?—But that does not matter. Do you know, Everard, that since you left me my feet have not passed outside these gardens?"

"That can be altered when you wish," he said quickly. "You can visit where you will. You can have a motor-car, even a house in town. I shall bring some wonderful doctors here, and they will make you quite strong again."

Her large eyes were lifted almost piteously to his.

"But how can I leave here?" she asked plaintively. "Every week, sometimes oftener, he calls to me. If I went away, his spirit would break loose and follow me. I must be here to wave my hand; then he goes away."

Dominey was conscious once more of that strange and most unexpected fit of emotion. He was unrecognisable even to himself. Never before in his life had his heart beaten as it was beating now. His eyes, too, were hot. He had travelled around the world in search of new things, only to find them in this strange, faded chamber, side by side with this suffering woman. Nevertheless, he said quietly:

"We must send you some place where the people are kinder and where life is pleasanter. Perhaps you love music and to see beautiful pictures. I think that we must try and keep you from thinking."

She sighed in a perplexed fashion.

"I wish that I could get it out of my blood that I want to kill you. Then you could take me right away. Other married people have lived together and hated each other. Why shouldn't we? We may forget even to hate."

Dominey staggered to his feet, walked to a window, threw it open and leaned out for a moment. Then he closed it and came back. This new element in the situation had been a shock to him. All the time she was watching him composedly.

"Well?" she asked, with a strange little smile. "What do you say? Would you like to hold as a wife's the hand which frightened you so last night?"

She held it out to him, soft and warm. Her fingers even returned the pressure of his. She looked at him pleasantly, and once more he felt like a man who has wandered into a strange country and has lost his bearings.

"I want you so much to be happy," he said hoarsely, "but you are not strong yet, Rosamund. We cannot decide anything in a hurry."

"How surprised you are to find that I am willing to be nice to you!" she murmured. "But why not? You cannot know why I have so suddenly changed my mind about you—and I have changed it. I have seen the truth these few minutes. There is a reason, Everard, why I should not kill you."

"What is it?" he demanded.

She shook her head with all the joy of a child who keeps a secret.

"You are clever," she said. "I will leave you to find it out. I am excited now, and I want you to go away for a little time. Please send Mrs. Unthank to me."

The prospect of release was a strange relief, mingled still more strangely with regret. He lingered over her hand.

"If you walk in your sleep tonight, then," he begged, "you will leave your dagger behind?"

"I have told you," she answered, as though surprised, "that I have abandoned my intention. I shall not kill you. Even though I may walk in my sleep—and sometimes the nights are so long—it will not be your death I seek."

# CHAPTER XI

Dominey left the room like a man in a dream, descended the stairs to his own part of the house, caught up a hat and stick and strode out into the sea mist which was fast enveloping the gardens. There was all the chill of the North Pole in that ice-cold cloud of vapour, but nevertheless his forehead remained hot, his pulses burning. He passed out of the postern gate which led from the walled garden on to a broad marsh, with dikes running here and there, and lapping tongues of sea water creeping in with the tide. He made his way seaward with uncertain steps until he reached a rough and stony road; here he hesitated for a moment, looked about him, and then turned back at right angles. Soon he came to a little village, a village of ancient cottages, with seasoned, red-brick tiles, trim little patches of garden, a church embowered with tall elm trees, a triangular green at the cross-roads. On one side a low, thatched building,—the Dominey Arms; on another, an ancient, square, stone house, on which was a brass plate. He went over and read the name, rang the bell, and asked the trim maidservant who answered it, for the doctor. Presently, a man of youthful middle-age presented himself in the surgery and bowed. Dominey was for a moment at a loss.

"I came to see Doctor Harrison," he ventured.

"Doctor Harrison retired from practice some years ago," was the courteous reply. "I am his nephew. My name is Stillwell."

"I understood that Doctor Harrison was still in the neighbourhood," Dominey said. "My name is Dominey—Sir Everard Dominey."

"I guessed as much," the other replied. "My uncle lives with me here, and to tell you the truth he was hoping that you would come and see him. He retains one patient only," Doctor

Stillwell added, in a graver tone. "You can imagine who that would be."

His caller bowed. "Lady Dominey, I presume."

The young doctor opened the door and motioned to his guest to precede him.

"My uncle has his own little apartment on the other side of the house," he said. "You must let me take you to him."

They moved across the pleasant white stone hall into a small apartment with French windows leading out to a flagged terrace and tennis lawn. An elderly man, broad-shouldered, with weather-beaten face, grey hair, and of somewhat serious aspect, looked around from the window before which he was standing examining a case of fishing flies.

"Uncle, I have brought an old friend in to see you," his nephew announced.

The doctor glanced expectantly at Dominey, half moved forward as though to greet him, then checked himself and shook his head doubtfully.

"You certainly remind me very much of an old friend, sir," he said, "but I can see now that you are not he. I do not believe that I have ever seen you before in my life."

There was a moment's somewhat tense silence. Then Dominey advanced a little stiffly and held out his hand.

"Come, Doctor," he said, "I can scarcely have changed as much as all that. Even these years of strenuous life—"

"You mean to tell me that I am speaking to Everard Dominey?" the doctor interposed.

"Without a doubt!"

The doctor shook hands coolly. His was certainly not the enthusiastic welcome of an old family attendant to the representative of a great family.

"I should certainly never have recognised you," he confessed.

"My presence here is nevertheless indisputable," Dominey continued. "Still attracted by your old pastime, I see, Doctor?"

"I have only taken up fly fishing," the other replied drily, "since I gave up shooting."

There was another somewhat awkward pause, which the younger man endeavoured to bridge over.

"Fishing, shooting, golf," he said; "I really don't know what we poor medical practitioners would do in the country without sport."

"I shall remind you of that later," Dominey observed. "I am told that the shooting is one of the only glories which has not passed away from Dominey."

"I shall look forward to the reminder," was the prompt response.

His uncle, who had been bending once more over the case of flies, turned abruptly around.

"Arthur," he said, addressing his nephew, "you had better start on your round. I dare say Sir Everard would like to speak to me privately."

"I wish to speak to you certainly," Dominey admitted, "but only professionally. There is no necessity—"

"I am late already, if you will excuse me," Doctor Stillwell interrupted. "I will be getting on. You must excuse my uncle, Sir Everard," he added in a lower tone, drawing him a little towards the door, "if his manners are a little gruff. He is devoted to Lady Dominey, and I sometimes think that he broods over her case too much."

Dominey nodded and turned back into the room to find the doctor, his hands in his old-fashioned breeches pockets, eying him steadfastly.

"I find it very hard to believe," he said a little curtly, "that you are really Everard Dominey."

"I am afraid you will have to accept me as a fact, nevertheless."

"Your present appearance," the old man continued, eying him appraisingly, "does not in any way bear out the description I had of you some years ago. I was told that you had become a broken-down drunkard."

"The world is full of liars," Dominey said equably. "You appear to have met with one, at least."

"You have not even," the doctor persisted, "the appearance of a man who has been used to excesses of any sort."

"Good old stock, ours," his visitor observed carelessly. "Plenty of two-bottle men behind my generation."

"You have also gained courage since the days when you fled from England. You slept at the Hall last night?"

"Where else? I also, if you want to know, occupied my own bedchamber—with results," Dominey added, throwing his head a little back, to display the scar on his throat, "altogether insignificant."

"That's just your luck," the doctor declared. "You've no right to have gone there without seeing me; no right, after all that has passed, to have even approached your wife."

"You seem rather a martinet as regards my domestic affairs," Dominey observed.

"That's because I know your history," was the blunt reply.

Uninvited, Dominey seated himself in an easy-chair.

"You were never my friend, Doctor," he said. "Let me suggest that we conduct this conversation on a purely professional basis."

"I was never your friend," came the retort, "because I have known you always as a selfish brute; because you were married to the sweetest woman on God's earth, gave up none of your bad habits, frightened her into insanity by reeling home with another man's blood on your hands, and then stayed away for over ten years instead of making an effort to repair the mischief you had done."

"This," observed Dominey, "is history, dished up in a somewhat partial fashion. I repeat my suggestion that we confine our conversation to the professional."

"This is my house," the other rejoined, "and you came to see me. I shall say exactly what I like to you, and if you don't like it you can get out. If it weren't for Lady Dominey's sake, you shouldn't have passed this threshold."

"Then for her sake," Dominey suggested in a softer tone, "can't you forget how thoroughly you disapprove of me? I am here now with only one object: I want you to point out to me any way in which we can work together for the improvement of my wife's health."

"There can be no question of a partnership between us."

"You refuse to help?"

"My help isn't worth a snap of the fingers. I have done all I can for her physically. She is a perfectly sound woman. The rest depends upon you, and you alone, and I am not very hopeful about it."

"Upon me?" Dominey repeated, a little taken aback.

"Fidelity," the doctor grunted, "is second nature with all good women. Lady Dominey is a good woman, and she is no exception to the rule. Her brain is starved because her heart is aching for love. If she could believe in your repentance and reform, if any atonement for the past were possible and were generously offered, I cannot tell what the result might be. They tell me that you are a rich man now, although heaven knows, when one considers what a lazy, selfish fellow you were, that sounds like a miracle. You could have the great specialists down. They couldn't help, but it might salve your conscience to pay them a few hundred guineas."

"Would you meet them?" Dominey asked anxiously. "Tell me whom to send for?"

"Pooh! Those days are finished with me," was the curt reply. "I would meet none of them. I am a doctor no longer. I have become a villager. I go to see Lady Dominey as an old friend."

"Give me your advice," Dominey begged. "Is it of any use sending for specialists?"

"Just for the present, none at all."

"And what about that horrible woman, Mrs. Unthank?"

"Part of your task, if you are really going to take it up. She stands between your wife and the sun."

"Then why have you suffered her to remain there all those years?" Dominey demanded.

"For one thing, because there has been no one to replace her," the doctor replied, "and for another, because Lady Dominey, believing that you slew her son, has some fantastic idea of giving her a home and shelter as a kind of expiation."

"You think there is no affection between the two?" Dominey asked.

"Not a scrap," was the blunt reply, "except that Lady Dominey is of so sweet and gentle a nature—"

The doctor paused abruptly. His visitor's fingers had strayed across his throat.

"That's a different matter," the former continued fiercely. "That's just where the weak spot in her brain remains. If you ask me, I believe it's pandered to by Mrs. Unthank. Come to think of it," he went on, "the Domineys were never cowards. If you've got your courage back, send Mrs. Unthank away, sleep with your doors wide open. If a single night passes without Lady Dominey coming to your room with a knife in her hand, she will be cured in time of that mania at any rate. Dare you do that?"

Dominey's hesitation was palpable,—also his agitation. The doctor grinned contemptuously.

"Still afraid!" he scoffed.

"Not in the way you imagine," his visitor replied. "My wife has already promised to make no further attempt upon my life."

"Well, you can cure her if you want to," the doctor declared, "and if you do, you will have the sweetest companion for life any man could have. But you'll have to give up the idea of town houses and racing and yachting, and grouse moors in Scotland, and all those sort of things I suppose you've been looking forward to. You'll have for some time, at any rate, to give every moment of your time to your wife."

Dominey moved uneasily in his chair.

"For the next few months," he said, "that would be impossible."

"Impossible!"

The doctor repeated the word, seemed to roll it round in his mouth with a sort of wondering scorn.

"I am not quite the idler I used to be," Dominey explained, frowning. "Nowadays, you cannot make money without assuming responsibilities. I am clearing off the whole of the mortgages upon the Dominey estates within the next few months."

"How you spend your time is your affair, not mine," the doctor muttered. "All that I say about the matter is that your wife's cure, if ever it comes to pass, is in your hands. And now—come over to me here, in the light of this window. I want to look at you."

Dominey obeyed with a little shrug of the shoulders. There was no sunshine, but the white north light was in its way searching. It showed the sprinkling of grey in his ruddy-brown hair, the suspicion of it in his closely trimmed moustache, but it could find no weak spot in his steady eyes, in the tan of his hard, manly complexion, or even in the set of his somewhat arrogant lips. The old doctor took up his box of flies again and jerked his head towards the door.

"You are a miracle," he said, "and I hate miracles. I'll come and see Lady Dominey in a day or so."

# CHAPTER XII

DOMINEY spent a curiously placid, and, to those with whom he was brought into contact, an entirely satisfactory afternoon. With Mr. Mangan by his side, murmuring amiable platitudes, and Mr. Johnson, his agent, opposite, revelling in the unusual situation of a satisfied landlord and delighted tenants, he made practically the entire round of the Dominey estates. They reached home late, but Dominey, although he seemed to be living in another world, was not neglectful of the claims of hospitality. Probably for the first time in their lives, Mr. Johnson and Lees, the bailiff, watched the opening of a magnum of champagne. Mr. Johnson cleared his throat as he raised his glass.

"It isn't only on my own account, Sir Everard," he said, "that I drink your hearty good health. I have your tenants too in my mind. They've had a rough time, some of them, and they've stood it like white men. So here's from them and me to you, sir, and may we see plenty of you in these parts."

Mr. Lees associated himself with these sentiments, and the glasses were speedily emptied and filled again.

"I suppose you know, Sir Everard," the agent observed, "that what you've promised to do today will cost a matter of ten to fifteen thousand pounds."

Dominey nodded.

"Before I go to bed tonight," he said, "I shall send a cheque for twenty thousand pounds to the estate account at your bank at Wells. The money is there waiting, put aside for just that one purpose and—well, you may just as well have it."

Agent and bailiff leaned back in the tonneau of their motor-car, half an hour later, with immense cigars in their mouths and a pleasant, rippling warmth in their veins. They had the sense of having drifted into fairyland. Their philosophy, however, met the situation.

"It's a fair miracle," Mr. Lees declared.

"A modern romance," Mr. Johnson, who reads novels, murmured. "Hello, here's a visitor for the Hall," he added, as a car swept by them.

"Comfortable-looking gent, too," Mr. Lees remarked.

The "comfortable-looking gent" was Otto Seaman, who presented himself at the Hall with a small dressing-bag and a great many apologies.

"Found myself in Norwich, Sir Everard," he explained. "I have done business there all my life, and one of my customers needed looking after. I finished early, and when I found that I was only thirty miles off you, I couldn't resist having a run across. If it is in any way inconvenient to put me up for the night, say so—"

"My dear fellow!" Dominey interrupted. "There are a score of rooms ready. All that we need is to light a fire, and an old-fashioned bed-warmer will do the rest. You remember Mr. Mangan?"

The two men shook hands, and Seaman accepted a little refreshment after his drive. He lingered behind for a moment after the dressing bell had rung.

"What time is that fellow going?" he asked.

"Nine o'clock tomorrow morning," Dominey replied.

"Not a word until then," Seaman whispered back. "I must not seem to be hanging after you too much—I really did not want to come—but the matter is urgent."

"We can send Mangan to bed early," Dominey suggested.

"I am the early bird myself," was the weary reply. "I was up all last night. Tomorrow morning will do."

Dinner that night was a pleasant and social meal. Mr. Mangan especially was uplifted. Everything to do with the Domineys for the last fifteen years had reeked of poverty. He had really had a hard struggle to make both ends meet. There had been disagreeable interviews with angry tenants, formal interviews with dissatisfied mortgagees, and remarkably little profit at the end of the year to set against these disagreeable episodes. The new situation was almost beatific. The concluding touch, perhaps, was in Parkins' congratulatory whisper as he set a couple of decanters upon the table.

"I have found a bin of Cockburn's *fifty-one*, sir," he announced, including the lawyer in his confidential whisper. "I thought you might like to try a couple of bottles, as Mr. Mangan seems rather a connoisseur, sir. The corks appear to be in excellent condition."

"After this," Mr. Mangan sighed, "it will be hard to get back to the austere life of a Pall Mall club!"

Seaman, very early in the evening, pleaded an extraordinary sleepiness and retired, leaving his host and Mangan alone over the port. Dominey, although an attentive host, seemed still a little abstracted. Even Mr. Mangan, who was not an observant man, was conscious that a certain hardness, almost arrogance of speech and manner, seemed temporarily to have left his patron.

"I can't tell you, Sir Everard," he said, as he sipped his first glass of wine, "what a pleasure it is to me to see, as it were, this recrudescence of an old family. If I might be allowed to say so, there's only one thing necessary to round the whole business off, as it were."

"And that?" Dominey asked unthinkingly.

"The return of Lady Dominey to health. I was one of the few, you may remember, privileged to make her acquaintance at the time of your marriage."

"I paid a visit this morning," Dominey said, "to the doctor who has been in attendance upon her since her marriage.

He agrees with me that there is no reason why Lady Dominey should not, in course of time, be restored to perfect health."

"I take the liberty of finishing my glass to that hope, Sir Everard," the lawyer murmured.

Both glasses were set down empty, only the stem of Dominey's was snapped in two. Mr. Mangan expressed his polite regrets.

"This old glass," he murmured, looking at his own admiringly, "becomes very fragile."

Dominey did not answer. His brain had served him a strange trick. In the shadows of the room he had fancied that he could see Stephanie Eiderstrom holding out her arms, calling to him to fulfill the pledges of long ago, and behind her—

"Have you ever been in love, Mangan?" Dominey asked his companion.

"I, sir? Well, I'm not sure," the man of the world replied, a little startled by the abruptness of the question. "It's an old-fashioned way of looking at things now, isn't it?"

Dominey relapsed into thoughtfulness.

"I suppose so," he admitted.

That night a storm rolled up from somewhere across that grey waste of waters, a storm heralded by a wind which came booming over the marshes, shaking the latticed windows of Dominey Hall, shrieking and wailing amongst its chimneys and around its many corners. Black clouds leaned over the land, and drenching streams of rain dashed against the loose-framed sashes of the windows. Dominey lit the tall candles in his bedroom, fastened a dressing-gown around him, threw himself into an easy-chair, and, fixing an electric reading lamp by his side, tried to read. Very soon the book slipped from his fingers. He became suddenly tense and watchful. His eyes counted one by one the panels in the wall by the left-hand side of the bed. The familiar click was twice repeated. For a moment a dark space appeared. Then a woman, stooping low, glided into the room. She came slowly towards him, drawn like a moth towards that semicircle of candle. Her hair hung down her back like a girl's, and the white dressing-gown which floated diaphanously about her was unexpectedly reminiscent of Bond Street.

"You are not afraid?" she asked anxiously. "See, I have nothing in my hands. I almost think that the desire has gone. You remember the little stiletto I had last night? Today I threw it into the well. Mrs. Unthank was very angry with me."

"I am not afraid," he assured her, "but—"

"Ah, but you will not scold me?" she begged. "It is the storm which terrifies me."

He drew a low chair for her into the little circle of light and arranged some cushions. As she sank into it, she suddenly looked up at him and smiled, a smile of rare and wonderful beauty. Dominey felt for a moment something like the stab of a knife at his heart.

"Sit here and rest," he invited. "There is nothing to fear."

"In my heart I know that," she answered simply. "These storms are part of our lives. They come with birth, and they shake the world when death seizes us. One should not be afraid, but I have been so ill, Everard. Shall I call you Everard still?"

"Why not?" he asked.

"Because you are not like Everard to me any more," she told him, "because something has gone from you, and something has come to you. You are not the same man. What is it? Had you troubles in Africa? Did you learn what life was like out there?"

He sat looking at her for a moment, leaning back in his chair, which he had pushed a few feet into the shadows. Her hair was glossy and splendid, and against it her skin seemed whiter and more delicate than ever. Her eyes were lustrous but plaintive, and with something of the child's fear of harm in them. She looked very young and very fragile to have been swayed through the years by an evil passion.

"I learned many things there, Rosamund," he told her quietly. "I learned a little of the difference between right doing and wrongdoing. I learned, too, that all the passions of life burn themselves out, save one alone."

She twisted the girdle of her dressing-gown in her fingers for a moment. His last speech seemed to have been outside the orbit of her comprehension or interest.

"You need not be afraid of me any more, Everard," she said, a little pathetically.

"I have no fear of you," he answered.

"Then why don't you bring your chair forward and come and sit a little nearer to me?" she asked, raising her eyes. "Do you hear the wind, how it shrieks at us? Oh, I am afraid!"

He moved forward to her side, and took her hand gently in his. Her fingers responded at once to his pressure. When he spoke, he scarcely recognised his own voice. It seemed to him thick and choked.

"The wind shall not hurt you, or anything else," he promised. "I have come back to take care of you."

She sighed, smiled like a tired child, and her eyes closed as her head fell farther back amongst the cushions.

"Stay just like that, please," she begged. "Something quite new is coming to me. I am resting. It is the sweetest rest I ever felt. Don't move, Everard. Let my fingers stay in yours—so."

The candles burned down in their sockets, the wind rose to greater furies, and died away only as the dawn broke through the storm clouds. A pale light stole into the room. Still the woman slept, and still her fingers seemed to keep their clutch upon his hand. Her breathing was all the time soft and regular. Her silky black eyelashes lay motionless upon her pale cheeks. Her mouth—a very perfectly shaped mouth—rested in quiet lines. Somehow he realised that about this slumber there was a new thing. With hot eyes and aching limbs he sat through the night. Dream after dream rose up and passed away before that little background of tapestried wall. When she opened her eyes and looked at him, the same smile parted her lips as the smile which had come there when she had passed away to sleep.

"I am so rested," she murmured. "I feel so well. I have had dreams, beautiful dreams."

The fire had burned out, and the room was chilly.

"You must go back to your own room now," he said.

Very slowly her fingers relaxed. She held out her arms.

"Carry me," she begged. "I am only half awake. I want to sleep again."

He lifted her up. Her fingers closed around his neck, her head fell back with a little sigh of content. He tried the folding doors, and, finding some difficulty in opening them, carried her out into the corridor, into her own room, and laid her upon the untouched bed.

"You are comfortable?" he asked.

"Quite," she murmured drowsily. "Kiss me, Everard."

Her hands drew his face down. His lips rested upon her forehead. Then he drew the bedclothes over her and fled.

## CHAPTER XIII

THERE WAS a cloud on Seaman's good-humoured face as, muffled up in their overcoats, he and his host walked up and down the terrace the next morning, after the departure of Mr. Mangan. He disclosed his mind a little abruptly.

"In a few minutes," he said, "I shall come to the great purpose of my visit. I have great and wonderful news for you. But it will keep."

"The time for action has arrived?" Dominey asked curiously. "I hope you will remember that as yet I am scarcely established here."

"It is with regard to your establishment here," Seaman explained drily, "that I desire to say a word. We have seen much of one another since we met in Cape Town. The passion and purpose of my life you have been able to judge. Of these interludes which are necessary to a human being, unless his system is to fall to pieces as dry dust, you have also seen something. I trust you will not misunderstand me when I say that apart from the necessities of my work, I am a man of sentiment."

"I am prepared to admit it," Dominey murmured a little idly.

"You have undertaken a great enterprise. It was, without a doubt, a miraculous piece of fortune which brought the Englishman, Dominey, to your camp just at the moment when you received your orders from headquarters. Your self-conceived plan has met with every encouragement from us. You will be placed in a unique position to achieve your final purpose. Now mark my words and do not misunderstand me. The very key-note of our progress is ruthlessness. To take even a single step forward towards the achievement of that purpose is worth the sacrifice of all the scruples and delicacies conceivable. But when a certain course of action is without profit to our purpose, I see ugliness in it. It distresses me."

"What the devil do you mean?" Dominey demanded.

"I sleep with one ear open," Seaman replied.

"Well?"

"I saw you leave your room early this morning," Seaman continued, "carrying Lady Dominey in your arms."

There were little streaks of pallor underneath the tan in Dominey's face. His eyes were like glittering metal. It was only when he had breathed once or twice quickly that he could command his voice.

"What concern is this of yours?" he demanded.

Seaman gripped his companion's arm.

"Look here," he said, "we are too closely allied for bluff. I am here to help you fill the shoes of another man, so far as regards his estates, his position, and character, which, by the by, you are rehabilitating. I will go further. I will admit that it is not my concern to interfere in any ordinary amour you might undertake, but—I shall tell you this, my friend, to your face—that to deceive a lady of weak intellect, however beautiful, to make use of your position as her supposed husband, is not, save in the vital interests of his country, the action of a Prussian nobleman."

Dominey's passion seemed to have burned itself out without expression. He showed not the slightest resentment at his companion's words.

"Have no fear, Seaman," he enjoined him. "The situation is delicate, but I can deal with it as a man of honour."

"You relieve me," Seaman confessed. "You must admit that the spectacle of last night was calculated to inspire me with uneasiness."

"I respect you for your plain words," Dominey declared. "The fact is, that Lady Dominey was frightened of the storm last night and found her way into my room. You may be sure that I treated her with all the respect and sympathy which our positions demanded."

"Lady Dominey," Seaman remarked meditatively, "seems to be curiously falsifying certain predictions."

"In what way?"

"The common impression in the neighbourhood here is that she is a maniac chiefly upon one subject—her detestation of you. She has been known to take an oath that you should die if you slept in this house again. You naturally, being a brave man, ignored all this, yet in the morning after your first night here there was blood upon your night clothes."

Dominey's eyebrows were slowly raised.

"You are well served here," he observed, with involuntary sarcasm.

"That, for your own sake as well as ours, is necessary," was the terse reply. "To continue, people of unsound mind are remarkably tenacious of their ideas. There was certainly nothing of the murderess in her demeanour towards you last night. Cannot you see that a too friendly attitude on her part might become fatal to our schemes?"

"In what way?"

"If ever your identity is doubted," Seaman explained, "the probability of which is, I must confess, becoming less every day, the fact that Lady Dominey seems to have so soon forgotten all her enmity towards you would be strong presumptive evidence that you are not the man you claim to be."

"Ingenious," Dominey assented, "and very possible. All this time, however, we speak on what you yourself admit to be a side issue."

"You are right," Seaman confessed. "Very well, then, listen. A great moment has arrived for you, my friend."

"Explain, if you please."

"I shall do so. You have seen proof, during the last few days, that you have an organisation behind you to whom money is dross. It is the same in diplomacy as in war. Germany will pay the price for what she intends to achieve. Ninety thousand pounds was yesterday passed to the credit of your account for the extinction of certain mortgages. In a few months' or a few years' time, some distant Dominey will benefit to that extent. We cannot recover the money. It is just an item in our day by day expenses."

"It was certainly a magnificent way of establishing me," Dominey admitted.

"Magnificent, but safest in the long run," Seaman declared. "If you had returned a poor man, everybody's hand would have been against you; suspicions, now absolutely unkindled, might have been formed; and, more important, perhaps, than either, you would not have been able to take your place in Society, which is absolutely necessary for the furtherance of our scheme."

"Is it not almost time," Dominey enquired, "that the way was made a little clearer for me?"

"That would have been my task this morning," Seaman replied, "but for the news I bring. In passing, however, let me promise you this. You will never be asked to stoop to the crooked ways of the ordinary spy. We want you for a different purpose."

"And the news?"

"What must be the greatest desire in your heart," Seaman said solemnly, "is to be granted. The Kaiser has expressed a desire to see you, to give you his instructions in person."

Dominey stopped short upon the terrace. He withdrew his arm from his companion's and stared at him blankly.

"The Kaiser?" he exclaimed. "You mean that I am to go to Germany?"

"We shall start at once," Seaman replied. "Personally, I do not consider the proceeding discreet or necessary. It has been decided upon, however, without consulting me."

"I consider it suicidal," Dominey protested. "What explanation can I possibly make for going to Germany, of all countries in the world, before I have had time to settle down here?"

"That of itself will not be difficult," his companion pointed out. "Many of the mines in which a share has been bought in your name are being run with German capital. It is easy to imagine that a crisis has arisen in the management of one of them. We require the votes of our fellow shareholders. You need not trouble your head about that. And think of the wonder of it! If only for a single day your sentence of banishment is lifted. You will breathe the air of the Fatherland once more."

"It will be wonderful," Dominey muttered.

"It will be for you," Seaman promised, "a breath of the things that are to come. And now, action. How I love action! That time-table, my friend, and your chauffeur."

It was arranged that the two men should leave during the morning for Norwich by motor-car and thence to Harwich. Dominey, having changed into travelling clothes, sent a messenger for Mrs. Unthank, who came to him presently in his study. He held out a chair to her, which she declined, however, to take.

"Mrs. Unthank," he said, "I should like to know why you have been content to remain my wife's attendant for the last ten years?"

Mrs. Unthank was startled by the suddenness of the attack.

"Lady Dominey has needed me," she answered after a moment's pause.

"Do you consider," he asked, "that you have been the best possible companion for her?"

"She has never been willing to accept any other," the woman replied.

"Are you very devoted to my wife?" he enquired.

Mrs. Unthank, grim and fierce though she was and appeared to be, was obviously disconcerted by Dominey's line of questions.

"If I weren't," she demanded, "should I have been here all these years?"

"I scarcely see," he continued, "what particular claim my wife has had upon you. I understand, moreover, that you are one of those who firmly believe that I killed your son. Is this attendance upon my wife a Christian act, then—the returning of good for evil?"

"Exactly what do you want to say to me, Sir Everard?" she asked harshly.

"I wish to say this," Dominey replied, "that I am determined to bring about my wife's restoration to health. For that reason I am going to have specialists down here, and above all things to change for a time her place of residence. My own feeling is that she will stand a much better chance of recovery without your attendance."

"You would dare to send me away?" the woman demanded.

"That is my intention," Dominey confessed. "I have not spoken to Lady Dominey yet, but I hope that very soon my influence over her will be such that she will be content to obey my wishes. I look upon your future from the financial point of view, as my care. I shall settle upon you the sum of three hundred pounds a year."

The woman showed her first sign of weakness. She began to shake. There was a curious look of fear in her eyes.

"I can't leave this place, Sir Everard," she cried. "I must stay here!"

"Why?" he demanded.

"Lady Dominey couldn't do without me," she answered sullenly.

"That," he replied, "is for her to decide. Personally, from enquiries I have made, I believe that you have encouraged in her that ridiculous superstition about the ghost of your son. I also believe that you have kept alive in her that spirit of unreasonable hatred which she has felt towards me."

"Unreasonable, you call it?" the woman almost shouted. "You, who came home to her with the blood on your hands of the man whom, if only you had kept away, she might one day have loved? Unreasonable, you call it?"

"I have finished what I had to say, Mrs. Unthank," Dominey declared. "I am compelled by important business to leave here for two or three days. On my return I shall embark upon the changes with which I have acquainted you. In the meantime," he added, watching a curious change in the woman's expression, "I have written this morning to Doctor Harrison, asking him to come up this afternoon and to keep Lady Dominey under his personal observation until my return."

She stood quite still, looking at him. Then she came a little nearer and leaned forward, as though studying his face.

"Eleven years," she muttered, "do change many men, but I never knew a man made out of a weakling."

"I have nothing more to say to you," Dominey replied, "except to let you know that I am coming to see my wife in the space of a few minutes."

The motor-horn was already sounding below when Dominey was admitted to his wife's apartment. She was dressed in a loose gown of a warm crimson colour, and she had the air of one awaiting his arrival expectantly. The passion of hatred seemed to have passed from her pale face and from the depths of her strangely soft eyes. She held out her hands towards him. Her brows were a little puckered. The disappointment of a child lurked in her manner.

"You are going away?" she murmured.

"In a very few moments," he told her. "I have been waiting to see you for an hour."

She made a grimace.

"It was Mrs. Unthank. I think that she hid my things on purpose. I was so anxious to see you."

"I want to talk to you about Mrs. Unthank," he said. "Should you be very unhappy if I sent her away and found some one younger and kinder to be your companion?"

The idea seemed to be outside the bounds of her comprehension.

"Mrs. Unthank would never go," she declared. "She stays here to listen to the voice. All night long sometimes she waits and listens, and it doesn't come. Then she hears it, and she is rested."

"And you?" he asked.

"I am afraid," she confessed. "But then, you see, I am not very strong."

"You are not fond of Mrs. Unthank?" he enquired anxiously.

"I don't think so," she answered, in a perplexed tone. "I think I am very much afraid of her. But it is no use, Everard! She would never go away."

"When I return," Dominey said, "we shall see."

She took his arm and linked her hands through it.

"I am so sorry that you are going," she murmured. "I hope you will soon come back. Will you come back—my husband?"

Dominey's nails cut into the flesh of his clenched hands.

"I will come back within three days," he promised.

"Do you know," she went on confidentially, "something has come into my mind lately. I spoke about it yesterday, but I did not tell you what it was. You need never be afraid of me any more. I understand."

"What do you understand?" he demanded huskily.

"The knowledge must have come to me," she went on, dropping her voice a little and whispering almost in his ear, "at the very moment when my dagger rested upon your throat, when I suddenly felt the desire to kill die away. You are very like him sometimes, but you are not Everard. You are not my husband at all. You are another man."

Dominey gave a little gasp. They both turned towards the door. Mrs. Unthank was standing there, her gaunt, hard face lit up with a gleam of something which was like triumph, her eyes glittering. Her lips, as though involuntarily, repeated her mistress' last words.

"Another man!"

# CHAPTER XIV

THERE WERE times during their rapid journey when Seaman, studying his companion, became thoughtful. Dominey seemed, indeed, to have passed beyond the boundaries of any ordinary reserve, to have become like a man immeshed in the toils of a past so absorbing that he moved as though in a dream, speaking only when necessary and comporting himself generally like one to whom all externals have lost significance. As they embarked upon the final stage of their travels, Seaman leaned forward in his seat in the sombrely upholstered, overheated compartment.

"Your home-coming seems to depress you, Von Ragastein," he said.

"It was not my intention," Dominey replied, "to set foot in Germany again for many years."

"The past still bites, eh?"

"Always."

The train sped on through long chains of vineyard-covered hills, out into a stretch of flat country, into forests of pines, in the midst of which were great cleared spaces, where, notwithstanding the closely drawn windows, the resinous odour from the fallen trunks seemed to permeate the compartment. Presently they slackened speed. Seaman glanced at his watch and rose.

"Prepare yourself, my friend," he said. "We descend in a few minutes."

Dominey glanced out of the window.

"But where are we?" he enquired.

"Within five minutes of our destination."

"But there is not a house in sight," Dominey remarked wonderingly.

"You will be received on board His Majesty's private train," Seaman announced. "The Kaiser, with his staff, is making one of his military tours. We are honoured by being permitted to travel back with him as far as the Belgian frontier."

They had come to a standstill now. A bearded and uniformed official threw open the door of their compartment, and they stepped onto the narrow wooden platform of a small station which seemed to have been recently built of fresh pine planks. The train, immediately they had alighted, passed on. Their journey was over.

A brief conversation was carried on between Seaman and the official, during which Dominey took curious note of his surroundings. Around the station, half hidden in some places by the trees and shrubs, was drawn a complete cordon of soldiers, who seemed to have recently disembarked from a military train which stood upon a siding. In the middle of it was a solitary saloon carriage, painted black, with much gold ornamentation, and having emblazoned upon the central panel the royal arms of Germany. Seaman, when he had finished his conversation, took Dominey by the arm and led him across the line towards it. An officer received them at the steps and bowed punctiliously to Dominey, at whom he gazed with much interest.

"His Majesty will receive you at once," he announced. "Follow me."

They boarded the train and passed along a richly carpeted corridor. Their guide paused and pointed to a small retiring-room, where several men were seated.

"Herr Seaman will find friends there," he said. "His Imperial Majesty will receive him for a few minutes later. The Baron von Ragastein will come this way."

Dominey was ushered now into the main saloon. His guide motioned him to remain near the entrance, and, himself advancing a few paces, stood at the salute before a seated figure who was bending over a map, which a stern-faced man in the uniform of a general had unrolled before him. The Kaiser glanced up at the sound of footsteps and whispered something in the general's ear. The latter clicked his heels together and retired. The Kaiser beckoned Dominey to advance.

"The Baron von Ragastein, your Majesty," the young officer murmured.

Dominey stood at attention for a moment and bowed a little awkwardly. The Kaiser smiled.

"It pleases me," he said, "to see a German officer ill at ease without his uniform. Count, you will leave us. Baron von Ragastein, be seated."

"Sir Everard Dominey, at your service, Majesty," Dominey replied, as he took the chair to which his august host pointed.

"Thorough in all things, I see," the latter observed. "Sit there and be at your ease. Good reports have reached me of your work in Africa."

"I did my best to execute your Majesty's will," Dominey ventured.

"You did so well," the Kaiser pronounced, "that my counsellors were unanimous in advising your withdrawal to what will shortly become the great centre of interest. From the moment of receiving our commands you appear to have displayed initiative. I gather that your personation of this English baronet has been successfully carried through?"

"Up to the present, your Majesty."

"Important though your work in Africa was," the Kaiser continued, "your present task is a far greater one. I wish to speak to you for these few minutes without reserve. First, though, drink a toast with me."

From a mahogany stand at his elbow, the Kaiser drew out a long-necked bottle of Moselle, filled two very beautiful glasses, passed one to his companion and raised the other.

"To the Fatherland!" he said.

"To the Fatherland!" Dominey repeated.

They set down their glasses, empty. The Kaiser threw back the grey military cloak which he was wearing, displaying a long row of medals and decorations. His fingers still toyed with the stem of his wineglass. He seemed for a moment to lose himself in thought. His hard and somewhat cruel mouth was tightly closed; there was a slight frown upon his forehead. He was sitting upright, taking no advantage of the cushioned back of his easy-chair, his eyes a little screwed up, the frown deepening. For quite five minutes there was complete silence. One might have gathered that, turning aside from great matters, he had been devoting himself entirely to the scheme in which Dominey was concerned.

"Von Ragastein," he said at last, "I have sent for you to have a few words concerning your habitation in England. I wish you to receive your impressions of your mission from my own lips."

"Your Majesty does me great honour," Dominey murmured.

"I wish you to consider yourself," the Kaiser continued, "as entirely removed from the limits, the authority and the duties of my espionage system. From you I look for other things. I desire you to enter into the spirit of your assumed position. As a typical English country gentleman I desire you to study the labour question, the Irish question, the progress of this National Service scheme, and other social movements of which you will receive notice in due time. I desire a list compiled of those writers who, in the Reviews, or by means of fiction, are encouraging the suspicions which I am inclined to fancy England has begun to entertain towards the Fatherland. These things are all on the fringe of your real mission. That, I believe, our admirable friend Seaman has already confided to you. It is to seek the friendship, if possible the intimacy, of Prince Terniloff."

The Kaiser paused, and once more his eyes wandered to the landscape which rolled away from the plate-glass windows of the car. They were certainly not the eyes of a dreamer, and yet in those moments they seemed filled with brooding pictures.

"The Prince has already received me graciously," Dominey confided.

"Terniloff is the dove of peace," the Kaiser pronounced. "He carries the sprig of olive in his mouth. My statesmen and coun-sellors would have sent to London an ambassador with sterner qualities. I preferred not. Terniloff is the man to gull fools, because he is a fool himself. He is a fit ambassador for a country which has not the wit to arm itself on land as well as by sea, when it sees a nation, mightier, more cultured, more splendidly led than its own, creeping closer every day."

"The English appear to put their whole trust in their navy, your Majesty," Dominey observed tentatively.

The eyes of his companion flashed. His lips curled contemp-tuously.

"Fools!" he exclaimed. "Of what use will their navy be when my sword is once drawn, when I hold the coast towns of Calais and Boulogne, when my cannon command the Straits of Dover! The days of insular nations are passed, passed as surely as the days of England's arrogant supremacy upon the seas."

The Kaiser refilled his glass and Dominey's.

"In some months' time, Von Ragastein," he continued, "you will understand why you have been enjoined to become the friend and companion of Terniloff. You will understand your mission a little more clearly than you do now. Its exact nature waits upon developments. You can at all times trust Seaman."

Dominey bowed and remained silent. His companion continued after another brief spell of silent brooding.

"Von Ragastein," he said, "my decree of banishment against you was a just one. The morals of my people are as sacred to me as my oath to win for them a mightier empire. You first of all betrayed the wife of one of the most influential noblemen of a State allied to my own, and then, in the duel that followed, you slew him."

"It was an accident, your Majesty," Dominey pleaded. "I had no intention of even wounding the Prince."

The Kaiser frowned. All manner of excuses were loathsome to him.

"The accident should have happened the other way," he rejoined sharply. "I should have lost a valuable servant, but it was your life which was forfeit, and not his. Still, they tell me that your work in Africa was well and thoroughly done. I give you this one great chance of rehabilitation. If your work in England commends itself to me, the sentence of exile under which you suffer shall be rescinded."

"Your Majesty is too good," Dominey murmured. "The work, for its own sake, will command my every effort, even without the hope of reward."

"That," the Kaiser said, "is well spoken. It is the spirit, I believe, with which every son of my Empire regards the future. I think that they, too, more especially those who surround my person, have felt something of that divine message which has come to me. For many years I have, for the sake of my people, willed peace. Now that the time draws near when Heaven has shown me another duty, I have no fear but that every loyal German will bow his head before the lightnings which will play around my sword and share with me the iron will to wield it. Your audience is finished, Baron von Ragastein. You will take your place with the gentlemen of my suite in the retiring-room. We shall proceed within a few minutes and leave you at the Belgian frontier."

Dominey rose, bowed stiffly and backed down the carpeted way. The Kaiser was already bending once more over the map. Seaman, who was waiting outside the door of the anteroom, called him in and introduced him to several members of the suite. One, a young man with a fixed monocle, scars upon his face, and a queer, puppet-like carriage, looked at him a little strangely.

"We met some years ago in Munich, Baron," he remarked.

"I acknowledge no former meetings with any one in this country," Dominey replied stiffly. "I obey the orders of my Imperial master when I wipe from my mind every episode or reminiscence of my former days."

The young man's face cleared, and Seaman, by his side, who had knitted his brows thoughtfully, nodded understandingly.

"You are certainly a great actor, Baron," he declared. "Even your German has become a little English. Sit down and join us in a glass of beer. Luncheon will be served to us here in a few minutes. You will not be recalled to the Presence until we set you down."

Dominey bowed stiffly and took his place with the others. The train had already started. Dominey gazed thoughtfully out of the window. Seaman, who was waiting about for his audience, patted him on the arm.

"Dear friend," he said, "I sympathise with you. You sorrow because your back is now to Berlin. Still, remember this, that the day is not far off when the sentence of exile against you will be annulled. You will have expiated that crime which, believe me, although I do not venture to claim a place amongst them, none of your friends and equals have ever regarded in the same light as His Imperial Majesty."

A smiling steward, in black livery with white facings, made his appearance and served them with beer in tall glasses. The senior officer there, who had now seated himself opposite to Dominey, raised his glass and bowed.

"To the Baron von Ragastein," he said, "whose acquaintance I regret not having made before today. May we soon welcome him back, a brother in arms, a companion in great deeds! Hoch!"

# CHAPTER XV

SIR EVERARD DOMINEY, Baronet, the latest and most popular recruit to Norfolk sporting society, stood one afternoon, some months after his return from Germany, at the corner of the long wood which stretched from the ridge of hills behind almost to the kitchen gardens of the Hall. At a reasonable distance on his left, four other guns were posted. On one side of him stood Middleton, leaning on his ash stick and listening to the approach of the beaters; on the other, Seaman, curiously out of place in his dark grey suit and bowler hat. The old keeper, whom time seemed to have cured of all his apprehensions, was softly garrulous and very happy.

"That do seem right to have a Squire Dominey at this corner," he observed, watching a high cock pheasant come crashing down over their heads. "I mind when the Squire, your father, sir, gave up this corner one day to Lord Wendermere, whom folks called one of the finest pheasant shots in England, and though they streamed over his head like starlings, he'd nowt but a few cripples to show for his morning's work."

"Come out with a bit of a twist from the left, don't they?" Dominey remarked, repeating his late exploit.

"They do that, sir," the old man assented, "and no one but a Dominey seems to have learnt the knack of dealing with them proper. That foreign Prince, so they say, is well on to his birds, but I wouldn't trust him at this corner."

The old man moved off a few paces to some higher ground, to watch the progress of the beaters through the wood. Seaman turned to his companion, and there was a note of genuine admiration in his tone.

"My friend," he declared, "you are a miracle. You seem to have developed the Dominey touch even in killing pheasants."

"You must remember that I have shot higher ones in Hungary," was the easy reply.

"I am not a sportsman," Seaman admitted. "I do not understand sport. But I do know this: there is an old man who has lived on this land since the day of his birth, who has watched you shoot, reverently, and finds even the way you hold your gun familiar."

"That twist of the birds," Dominey explained, "is simply a local superstition. The wood ends on the slant, and they seem to be flying more to the left than they really are."

Seaman gazed steadfastly for a moment along the side of the wood.

"Her Grace is coming," he said. "She seems to share the Duke's dislike of me, and she is too great a lady to conceal her feelings. Just one word before I go. The Princess Eiderstrom arrives this afternoon."

Dominey frowned, then, warned by the keeper's shout, turned around and killed a hare.

"My friend," he said, with a certain note of challenge in his tone, "I am not certain that you have told me all that you know concerning the Princess's visit."

Seaman was thoughtful for a brief space of time.

"You are right," he admitted, "I have not. It is a fault which I will repair presently."

He strolled away to the next stand, where Mr. Mangan was displaying an altogether different standard of proficiency. The Duchess came up to Dominey a few minutes later.

"I told Henry I shouldn't stop with him another moment," she declared. "He has fired off about forty cartridges and wounded one hare."

"Henry is not keen," Dominey remarked, "although I think you are a little hard on him, are you not? I saw him bring down a nice cock just now. So far as regards the birds, it really does not matter. They are all going home."

The Duchess was very smartly tailored in clothes of brown heather mixture. She wore thick shoes and gaiters and a small hat. She was looking very well but a little annoyed.

"I hear," she said, "that Stephanie is coming today."

Dominey nodded, and seemed for a moment intent on watching the flight of a pigeon which kept tantalisingly out of range.

"She is coming down for a few days," he assented. "I am afraid that she will be bored to death."

"Where did you become so friendly with her?" his cousin asked curiously.

"The first time we ever met," Dominey replied, "was in the Carlton grill room, a few days after I landed in England. She mistook me for some one else, and we parted with the usual apologies. I met her the same night at Carlton House Terrace—she is related to the Terniloffs—and we came across one another pretty often after that, during the short time I was in town."

"Yes," the Duchess murmured meditatively. "That is another of the little surprises you seem to have all ready dished up for us. How on earth did you become so friendly with the German Ambassador?"

Dominey smiled tolerantly.

"Really," he replied, "there is not anything so very extraordinary about it, is there? Mr. Seaman, my partner in one or two mining enterprises, took me to call upon him. He is very interested in East Africa, politically and as a sportsman. Our conversations seemed to interest him and led to a certain intimacy,—of which I may say that I am proud. I have the greatest respect and liking for the Prince."

"So have I," Caroline agreed. "I think he's charming. Henry declares that he must be either a fool or a knave."

"Henry is blinded by prejudice," Dominey declared a little impatiently. "He cannot imagine a German who feasts with any one else but the devil."

"Don't get annoyed, dear," she begged, resting her fingers for a moment upon his coat sleeve. "I admire the Prince immensely. He is absolutely the only German I ever met whom one felt instinctively to be a gentleman.—Now what are you smiling at?"

Dominey turned a perfectly serious face towards her. "Not guilty," he pleaded.

"I saw you smile."

"It was just a quaint thought. You are rather sweeping, are you not, Caroline?"

"I'm generally right," she declared.—"To return to the subject of Stephanie."

"Well?"

"Do you know whom she mistook you for in the Carlton grill room?"

"Tell me?" he answered evasively.

"She mistook you for a Baron Leopold von Ragastein," Caroline continued drily. "Von Ragastein was her lover in Hungary. He fought a duel with her husband and killed him. The Kaiser was furious and banished him to East Africa."

Dominey picked up his shooting-stick and handed his gun to Middleton. The beaters were through the wood.

"Yes, I remember now," he said. "She addressed me as Leopold."

"I still don't see why it was necessary to invite her here," his companion observed a little petulantly. "She may—call you Leopold again!"

"If she does, I shall be deaf," Dominey promised. "But seriously, she is a cousin of the Princess Terniloff, and the two women are devoted to one another. The Princess hates shooting parties, so I thought they could entertain one another."

"Bosh! Stephanie will monopolise you all the time! That's what she's coming for."

"You are not suggesting that she intends seriously to put me in the place of my double?" Dominey asked, with mock alarm.

"Oh, I shouldn't wonder! And she's an extraordinarily attractive woman. I'm full of complaints, Everard. There's that other horrible little man, Seaman. You know that the very sight of him makes Henry furious. I am quite sure that he never expected to sit down at the same table with him."

"I am really sorry about that," Dominey assured her, "but you see His Excellency takes a great interest in him on account of this Friendship League, of which Seaman is secretary, and he particularly asked to have him here."

"Well, you must admit that the situation is a little awkward for Henry," she complained. "Next to Lord Roberts, Henry is practically the leader of the National Service movement here; he hates Germany and distrusts every German he ever met, and in a small house party like this we meet the German Ambassador and a man who is working hard to lull to sleep the very sentiments which Henry is endeavouring to arouse."

"It sounds very pathetic," Dominey admitted, with a smile, "but even Henry likes Terniloff, and after all it is stimulating to meet one's opponents sometimes."

"Of course he likes Terniloff," Caroline assented, "but he hates the things he stands for. However, I'd have forgiven you everything if only Stephanie weren't coming. That woman is really beginning to irritate me. She always seems to be making mysterious references to some sentimental past in which you both are concerned, and for which there can be no foundation at all except your supposed likeness to her exiled lover. Why, you never met her until that day at the Carlton!"

"She was a complete stranger to me," Dominey asserted.

"Then all I can say is that you have been unusually rapid if you've managed to create a past in something under three months!" Caroline pronounced suspiciously. "I call her coming here a most bare-faced proceeding, especially as this is practically a bachelor establishment."

They had arrived at the next stand, and conversation was temporarily suspended. A flight of wild duck were put out from a pool in the wood, and for a few minutes every one was busy. Middleton watched his master with unabated approval.

"You're most as good as the old Squire with them high duck, Sir Everard," he said. "That's true very few can touch 'em when they're coming out nigh to the pheasants. They can't believe in the speed of 'em."

"Do you think Sir Everard shoots as well as he did before he went to Africa?" Caroline asked.

Middleton touched his hat and turned to Seaman, who was standing in the background.

"Better, your Grace," he answered, "as I was saying to this gentleman here, early this morning. He's cooler like and swings more level. I'd have known his touch on a gun anywhere, though."

There was a glint of admiration in Seaman's eyes. The beaters came through the wood, and the little party of guns gossiped together while the game was collected. Terniloff, his usual pallor chased away by the bracing wind and the pleasure of the sport, was affable and even loquacious. He had great estates of his own in Saxony and was explaining to the Duke his manner of shooting them. Middleton glanced at his horn-rimmed watch.

"There's another hour's good light, sir," he said. "Would you care about a partridge drive, or should we go through the home copse?"

"If I might make a suggestion," Terniloff observed diffidently, "most of the pheasants went into that gloomy-looking wood just across the marshes."

There was a moment's rather curious silence. Dominey had turned and was looking towards the wood in question, as though fascinated by its almost sinister-like blackness and density. Middleton had dropped some game he was carrying and was muttering to himself.

"We call that the Black Wood," Dominey said calmly, "and I am rather afraid that the pheasants who find their way there claim sanctuary. What do you think, Middleton?"

The old man turned his head slowly and looked at his master. Somehow or other, every scrap of colour seemed to have faded out of his bronzed face. His eyes were filled with that vague horror of the supernatural common amongst the peasant folk of various localities. His voice shook. The old fear was back again.

"You wouldn't put the beaters in there, Squire?" he faltered; "not that there's one of them would go."

"Have we stumbled up against a local superstition?" the Duke enquired.

"That's not altogether local, your Grace," Middleton replied, "as the Squire himself will tell you. I doubt whether there's a beater in all Norfolk would go through the Black Wood, if you paid him red gold for it.—Here, you lads."

He turned to the beaters, who were standing waiting for instructions a few yards away. There were a dozen of them, stalwart men for the most part, clad in rough smocks and breeches and carrying thick sticks.

"There's one of the gentlemen here," Middleton announced, addressing them, "who wants to know if you'd go through the Black Wood of Dominey for a sovereign apiece, eh?—Watch their faces, your Grace.—Now then, lads?"

There was no possibility of any mistake. The very suggestion seemed to have taken the healthy sunburn from their cheeks. They fumbled with their sticks uneasily. One of them touched his hat and spoke to Dominey.

"I'm one as 'as seen it, sir, as well as heard," he said. "I'd sooner give up my farm than go nigh the place."

Caroline suddenly passed her arm through Dominey's. There was a note of distress in her tone.

"Henry, you're an idiot!" she exclaimed. "It was my fault, Everard. I'm so sorry. Just for one moment I had forgotten. I ought to have stopped Henry at once. The poor man has no memory."

Dominey's arm responded for a moment to the pressure of her fingers. Then he turned to the beaters.

"Well, no one is going to ask you to go to the Black Wood," he promised. "Get round to the back of Hunt's stubbles, and bring them into the roots and then over into the park. We will line the park fence. How is that, Middleton, eh?"

The keeper touched his hat and stepped briskly off.

"I'll just have a walk with them myself, sir," he said. "Them birds do break at Fuller's corner. I'll see if I can flank them. You'll know where to put the guns, Squire."

Dominey nodded. One and all the beaters were walking with most unaccustomed speed towards their destination. Their backs were towards the Black Wood. Terniloff came up to his host.

"Have I, by chance, been terribly tactless?" he asked.

Dominey shook his head.

"You asked a perfectly natural question, Prince," he replied. "There is no reason why you should not know the truth. Near that wood occurred the tragedy which drove me from England for so many years."

"I am deeply grieved," the Prince began—

"It is false sentiment to avoid allusions to it," Dominey interrupted. "I was attacked there one night by a man who had some cause for offence against me. We fought, and I reached home in a somewhat alarming state. My condition terrified my wife so much that she has been an invalid ever since. But here is the point which has given birth to all these superstitions, and which made me for many years a suspected person. The man with whom I fought has never been seen since."

Terniloff was at once too fascinated by the story and puzzled by his host's manner of telling it to maintain his apologetic attitude.

"Never seen since!" he repeated.

"My own memory as to the end of our fight is uncertain," Dominey continued. "My impression is that I left my assailant unconscious upon the ground."

"Then it is his ghost, I imagine, who haunts the Black Wood?"

Dominey shook himself as one who would get rid of an unwholesome thought.

"The wood itself, Prince," he explained, as they walked along, "is a noisome place. There are quagmires even in the middle of it, where a man may sink in and be never heard of again. Every sort of vermin abounds there, every unclean insect and bird is to be found in the thickets. I suppose the character of the place has encouraged the local superstition in which every one of those men firmly believes."

"They absolutely believe the place to be haunted, then?"

"The superstition goes further," Dominey continued. "Our locals say that somewhere in the heart of the wood, where I believe that no human being for many years has dared to penetrate, there is living in the spiritual sense some sort of a demon who comes out only at night and howls underneath my windows."

"Has any one ever seen it?"

"One or two of the villagers; to the best of my belief, no one else," Dominey replied.

Terniloff seemed on the point of asking more questions, but the Duke touched him on the arm and drew him on one side, as though to call his attention to the sea fogs which were rolling up from the marshes.

"Prince," he whispered, "the details of that story are inextricably mixed up with the insanity of Lady Dominey. I am sure you understand."

The Prince, a diplomatist to his fingertips, appeared shocked, although a furtive smile still lingered upon his lips.

"I regret my *faux pas* most deeply," he murmured. "Sir Everard," he went on, "you promised to tell me of some of your days with a shotgun in South Africa. Isn't there a bird there which corresponds with your partridges?"

Dominey smiled.

"If you can kill the partridges which Middleton is going to send over in the next ten minutes," he said, "you could shoot anything of the sort that comes along in East Africa, with a catapult. If you stand just a few paces there to the left, Henry, Terniloff by the gate, Stillwell up by the left-hand corner, Mangan next, Eddy next, and I shall be just beyond towards the oak clump. Will you walk with me, Caroline?"

His cousin took his arm as they walked off and pressed it.

"Everard, I congratulate you," she said. "You have conquered your nerve absolutely. You did a simple and a fine thing to tell the whole story. Why, you were almost matter-of-fact. I could even have imagined you were telling it about some one else."

Her host smiled enigmatically.

"Curious that it should have struck you like that," he remarked. "Do you know, when I was telling it I had the same feeling.—Do you mind crouching down a little now? I am going to blow the whistle."

# CHAPTER XVI

EVEN in the great dining-room of Dominey Hall, the mahogany table which was its great glory was stretched that evening to its extreme capacity. Besides the house party, which included the Right Honourable Gerald Watson, a recently appointed Cabinet Minister, there were several guests from the neighbourhood—the Lord Lieutenant of the County and other notabilities. Caroline, with the Lord Lieutenant on one side of her and Terniloff on the other, played the part of hostess adequately but without enthusiasm. Her eyes seldom left for long the other end of the table, where Stephanie, at Dominey's left hand, with her crown of exquisitely coiffured red-gold hair, her marvellous jewellery, her languorous grace of manner, seemed more like one of the beauties of an ancient Venetian Court than a modern Hungarian Princess gowned in the Rue de la Paix. Conversation remained chiefly local and concerned the day's sport and kindred topics. It was not until towards the close of the meal that the Duke succeeded in launching his favourite bubble.

"I trust, Everard," he said, raising his voice a little as he turned towards his host, "that you make a point of inculcating the principles of National Service into your tenantry here."

Dominey's reply was a little dubious.

"I am afraid they do not take to the idea very kindly in this part of the world," he confessed. "Purely agricultural districts are always a little difficult."

"It is your duty as a landowner," the Duke insisted, "to alter their point of view. There is not the slightest doubt," he added, looking belligerently over the top of his *pince nez* at Seaman, who was seated at the opposite side of the table, "that before long we shall find ourselves—and in a shocking state of unpreparedness, mind you—at war with Germany."

Lady Maddeley, the wife of the Lord Lieutenant, who sat at his side, seemed a little startled. She was probably one of the only people present who was not aware of the Duke's foible.

"Do you really think so?" she asked. "The Germans seem such civilised people, so peaceful and domestic in their home life, and that sort of thing."

The Duke groaned. He glanced down the table to be sure that Prince Terniloff was out of hearing.

"My dear Lady Maddeley," he declared, "Germany is not governed like England. When the war comes, the people will have had nothing to do with it. A great many of them will be just as surprised as you will be, but they will fight all the same."

Seaman, who had kept silence during the last few moments with great difficulty, now took up the Duke's challenge.

"Permit me to assure you, madam," he said, bowing across the table, "that the war with Germany of which the Duke is so afraid will never come. I speak with some amount of knowledge because I am a German by birth, although naturalised in this country. I have as many and as dear friends in Berlin as in London, and with the exception of my recent absence in Africa, where I had the pleasure to meet our host, I spend a great part of my time going back and forth between the two capitals. I have also the honour to be the secretary of a society for the promotion of a better understanding between the citizens of Germany and England."

"Rubbish!" the Duke exclaimed. "The Germans don't want a better understanding. They only want to fool us into believing that they do."

Seaman looked a little pained. He stuck to his guns, however.

"His Grace and I," he observed, "are old opponents on this subject."

"We are indeed," the Duke agreed. "You may be an honest man, Mr. Seaman, but you are a very ignorant one upon this particular topic."

"You are probably both right in your way," Dominey intervened, very much in the manner of a well-bred host making his usual effort to smooth over two widely divergent points of view. "There is no doubt a war party in Germany and a peace party, statesmen who place economic progress first, and others who are tainted with a purely military lust for conquest. In this country it is very hard for us to strike a balance between the two."

Seaman beamed his thanks upon his host.

"I have friends," he said impressively, "in the very highest circles of Germany, who are continually encouraging my work here, and I have received the benediction of the Kaiser himself upon my efforts to promote a better feeling in this country. And if you will forgive my saying so, Duke, it is such ill-advised and ill-founded statements as you are constantly making about my country which become the only bar to a better understanding between us."

"I have my views," the Duke snapped, "and they have become convictions. I shall continue to express them at all times and with all the eloquence at my command."

The Ambassador, to whom portions of this conversation had now become audible, leaned a little forward in his place.

"Let me speak first as a private individual," he begged, "and express my well-studied opinion that war between our two countries would be simply race suicide, an indescribable and an abominable crime. Then I will remember what I represent over here, and I will venture to add in my ambassadorial capacity that I come with an absolute and heartfelt mandate of peace. My task over here is to secure and ensure it."

Caroline flashed a warning glance at her husband.

"How nice of you to be so frank, Prince!" she said. "The Duke sometimes forgets, in the pursuit of his hobby, that a private dinner table is not a platform. I insist upon it that we discuss something of more genuine interest."

"There isn't a more vital subject in the world," the Duke declared, resigning himself, however, to silence.

"We will speak," the Ambassador suggested, "of the way in which our host brought down those tall pheasants."

"You will tell me, perhaps," Seaman suggested to the lady on his right, "how you English women have been able to secure for yourselves so much more liberty than our German wives enjoy?"

"Later on," Stephanie whispered to her host, with a little tremble in her voice, "I have a surprise for you."

After dinner, Dominey's guests passed naturally enough to the relaxations which each preferred. There were two bridge tables, Terniloff and the Cabinet Minister played billiards, and Seaman, with a touch which amazed every one, drew strange music from the yellow keys of the old-fashioned grand piano in the drawing-room. Stephanie and her host made a slow progress through the hall and picture gallery. For some time their conversation was engaged solely with the objects to which Dominey drew his companion's attention. When they had passed out of possible hearing, however, of any of the other guests, Stephanie's fingers tightened upon her companion's arm.

"I wish to speak to you alone," she said, "without the possibility of any one overhearing."

Dominey hesitated and looked behind.

"Your guests are well occupied," she continued a little impatiently, "and in any case I am one of them. I claim your attention."

Dominey threw open the door of the library and turned on a couple of the electric lights. She made her way to the great open fireplace, on which a log was burning, looked down into the shadows of the room and back again into her host's face.

"For one moment," she begged, "turn on all the lights. I wish to be sure that we are alone."

Dominey did as he was bidden. The furthermost corners of the room, with its many wings of book-filled shelves, were illuminated. She nodded.

"Now turn them all out again except this one," she directed, "and wheel me up an easy-chair.—No, I choose this settee. Please seat yourself by my side."

"Is this going to be serious?" he asked, with some slight disquietude.

"Serious but wonderful," she murmured, lifting her eyes to his. "Will you please listen to me, Leopold?"

She was half curled up in a corner of the settee, her head resting slightly upon her long fingers, her brown eyes steadily fixed upon her companion. There was an atmosphere about her of serious yet of tender things. Dominey's face seemed to fall into more rigid lines as he realised the appeal of her eyes.

"Leopold," she began, "I left this country a few weeks ago, feeling that you were a brute, determined never to see you again, half inclined to expose you before I went as an impostor and a charlatan. Germany means little to me, and a patriotism which took no account of human obligations left me absolutely unresponsive. I meant to go home and never to return to London. My heart was bruised, and I was very unhappy."

She paused, but her companion made no sign. She paused for so long, however, that speech became necessary.

"You are speaking, Princess," he said calmly, "to one who is not present. My name is no longer Leopold."

She laughed at him with a curious mixture of tenderness and bitterness.

"My friend," she continued, "I am terrified to think, besides your name, how much of humanity you have lost in your new identity. To proceed, it suited my convenience to remain for a few days in Berlin, and I was therefore compelled to present myself at Potsdam. There I received a great surprise. Wilhelm spoke to me of you, and though, alas! my heart is still bruised, he helped me to understand."

"Is this wise?" he asked a little desperately.

She ignored his words.

"I was taken back into favour at Court," she went on. "For that I owe to you my thanks. Wilhelm was much impressed by your recent visit to him, and by the way in which you have established yourself here. He spoke also with warm commendations of your labours in Africa, which he seemed to appreciate all the more as you were sent there an exile. He asked me, Leopold," she added, dropping her voice a little, "if my feelings towards you remained unchanged."

Dominey's face remained unrelaxed. Persistently he refused the challenge of her eyes.

"I told him the truth," she proceeded. "I told him how it all began, and how it must last with me—to the end. We spoke even of the duel. I told him what both your seconds had explained to me,—that turn of the wrist, Conrad's wild lunge, how he literally threw himself upon the point of your sword. Wilhelm understands and forgives, and he has sent you this letter."

She drew a small grey envelope from her pocket. On the seal were the Imperial Hohenzollern arms. She passed it to him.

"Leopold," she whispered, "please read that."

He shook his head, although he accepted the letter with reluctant fingers.

"Leopold again," he muttered. "It is not for me."

"Read the superscription," she directed.

He obeyed her. It was addressed in a strange, straggling handwriting to *Sir Everard Dominey, Baronet*. He broke the seal unwillingly and drew out the letter. It was dated barely a fortnight back. There was neither beginning nor ending; just a couple of sentences scrawled across the thick notepaper:

> "It is my will that you offer your hand in marriage to the Princess Stephanie of Eiderstrom. Your union shall be blessed by the Church and approved by my Court."
>
> "WILHELM."

Dominey sat as a man enthralled with silence. She watched him.

"Not on your knees yet?" she asked, with faint but somewhat resentful irony. "Can it be, Leopold, that you have lost your love for me? You have changed so much and in so many ways. Has the love gone?"

Even to himself his voice sounded harsh and unnatural, his words instinct with the graceless cruelty of a clown.

"This is not practical," he declared. "Think! I am as I have been addressed here, and as I must remain yet for months to come—Everard Dominey, an Englishman and the owner of this house—the husband of Lady Dominey."

"Where is your reputed wife?" Stephanie demanded, frowning.

"In the nursing home where she has been for the last few months," he replied. "She has already practically recovered. She cannot remain there much longer."

"You must insist upon it that she does."

"I ask you to consider the suspicions which would be excited by such a course," Dominey pleaded earnestly, "and further, can you explain to me in what way I, having already, according to the belief of everybody, another wife living, can take advantage of this mandate?"

She looked at him wonderingly.

"You make difficulties? You sit there like the cold Englishman whose place you are taking, you whose tears have fallen before now upon my hand, whose lips—"

"You speak of one who is dead," Dominey interrupted, "dead until the coming of great events may bring him to life again. Until that time your lover must be dumb."

Then her anger blazed out. She spoke incoherently, passionately, dragged his face down to hers and clenched her fist the next moment as though she would have struck it. She broke down with a storm of tears.

"Not so hard—not so hard, Leopold!" she implored. "Oh! yours is a great task, and you must carry it through to the end, but we have his permission—there can be found a way— we could be married secretly. At least your lips—your arms! My heart is starved, Leopold."

He rose to his feet. Her arms were still twined about his neck, her lips hungry for his kisses, her eyes shining up into his.

"Have pity on me, Stephanie," he begged. "Until our time has come there is dishonour even in a single kiss. Wait for the day, the day you know of."

She unwound her arms and shivered slightly. Her hurt eyes regarded him wonderingly.

"Leopold," she faltered, "what has changed you like this? What has dried up all the passion in you? You are a different man. Let me look at you."

She caught him by the shoulders, dragged him underneath the electric globe, and stood there gazing into his face. The great log upon the hearth was spluttering and fizzing. Through the closed door came the faint wave of conversation and laughter from outside. Her breathing was uneven, her eyes were seeking to rend the mask from his face.

"Can you have learned to care for any one else?" she muttered. "There were no women in Africa. This Rosamund Dominey, your reputed wife—they tell me that she is beautiful, that you have been kindness itself to her, that her health has improved since your coming, that she adores you. You wouldn't dare—"

"No," he interrupted, "I should not dare."

"Then what are you looking at?" she demanded. "Tell me that?"

His eyes were following the shadowed picture which had passed out of the room. He saw once more the slight, girlish form, the love-seeking light in those pleading dark eyes, the tremulous lips, the whole sweet appeal for safety from a frightened child to him, the strong man. He felt the clinging touch of those soft fingers laid upon his, the sweetness of those marvellously awakened emotions, so cruelly and drearily stifled through a cycle of years. The woman's passion by his side seemed suddenly tawdry and unreal, the seeking of her lips for his something horrible. His back was towards the door, and it was her cry of angry dismay which first apprised him of a welcome intruder. He swung around to find Seaman standing upon the threshold—Seaman, to him a very angel of deliverance.

"I am indeed sorry to intrude, Sir Everard," the newcomer declared, with a shade of genuine concern on his round, good-humoured face. "Something has happened which I thought you ought to know at once. Can you spare me a moment?"

The Princess swept past them without a word of farewell or a backward glance. She had the carriage and the air of an insulted queen. A shade of deeper trouble came into Seaman's face as he stepped respectfully on one side.

"What is it that has happened?" Dominey demanded.

"Lady Dominey has returned," was the quiet reply.

# CHAPTER XVII

IT SEEMED to Dominey that he had never seen anything more pathetic than that eager glance, half of hope, half of apprehension, flashed upon him from the strange, tired eyes of the woman who was standing before the log fire in a little recess of the main hall. By her side stood a pleasant, friendly looking person in the uniform of a nurse; a yard or two behind, a maid carrying a jewel case. Rosamund, who had thrown back her veil, had been standing with her foot upon the fender. Her whole expression changed as Dominey came hastily towards her with outstretched hands.

"My dear child," he exclaimed, "welcome home!"

"Welcome?" she repeated, with a little glad catch in her throat. "You mean it?"

With a self-control of which he gave no sign, he touched the lips which were raised so eagerly to his as tenderly and reverently as though this were some strange child committed to his care.

"Of course I mean it," he answered heartily. "But what possessed you to come without giving us notice? How was this, nurse?"

"Her ladyship has had no sleep for two nights," the latter replied. "She has been so much better that we dreaded the thought of a relapse, so Mrs. Coulson, our matron, thought it best to let her have her own way about coming. Instead of telegraphing to you, unfortunately, we telegraphed to Doctor Harrison, and I believe he is away."

"Is it very wrong of me?" Rosamund asked, clinging to Dominey's arm. "I had a sudden feeling that I must get back here. I wanted to see you again. Every one has been so sweet and kind at Falmouth, especially Nurse Alice here, but they weren't quite the same thing. You are not angry? These people who are staying here will not mind?"

"Of course not," he assured her cheerfully. "They will be your guests. Tomorrow you must make friends with them all."

"There was a very beautiful woman," she said timidly, "with red hair, who passed by just now. She looked very angry. That was not because I have come?"

"Why should it be?" he answered. "You have a right here—a better right than any one."

She drew a long sigh of contentment.

"Oh, but this is wonderful!" she cried. "And you, dear—I shall call you Everard, mayn't I?—you look just as I hoped you might. Will you take me upstairs, please? Nurse, you can follow us."

She leaned heavily on his arm and even loitered on the way, but her steps grew lighter as they approached her own apartment. Finally, as they reached the corridor, she broke away from him and tripped on with the gaiety almost of a child to the door of her room. Then came a little cry of disappointment as she flung open the door. Several maids were there, busy with a refractory fire and removing the covers from the furniture, but the room was half full of smoke and entirely unprepared.

"Oh, how miserable!" she exclaimed. "Everard, what shall I do?"

He threw open the door of his own apartment. A bright fire was burning in the grate, the room was warm and comfortable. She threw herself with a little cry of delight into the huge Chesterfield drawn up to the edge of the hearthrug. "I can stay here, Everard, can't I, until you come up to bed?" she pleaded. "And then you can sit and talk to me, and tell me who is here and all about the people. You have no idea how much better I am. All my music has come back to me, and they say that I play bridge ever so well. I shall love to help you entertain."

The maid was slowly unfastening her mistress's boots. Rosamund held up her foot for him to feel.

"See how cold I am!" she complained. "Please rub it. I am going to have some supper up here with nurse. Will one of you maids please go down and see about it? What a lot of nice new things you have, Everard!" she added, looking around. "And that picture of me from the drawing-room, on the table!" she cried, her eyes suddenly soft with joy. "You dear thing! What made you bring that up?"

"I wanted to have it here," he told her.

"I'm not so nice as that now," she sighed, a little wistfully.

"Do not believe it," he answered. "You have not changed in the least. You will be better-looking still when you have been here for a few months."

She looked at him almost shyly—tenderly, yet still with that gleam of aloofness in her eyes.

"I think," she murmured, "I shall be just what you want me to be. I think you could make me just what you want. Be very kind to me, please," she begged, stretching her arms out to him. "I suppose it is because I have been ill so long, but I feel so helpless, and I love your strength and I want you to take care of me. Your own hands are quite cold," she added anxiously. "You look pale, too. You're not ill, Everard?"

"I am very well," he assured her, struggling to keep his voice steady. "Forgive me now, won't you, if I hurry away. There are guests here—rather important guests. Tomorrow you must come and see them all."

"And help you?"

"And help me."

Dominey made his escape and went reeling down the corridor. At the top of the great quadrangular landing he stopped and stood with half-closed eyes for several moments. From downstairs he could hear the sound of pleasantly raised voices, the music of a piano in the distance, the click of billiard balls. He waited until he had regained his self-possession. Then, as he was on the point of descending, he saw Seaman mounting the stairs. At a gesture he waited for him, waited until he came, and, taking him by the arm, led him to a great settee in a dark corner. Seaman had lost his usual blitheness. The good-humoured smile played no longer about his lips.

"Where is Lady Dominey?" he asked.

"In my room, waiting until her own is prepared."

Seaman's manner was unusually grave.

"My friend," he said, "you know very well that when we walk in the great paths of life I am unscrupulous. In those other hours, alas! I have a weakness.—I love women."

"Well?" Dominey muttered.

"I will admit," the other continued, "that you are placed in a delicate and trying position. Lady Dominey seems disposed to offer to you the affection which, notwithstanding their troubles together, she doubtless felt for her husband. I risk your anger, my friend, but I warn you to be very careful how you encourage her."

A light flashed in Dominey's eyes. For the moment angry words seemed to tremble upon his lips. Seaman's manner, however, was very gentle. He courted no offence.

"If you were to take advantage of your position with—with any other, I would shrug my shoulders and stand on one side, but this mad Englishman's wife, or rather his widow, has been mentally ill. She is still weak-minded, just as she is tender-hearted. I watched her as she passed through the hall with you just now. She turns to you for love as a flower to the sun after a long spell of cold, wet weather. Von Ragastein, you are a man of honour.

You must find means to deal with this situation, however difficult it may become."

Dominey had recovered from his first wave of weakness. His companion's words excited no sentiment of anger. He was conscious even of regarding him with a greater feeling of kindness than ever before.

"My friend," he said, "you have shown me that you are conscious of one dilemma in which I find myself placed, and which I must confess is exercising me to the utmost. Let me now advise you of another. The Princess Eiderstrom has brought me an autographed letter from the Kaiser, commanding me to marry her."

"The situation," Seaman declared grimly, "but for its serious side, would provide all the elements for a Palais Royal farce. For the present, however, you have duties below. I have said the words which were thumping against the walls of my heart."

Their descent was opportune. Some of the local guests were preparing to make their departure, and Dominey was in time to receive their adieux. They all left messages for Lady Dominey, spoke of a speedy visit to her, and expressed themselves as delighted to hear of her return and recovery. As the last car rolled away, Caroline took her host's arm and led him to a chimney seat by the huge log fire in the inner hall.

"My dear Everard," she said, "you really are a very terrible person."

"Exactly why?" he demanded.

"Your devotion to my sex," she continued, "is flattering but far too catholic. Your return to England appears to have done what we understood to be impossible—restored your wife's reason. A fiery-headed Hungarian Princess has pursued you down here, and has now gone to her room in a tantrum because you left her side for a few minutes to welcome your wife. And there remains our own sentimental little flirtation, a broken and, alas, a discarded thing! There is no doubt whatever, Everard, that you are a very bad lot."

"You are distressing me terribly," Dominey confessed, "but all the same, after a somewhat agitated evening I must admit that I find it pleasant to talk with some one who is not wielding the lightnings. May I have a whisky and soda?"

"Bring me one, too, please," Caroline begged. "I fear that it will seriously impair the note which I had intended to strike in our conversation, but I am thirsty. And a handful of those Turkish cigarettes, too. You can devote yourself to me with a perfectly clear conscience. Your most distinguished guest has found a task after his own heart. He has got Henry in a corner of the billiard-room and is trying to convince him of what I am sure the dear man really believes himself—that Germany's intentions towards England are of a particularly dovelike nature. Your Right Honourable guest has gone to bed, and Eddy Pelham is playing billiards with Mr. Mangan. Every one is happy. You can devote yourself to soothing my wounded vanity, to say nothing of my broken heart."

"Always gibing at me," Dominey grumbled.

"Not always," she answered quietly, raising her eyes for a moment. "There was a time, Everard, before that terrible tragedy—the last time you stayed at Dunratter—when I didn't gibe."

"When, on the contrary, you were sweetness itself," he reflected.

She sighed reminiscently.

"That was a wonderful month," she murmured. "I think it was then for the first time that I saw traces of something in you which I suppose accounts for your being what you are today."

"You think that I have changed, then?"

She looked him in the eyes.

"I sometimes find it difficult to believe," she admitted, "that you are the same man."

He turned away to reach for his whisky and soda.

"As a matter of curiosity," he asked, "why?"

"To begin with, then," she commented, "you have become almost a precisian in your speech. You used to be rather slangy at times."

"What else?"

"You used always to clip your final g's."

"Shocking habit," he murmured. "I cured myself of that by reading aloud in the bush.—Go on, please?"

"You carry yourself so much more stiffly. Sometimes you have the air of being surprised that you are not in uniform."

"Trifles, all these things," he declared. "Now for something serious?"

"The serious things are pretty good," she admitted. "You used to drink whiskies and sodas at all hours of the day, and quite as much wine as was good for you at dinner time. Now, although you are a wonderful host, you scarcely take anything yourself."

"You should see me at the port," he told her, "when you ladies are well out of the way! Some more of the good, please?"

"All your best qualities seem to have come to the surface," she went on, "and I think that the way you have come back and faced it all is simply wonderful. Tell me, if that man's body should be discovered after all these years, would you be charged with manslaughter?"

He shook his head. "I do not think so, Caroline."

"Everard."

"Well?"

"Did you kill Roger Unthank?"

A portion of the burning log fell onto the hearth. Then there was silence. They heard the click of the billiard balls in the adjoining room. Dominey leaned forward and with a pair of small tongs replaced the burning wood upon the fire. Suddenly he felt his hands clasped by his companion's.

"Everard dear," she said, "I am so sorry. You came to me a little tired tonight, didn't you? I think that you needed sympathy, and here I am asking you once more that horrible question. Forget it, please. Talk to me like your old dear self. Tell me about Rosamund's return? Is she really recovered, do you think?"

"I saw her only for a few minutes," Dominey replied, "but she seemed to me absolutely better. I must say that the weekly reports I have received from the nursing home quite prepared me for a great improvement. She is very frail, and her eyes still have that restless look, but she talks quite coherently."

"What about that horrible woman?"

"I have pensioned Mrs. Unthank. To my surprise I hear that she is still living in the village."

"And your ghost?"

"Not a single howl all the time that Rosamund has been away."

"There is one thing more," Caroline began hesitatingly.

That one thing lacked forever the clothing of words. There came a curious, almost a dramatic interruption. Through the silence of the hall there pealed the summons of the great bell which hung over the front door. Dominey glanced at the clock in amazement.

"Midnight!" he exclaimed. "Who on earth can be coming here at this time of night!"

Instinctively they both rose to their feet. A manservant had turned the great key, drawn the bolts, and opened the door with difficulty. Little flakes of snow and a gust of icy wind swept into the hall, and following them the figure of a man, white from head to foot, his hair tossed with the wind, almost unrecognisable after his struggle.

"Why, Doctor Harrison!" Dominey cried, taking a quick step forward. "What brings you here at this time of night!"

The doctor leaned upon his stick for a moment. He was out of breath, and the melting snow was pouring from his clothes on to the oak floor. They relieved him of his coat and dragged him towards the fire.

"I must apologise for disturbing you at such an hour," he said, as he took the tumbler which Dominey pressed into his hand. "I have only just received Lady Dominey's telegram. I had to see you—at once."

# CHAPTER XVIII

THE DOCTOR, with his usual bluntness, did not hesitate to make it known that this unusual visit was of a private nature. Caroline promptly withdrew, and the two men were left alone in the great hall. The lights in the billiard-room and drawing-room were extinguished. Every one in the house except a few servants had retired.

"Sir Everard," the doctor began, "this return of Lady Dominey's has taken me altogether by surprise. I had intended tomorrow morning to discuss the situation with you."

"I am most anxious to hear your report," Dominey said.

"My report is good," was the confident answer. "Although I would not have allowed her to have left the nursing home so suddenly had I known, there was nothing to keep her there. Lady Dominey, except for one hallucination, is in perfect health, mentally and physically."

"And this one hallucination?"

"That you are not her husband."

Dominey was silent for a moment. Then he laughed a little unnaturally.

"Can a person be perfectly sane," he asked, "and yet be subject to an hallucination which must make the whole of her surroundings seem unreal?"

"Lady Dominey is perfectly sane," the doctor answered bluntly, "and as for that hallucination, it is up to you to dispel it."

"Perhaps you can give me some advice?" Dominey suggested.

"I can, and I am going to be perfectly frank with you," the doctor replied. "To begin with then, there are certain obvious changes in you which might well minister to Lady

Dominey's hallucination. For instance, you have been in England now some eight months, during which time you have revealed an entirely new personality. You seem to have got rid of every one of your bad habits, you drink moderately, as a gentleman should, you have subdued your violent temper, and you have collected around you, where your personality could be the only inducement, friends of distinction and interest. This is not at all what one expected from the Everard Dominey who scuttled out of England a dozen years ago."

"You are excusing my wife," Dominey remarked.

"She needs no excuses," was the brusque reply. "She has been a long-enduring and faithful woman, suffering from a cruel illness, brought on, to take the kindest view of it, through your clumsiness and lack of discretion. Like all good women, forgiveness is second nature to her. It has now become her wish to take her proper place in life."

"But if her hallucination continues," Dominey asked, "if she seriously doubts that I am indeed her husband, how can she do that?"

"That is the problem you and I have to face," the doctor said sternly. "The fact that your wife has been willing to return here to you, whilst still subject to that hallucination, is a view of the matter which I can neither discuss nor understand. I am here tonight, though, to lay a charge upon you. You have to remember that your wife needs still one step towards a perfect recovery, and until that step has been surmounted you have a very difficult but imperative task."

Dominey set his teeth for a moment. He felt the doctor's keen grey eyes glowering from under his shaggy eyebrows as he leaned forward, his hands upon his knees.

"You mean," Dominey suggested quietly, "that until that hallucination has passed we must remain upon the same terms as we have done since my arrival home."

"You've got it," the doctor assented. "It's a tangled-up position, but we've got to deal with it—or rather you have. I can assure you," he went on, "that all her other delusions have gone. She speaks of the ghost of Roger Unthank, of the cries at night, of his mysterious death, as parts of a painful past. She is quite conscious of her several attempts upon your life and bitterly regrets them. Now we come to the real danger. She appears to be possessed of a passionate devotion towards you, whilst still believing that you are not her husband."

Dominey pushed his chair back from the fire as though he felt the heat. His eyes seemed glued upon the doctor's.

"I do not pretend," the latter continued gravely, "to account for that, but it is my duty to warn you, Sir Everard, that that devotion may lead her to great lengths. Lady Dominey is naturally of an exceedingly affectionate disposition, and this return to a stronger condition of physical health and a fuller share of human feelings has probably reawakened all those tendencies which her growing fondness for you and your position as her reputed husband make perfectly natural. I warn you, Sir Everard, that you may find your position an exceedingly difficult one, but, difficult though it may be, there is a plain duty before you. Keep and encourage your wife's affection if you can, but let it be a charge upon you that whilst the hallucination remains that affection must never pass certain bounds. Lady Dominey is a good and a sweet woman. If she woke up one morning with that hallucination still in her mind, and any sense of guilt on her conscience, all our labours for these last months might well be wasted, and she herself might very possibly end her days in a madhouse."

"Doctor," Dominey said firmly. "I appreciate every word you say. You can rely upon me."

The doctor looked at him.

"I believe I can," he admitted, with a sigh of relief. "I am glad of it."

"There is just one more phase of the position," Dominey went on, after a pause. "Supposing this hallucination of hers should pass? Supposing she should suddenly become convinced that I am her husband?"

"In that case," the doctor replied earnestly, "the position would be exactly reversed, and it would be just as important for you not to check the affection which she might offer to you as it would be in the other case for you to accept it. The moment she realises, with her present predispositions, that you really are her lawful husband, that moment will be the beginning of a new life for her."

Somehow they both seemed to feel that the last words had been spoken. After a brief pause, the doctor helped himself to a farewell drink, filled his pipe and stood up. The car which Dominey had ordered from the garage was already standing at the door. It was curious how both of them seemed disinclined to refer again even indirectly to the subject which they had been discussing.

"Very good of you to send me back," the doctor said gruffly. "I started out all right, but it was a drear walk across the marshes."

"I am very grateful to you for coming," Dominey replied, with obvious sincerity. "You will come and have a look at the patient in a day or two?"

"I'll stroll across as soon as you've got rid of some of this houseful," the doctor promised. "Good night!"

The two men parted, and curiously enough Dominey was conscious that with those few awkward words of farewell some part of the incipient antagonism between them had been buried. Left to himself, he wandered for some moments up and down the great, dimly lit hall. A strange restlessness seemed to have fastened itself upon him. He stood for a time by the dying fire, watching the grey ashes, stirred uneasily by the wind which howled down the chimney. Then he strolled to a different part of the hall, and one by one he turned on, by means of the electric switches, the newly installed lights which hung above the sombre oil pictures upon the wall. He looked into the faces of some of these dead Domineys, trying to recall what he had heard of their history, and dwelling longest upon a gallant of the Stuart epoch, whose misdeeds had supplied material for every intimate chronicler of those days. When at last the sight of a sleepy manservant hovering in the background forced his steps upstairs, he still lingered for a few moments in the corridor and turned the handle of his bedroom door with almost reluctant fingers. His heart gave a great jump as he realised that there was some one there. He stood for a moment upon the threshold, then laughed shortly to himself at his foolish imagining. It was his servant who was patiently awaiting his arrival.

"You can go to bed, Dickens," he directed. "I shall not want you again tonight. We shoot in the morning."

The man silently took his leave, and Dominey commenced his preparations for bed. He was in no humour for sleep, however, and, still attired in his shirt and trousers, he wrapped a dressing-gown around him, drew a reading lamp to his side, and threw himself into an easy-chair, a book in his hand. It was some time before he realised that the volume was upside down, and even when he had righted it, the words he saw had no meaning for him. All the time a queer procession of women's faces was passing before his eyes—Caroline, with her half-flirtatious, wholly sentimental *bon camaraderie*; Stephanie, with her voluptuous figure and passion-lit eyes; and then, blotting the others utterly out of his thoughts and memory, Rosamund, with all the sweetness of life shining out of her eager face. He saw her as she had come to him last, with that little unspoken cry upon her tremulous lips, and the haunting appeal in her soft eyes. All other memories faded away. They were as though they had never been. Those dreary years of exile in Africa, the day by day tension of his precarious life, were absolutely forgotten. His heart was calling all the time for an unknown boon. He felt himself immeshed in a world of cobwebs, of weakness more potent than all his boasted strength. Then he suddenly felt that the madness which he had begun to fear had really come. It was the thing for which he longed yet dreaded most—the faint click, the soft withdrawal of the panel, actually pushed back by a pair of white hands. Rosamund herself was there. Her eyes shone at him, mystically, wonderfully. Her lips were parted in a delightful smile, a smile in which there was a spice of girlish mischief. She turned for a moment to close the panel. Then she came towards him with her finger upraised.

"I cannot sleep," she said softly. "Do you mind my coming for a few minutes?"

"Of course not," he answered. "Come and sit down."

She curled up in his easy-chair.

"Just for a moment," she murmured contentedly. "Give me your hands, dear. But how cold! You must come nearer to the fire yourself."

He sat on the arm of her chair, and she stroked his head with her hands.

"You were not afraid, then," she asked, "when you saw me come through the panel?"

"I should never be afraid of any harm that you might bring me, dear," he assured her.

"Because all that foolishness is really gone," she continued eagerly. "I know that whatever happened to poor Roger, it was not you who killed him. Even if I heard his ghost calling again tonight, I should have no fear. I can't think why I ever wanted to hurt you, Everard. I am sure that I always loved you."

His arm went very softly around her. She responded to his embrace without hesitation. Her cheek rested upon his shoulder, he felt the warmth of her arm through her white, fur-lined dressing-gown.

"Why do you doubt any longer then," he asked hoarsely, "that I am your husband?"

She sighed.

"Ah, but I know you are not," she answered. "Is it wrong of me to feel what I do for you, I wonder? You are so like yet so unlike him. He is dead. He died in Africa. Isn't it strange that I should know it? But I do!"

"But who am I then?" he whispered.

She looked at him pitifully.

"I do not know," she confessed, "but you are kind to me, and when I feel you are near I am happy. It is because I wanted to see you that I would not stay any longer at the nursing home. That must mean that I am very fond of you."

"You are not afraid," he asked, "to be here alone with me?"

She put her other arm around his neck and drew his face down.

"I am not afraid," she assured him. "I am happy.—But, dear, what is the matter? A moment ago you were cold. Now your head is wet, your hands are burning. Are you not happy because I am here?"

Her lips were seeking his. His own touched them for a moment. Then he kissed her on both cheeks. She made a little grimace.

"I am afraid," she said, "that you are not really fond of me."

"Can't you believe," he asked hoarsely, "that I am really Everard—your husband? Look at me. Can't you feel that you have loved me before?"

She shook her head a little sadly.

"No, you are not Everard," she sighed; "but," she added, her eyes lighting up, "you bring me love and happiness and life, and—"

A few seconds before, Dominey felt from his soul that he would have welcomed an earthquake, a thunderbolt, the crumbling of the floor beneath his feet to have been spared the torture of her sweet importunities. Yet nothing so horrible as this interruption which really came could ever have presented itself before his mind. Half in his arms, with her head thrown back, listening—he, too, horrified, convulsed for a moment even with real physical fear—they heard the silence of the night broken by that one awful cry, the cry of a man's soul in torment, imprisoned in the jaws of a beast. They listened to it together until its echoes died away. Then what was, perhaps, the most astonishing thing of all, she nodded her head slowly, unperturbed, unterrified.

"You see," she said, "I must go back. He will not let me stay here. He must think that you are Everard. It is only I who know that you are not."

She slipped from the chair, kissed him, and, walking quite firmly across the floor, touched the spring and passed through the panel. Even then she turned around and waved a little good-bye to him. There was no sign of fear in her face; only a little dumb disappointment. The panel glided to and shut out the vision of her. Dominey held his head like a man who fears madness.

## CHAPTER XIX

DAWN the next morning was heralded by only a thin line of red parting the masses of black-grey snow clouds which still hung low down in the east. The wind had dropped, and there was something ghostly about the still twilight as Dominey issued from the back regions and made his way through the untrodden snow round to the side of the house underneath Rosamund's window. A little exclamation broke from his lips as he stood there. From the terraced walk, down the steps, and straight across the park to the corner of the Black Wood, were fresh tracks. The cry had been no fantasy. Somebody or something had passed from the Black Wood and back again to this spot in the night.

Dominey, curiously excited by his discovery, examined the footmarks eagerly, then followed them to the corner of the wood. Here and there they puzzled him. They were neither like human footsteps nor the track of any known animal. At the edge of the wood they seemed to vanish into the heart of a great mass of brambles, from which here and there the snow had been shaken off. There was no sign of any pathway; if ever there had been one, the neglect of years had obliterated it. Bracken, brambles, shrubs and bushes had grown up and degenerated, only to be succeeded by a ranker and more dense form of undergrowth. Many of the trees, although they were still plentiful, had been blown down and left to rot on the ground. The place was silent except for the slow drip of falling snow from the drooping leaves. He took one more cautious step forward and found himself slowly sinking. Black mud was oozing up through the snow where he had set his feet. He was just able to scramble back. Picking his way with great caution, he commenced a leisurely perambulation of the whole of the outside of the wood.

Heggs, the junior keeper, an hour or so later, went over the gun rack once more, tapped the empty cases, and turned towards Middleton, who was sitting in a chair before the fire, smoking his pipe.

"I can't find master's number two gun, Mr. Middleton," he announced. "That's missing."

"Look again, lad," the old keeper directed, removing the pipe from his mouth. "The master was shooting with it yesterday. Look amongst those loose 'uns at the far end of the rack. It must be somewhere there."

"Well, that isn't," the young man replied obstinately.

The door of the room was suddenly opened, and Dominey entered with the missing gun under his arm. Middleton rose to his feet at once and laid down his pipe. Surprise kept him temporarily silent.

"I want you to come this way with me for a moment," his master ordered.

The keeper took up his hat and stick and followed. Dominey led him to where the tracks had halted on the gravel outside Rosamund's window and pointed across to the Black Wood.

"What do you make of those?" he enquired.

Middleton did not hesitate. He shook his head gravely.

"Was anything heard last night, sir?"

"There was an infernal yell underneath this window."

"That was the spirit of Roger Unthank, for sure," Middleton pronounced, with a little shudder. "When he do come out of that wood, he do call."

"Spirits," his master pointed out, "do not leave tracks like that behind."

Middleton considered the matter.

"They do say hereabout," he confided, "that the spirit of Roger Unthank have been taken possession of by some sort of great animal, and that it do come here now and then to be fed."

"By whom?" Dominey enquired patiently.

"Why, by Mrs. Unthank."

"Mrs. Unthank has not been in this house for many months. From the day she left until last night, so far as I can gather, nothing has been heard of this ghost, or beast, or whatever it is."

"That do seem queer, surely," Middleton admitted.

Dominey followed the tracks with his eyes to the wood and back again.

"Middleton," he said, "I am learning something about spirits. It seems that they not only make tracks, but they require feeding. Perhaps if that is so they can feel a charge of shot inside them."

The old man seemed for a moment to stiffen with slow horror.

"You wouldn't shoot at it, Squire?" he gasped.

"I should have done so this morning if I had had a chance," Dominey replied. "When the weather is a little drier, I am going to make my way into that wood, Middleton, with a rifle under my arm."

"Then as God's above, you'll never come out, Squire!" was the solemn reply.

"We will see," Dominey muttered. "I have hacked my way through some queer country in Africa."

"There's nowt like this wood in the world, sir," the old man asserted doggedly. "The bottom's rotten from end to end and the top's all poisonous. The birds die there on the trees. It's chockful of reptiles and unclean things, with green and purple fungi, two feet high, with poison in the very sniff of them. The man who enters that wood goes to his grave."

"Nevertheless," Dominey said firmly, "within a very short time I am going to solve the mystery of this nocturnal visitor."

They returned to the house, side by side. Just before they entered, Dominey turned to his companion.

"Middleton," he said, "you keep up the good old customs, I suppose, and spend half an hour at the 'Dominey Arms' now and then?"

"Most every night of my life, sir," the old man replied, "from eight till nine. I'm a man of regular habits, and that do seem right to me that with the work done right and proper a man should have his relaxation."

"That is right, John," Dominey assented. "Next time you are there, don't forget to mention that I am going to have that wood looked through. I should like it to get about, you understand?"

"That'll fair flummox the folk," was the doubtful reply, "but I'll let 'em know, Squire. There'll be a rare bit of talk, I can promise you that."

Dominey handed over his gun, went to his room, bathed and changed, and descended for breakfast. There was a sudden hush as he entered, which he very well understood. Every one began to talk about the prospect of the day's sport. Dominey helped himself from the sideboard and took his place at the table.

"I hope," he said, "that our very latest thing in ghosts did not disturb anybody."

"We all seem to have heard the same thing," the Cabinet Minister observed, with interest,—"a most appalling and unearthly cry. I have lately joined every society connected with spooks and find them a fascinating study."

"If you want to investigate," Dominey observed, as he helped himself to coffee, "you can bring out a revolver and prowl about with me one night. From the time when I was a kid, before I went to Eton, up till when I left here for Africa, we had a series of highly respectable and well-behaved ghosts, who were a credit to the family and of whom we were somewhat proud. This latest spook, however, is something quite outside the pale."

"Has he a history?" Mr. Watson asked, with interest.

"I am informed," Dominey replied, "that he is the spirit of a schoolmaster who once lived here, and for whose departure from the world I am supposed to be responsible. Such a spook is neither a credit nor a comfort to the family."

Their host spoke with such an absolute absence of emotion that every one was conscious of a curious reluctance to abandon a subject full of such fascinating possibilities. Terniloff was the only one, however, who made a suggestion.

"We might have a battue in the wood," he proposed.

"I am not sure," Dominey told them, "that the character of the wood is not more interesting than the ghost who is supposed to dwell in it. You remember how terrified the beaters were yesterday at the bare suggestion of entering it? For generations it has been held unclean. It is certainly most unsafe. I went in over my knees on the outskirts of it this morning.—Shall we say half-past ten in the gun room?"

Seaman followed his host out of the room.

"My friend," he said, "you must not allow these local circumstances to occupy too large a share of your thoughts. It is true that these are the days of your relaxation. Still, there is the Princess for you to think of. After all, she has us in her power. The merest whisper in Downing Street, and behold, catastrophe!"

Dominey took his friend's arm.

"Look here, Seaman," he rejoined, "it's easy enough to say there is the Princess to be considered, but will you kindly tell me what on earth more I can do to make her see the position? Necessity demands that I should be on the best of terms with Lady Dominey and that I should not make myself in any way conspicuous with the Princess."

"I am not sure," Seaman reflected, "that the terms you are on with Lady Dominey matter very much to any one. So far as regards the Princess, she is an impulsive and passionate person, but she is also *grande dame* and a diplomatist. I see no reason why you should not marry her secretly in London, in the name of Everard Dominey, and have the ceremony repeated under your rightful name later on."

They had paused to help themselves to cigarettes, which were displayed with a cabinet of cigars on a round table in the hall. Dominey waited for a moment before he answered.

"Has the Princess confided to you that that is her wish?" he asked.

"Something of the sort," Seaman acknowledged. "She wishes the suggestion, however, to come from you."

"And your advice?"

Seaman blew out a little cloud of cigar smoke.

"My friend," he confessed, "I am a little afraid of the Princess. I ask you no questions as to your own feelings with regard to her. I take it for granted that as a man of honour it will be your duty to offer her your hand in marriage, sooner or later. I see no harm in anticipating a few months, if by that means we can pacify her. Terniloff would arrange it at the Embassy. He is devoted to her, and it will strengthen your position with him."

Dominey turned away towards the stairs.

"We will discuss this again before we leave," he said gloomily.

Dominey was admitted at once by her maid into his wife's sitting-room. Rosamund, in a charming morning robe of pale blue lined with grey fur, had just finished breakfast. She held out her hands to him with a delighted little cry of welcome.

"How nice of you to come, Everard!" she exclaimed. "I was hoping I should see you for a moment before you went off."

He raised her fingers to his lips and sat down by her side. She seemed entirely delighted by his presence, and he felt instinctively that she was quite unaffected by the event of the night before.

"You slept well?" he enquired.

"Perfectly," she answered.

He tackled the subject bravely, as he had made up his mind to on every opportunity.

"You do not lie awake thinking of our nocturnal visitor, then?"

"Not for one moment. You see," she went on conversationally, "if you were really Everard, then I might be frightened, for some day or other I feel that if Everard comes here, the spirit of Roger Unthank will do him some sort of mischief."

"Why?" he asked.

"You don't know about these things, of course," she went on, "but Roger Unthank was in love with me, although I had scarcely ever spoken to him, before I married Everard. I think I told you that much yesterday, didn't I? After I was married, the poor man nearly went out of his mind. He gave up his work and used to haunt the park here. One evening Everard caught him and they fought, and Roger Unthank was never seen again. I think that any one around here would tell you," she went on, dropping her voice a little, "that Everard killed Roger and threw him into one of those swampy places near the Black Wood, where a body sinks and sinks and nothing is ever seen of it again."

"I do not believe he did anything of the sort," Dominey declared.

"Oh, I don't know," she replied doubtfully. "Everard had a terrible temper, and that night he came home covered with blood, looking—awful! It was the night when I was taken ill."

"Well, no more tragedies," he insisted. "I have come up to remind you that we have guests here. When are you coming down to see them?"

She laughed like a child.

"You say 'we' just as though you were really my husband," she declared.

"You must not tell any one else of your fancy," he warned her.

She acquiesced at once.

"Oh, I quite understand," she assured him. "I shall be very, very careful. And, Everard, you have such clever guests, not at all the sort of people my Everard would have had here, and I have been out of the world for so long, that I am afraid I sha'n't be able to talk to them. Nurse Alice is tremendously impressed. I am sure I should be terrified to sit at the end of the table, and Caroline will hate not being hostess any longer. Let me come down at tea-time and after dinner, and slip into things gradually. You can easily say that I am still an invalid, though of course I'm not at all."

"You shall do exactly as you choose," he promised, as he took his leave.

So when the shooting party tramped into the hall that afternoon, a little weary, but flushed with exercise and the pleasure of the day's sport, they found, seated in a corner of the room, behind the great round table upon which tea was set out, a rather pale but extraordinarily childlike and fascinating woman, with large, sweet eyes which seemed to be begging for their protection and sympathy as she rose hesitatingly to her feet. Dominey was by her side in a moment, and his first few words of introduction brought every one around her. She said very little, but what she said was delightfully natural and gracious.

"It has been so kind of you," she said to Caroline, "to help my husband entertain his guests. I am very much better, but I have been ill for so long that I have forgotten a great many things, and I should be a very poor hostess. But I want to make tea for you, please, and I want you all to tell me how many pheasants you have shot."

Terniloff seated himself on the settee by her side.

"I am going to help you in this complicated task," he declared. "I am sure those sugar tongs are too heavy for you to wield alone."

She laughed at him gaily.

"But I am not really delicate at all," she assured him. "I have had a very bad illness, but I am quite strong again."

"Then I will find some other excuse for sitting here," he said. "I will tell you all about the high pheasants your husband killed, and about the woodcock he brought down after we had all missed it."

"I shall love to hear about that," she assented. "How much sugar, please, and will you pass those hot muffins to the Princess? And please touch that bell. I shall want more hot water. I expect you are all very thirsty. I am so glad to be here with you."

## CHAPTER XX

ARM IN ARM, Prince Terniloff and his host climbed the snow-covered slope at the back of a long fir plantation, towards the little beflagged sticks which indicated their stand. There was not a human being in sight, for the rest of the guns had chosen a steeper but somewhat less circuitous route.

"Von Ragastein," the Ambassador said, "I am going to give myself the luxury of calling you by your name. You know my one weakness, a weakness which in my younger days very nearly drove me out of diplomacy. I detest espionage in every shape and form, even where it is necessary. So far as you are concerned, my young friend," he went on, "I think your position ridiculous. I have sent a private despatch to Potsdam, in which I have expressed that opinion."

"So far," Dominey remarked, "I have not been overworked."

"My dear young friend," the Prince continued, "you have not been overworked because there has been no legitimate work for you to do. There will be none. There could be no possible advantage accruing from your labours here to compensate for the very bad effect which the discovery of your true name and position would have in the English Cabinet."

"I must ask you to remember," Dominey begged, "that I am here as a blind servant of the Fatherland. I simply obey orders."

"I will grant that freely," the Prince consented. "But to continue. I am now at the end of my first year in this country. I feel able to congratulate myself upon a certain measure of success. From that part of the Cabinet with whom I have had to do, I have received nothing but encouragement in my efforts to promote a better understanding between our two countries."

"The sky certainly seems clear enough just now," agreed Dominey.

"I have convinced myself," the Prince said emphatically, "that there is a genuine and solid desire for peace with Germany existing in Downing Street. In every argument I have had, in every concession I have asked for, I have been met with a sincere desire to foster the growing friendship between our countries. I am proud of my work here, Von Ragastein. I believe that I have brought Germany and England nearer together than they have been since the days of the Boer War."

"You are sure, sir," Dominey asked, "that you are not confusing personal popularity with national sentiment?"

"I am sure of it," the Ambassador answered gravely. "Such popularity as I may have achieved here has been due to an appreciation of the more healthy state of world politics now existing. It has been my great pleasure to trace the result of my work in a manuscript of memoirs, which some day, when peace is firmly established between our two countries, I shall cause to be published. I have put on record there evidences of the really genuine sentiment in favour of peace which I have found amongst the present Cabinet."

"I should esteem it an immense privilege," Dominey said, "to be given a private reading of these memoirs."

"That may be arranged," was the suave reply. "In the meantime, Von Ragastein, I want you to reconsider your position here."

"My position is not voluntary," Dominey repeated. "I am acting under orders."

"Precisely," the other acquiesced, "but matters have changed very much during the last six months. Even at the risk of offending France, England is showing wonderful pliability with regard to our claims in Morocco. Every prospect of disagreement between our two countries upon any vital matter has now disappeared."

"Unless," Dominey said thoughtfully, "the desire for war should come, not from Downing Street but from Potsdam."

"We serve an honourable master," Terniloff declared sternly, "and he has shown me his mind. His will is for peace, and for the great triumphs to which our country is already entitled by reason of her supremacy in industry, in commerce, in character and in genius. These are the weapons which will make Germany the greatest Power in the world. No empire has ever hewn its way to permanent glory by the sword alone. We have reached our stations, I see. Come to me after this drive is finished, my host. All that I have said so far has been by way of prelude."

The weather had turned drier, the snow was crisp, and a little party of women from the Hall reached the guns before the beaters were through the wood. Caroline and Stephanie both took their places by Dominey's side. The former, however, after a few minutes passed on to Terniloff's stand. Stephanie and Dominey were alone for the first time since their stormy interview in the library.

"Has Maurice been talking to you?" she asked a little abruptly.

"His Excellency and I are, to tell you the truth," Dominey confessed, "in the midst of a most interesting conversation."

"Has he spoken to you about me?"

"Your name has not yet been mentioned."

She made a little grimace. In her wonderful furs and Russian turban hat she made rather a striking picture against the background of snow.

"An interesting conversation in which my name has not been mentioned!" she repeated satirically.

"I think you were coming into it before very long," Dominey assured her. "His Excellency warned me that all he had said so far was merely the prelude to a matter of larger importance."

Stephanie smiled.

"Dear Maurice is so diplomatic," she murmured. "I am perfectly certain he is going to begin by remonstrating with you for your shocking treatment of me."

Their conversation was interrupted for a few minutes by the sport. Dominey called the faithful Middleton to his side for a further supply of cartridges. Stephanie bided her time, which came when the beaters at last emerged from the wood.

"Shocking," Stephanie repeated, reverting to their conversation, "is the mildest word in my vocabulary which I can apply to your treatment of me. Honestly, Leopold, I feel bruised all over inside. My pride is humbled."

"It is because you look at the matter only from a feminine point of view," Dominey persisted.

"And you," she answered in a low tone, "once the fondest and the most passionate of lovers, only from a political one. You think a great deal, of your country, Leopold. Have I no claims upon you?"

"Upon Everard Dominey, none," he insisted. "When the time comes, and Leopold von Ragastein can claim all that is his right, believe me, you will have no cause to complain of coldness or dilatoriness. He will have only one thought, only one hope—to end the torture of these years of separation as speedily as may be."

The strained look passed from her face. Her tone became more natural.

"But, dear," she pleaded, "there is no need to wait. Your Sovereign gives you permission. Your political chief will more than endorse it."

"I am on the spot," Dominey replied, "and believe me I know what is safest and best. I cannot live as two men and keep my face steadfast to the world. The Prince, however, has not spoken to me yet. I will hear what he has to say."

Stephanie turned a little haughtily away.

"You are putting me in the position of a suppliant!" she exclaimed. "Tonight we must have an understanding."

The little party moved on all together to another cover. Rosamund had joined them and hung on to Dominey's arm with delight. The brisk walk across the park had brought colour to her cheeks. She walked with all the free and vigorous grace of a healthy woman. Dominey found himself watching her, as she deserted him a little later on to stand by Terniloff's side, with a little thrill of tangled emotions. He felt a touch on his arm. Stephanie, who was passing with another of the guns, paused to whisper in his ear:

"There might be a greater danger—one that has evaded even your cautious mind—in overplaying your part!"

Dominey was taken possession of by Caroline on their walk to the next stand. She planted herself on a shooting stick by his side and commenced to take him roundly to task.

"My dear Everard," she said, "you are one of the most wonderful examples of the reformed rake I ever met! You have even acquired respectability. For heaven's sake, don't disappoint us all!"

"I seem to be rather good at that," Dominey observed a little drearily.

"Well, you are the master of your own actions, are you not?" she asked. "What I want to say in plain words is, don't go and make a fool of yourself with Stephanie."

"I have not the least intention of doing anything of the sort."

"Well, she has! Mark my words, Everard, I know that woman. She is clever and brilliant and anything else you like, but for some reason or other she has set her mind upon you. She looks at dear little Rosamund as though she hadn't a right to exist. Don't look so sorry for yourself. You must have encouraged her."

Dominey was silent. Fortunately, the exigencies of the next few minutes demanded it. His cousin waited patiently until there came a pause in the shooting.

"Now let me hear what you have to say for yourself, sir? So far as I can see, you've been quite sweet to your wife, and she adores you. If you want to have an affair with the Princess, don't begin it here. You'll have your wife ill again if you make her jealous."

"My dear Caroline, there will be no affair between Stephanie and me. Of that you may rest assured."

"You mean to say that this is altogether on her side, then?" Caroline persisted.

"You exaggerate her demeanour," he replied, "but even if what you suggest were true—"

"Oh, I don't want a lot of protestations!" she interrupted. "I am not saying that you encourage her much, because I don't believe you do. All I want to point out is that, having really brought your wife back almost to health, you must be extraordinarily and wonderfully careful. If you want to talk nonsense with Stephanie, do it in Belgrave Square."

Dominey was watching the gyrations of a falling pheasant. His left hand was stretched out towards the cartridge bag which Caroline was holding. He clasped her fingers for a moment before he helped himself.

"You are rather a dear," he said. "I would not do anything to hurt Rosamund for the world."

"If you can't get rid of your old tricks altogether and must flirt," she remarked, "well, I'm always somewhere about. Rosamund wouldn't mind me, because there are a few grey hairs in my sandy ones.—And here comes your man across the park—looks as though he had a message for you. So long as nothing has happened to your cook, I feel that I could face ill tidings with composure."

Dominey found himself watching with fixed eyes the approach of his rather sad-faced manservant through the snow. Parkins was not dressed for such an enterprise, nor did he seem in any way to relish it. His was the stern march of duty, and, curiously enough, Dominey felt from the moment he caught sight of him that he was in some respects a messenger of Fate. Yet the message which he delivered, when at last he reached his master's side, was in no way alarming.

"A person of the name of Miller has arrived here, sir," he announced, "from Norwich. He is, I understand, a foreigner of some sort, who has recently landed in this country. I found it a little difficult to understand him, but her Highness's maid conversed with him in German, and I understand that he either is or brings you a message from a certain Doctor Schmidt, with whom you were acquainted in Africa."

The warning whistle blew at that moment, and Dominey swung round and stood at attention. His behaviour was perfectly normal. He let a hen pheasant pass over his head, and brought down a cock from very nearly the limit distance. He reloaded before he turned to Parkins.

"Is this person in a hurry?" he said.

"By no means, sir," the man replied. "I told him that you would not be back until three or four o'clock, and he is quite content to wait."

Dominey nodded.

"Look after him yourself then, Parkins," he directed. "We shall not be shooting late today. Very likely I will send Mr. Seaman back to talk to him."

The man raised his hat respectfully and turned back towards the house. Caroline was watching her companion curiously.

"Do you find many of your acquaintances in Africa look you up, Everard?" she asked.

"Except for Seaman," Dominey replied, looking through the barrels of his gun, "who really does not count because we crossed together, this is my first visitor from the land of fortune. I expect there will be plenty of them by and by, though. Colonials have a wonderful habit of sticking to one another."

# CHAPTER XXI

THERE WAS nothing in the least alarming about the appearance of Mr. Ludwig Miller. He had been exceedingly well entertained in the butler's private sitting-room and had the air of having done full justice to the hospitality which had been offered him. He rose to his feet at Dominey's entrance and stood at attention. But for some slight indications of military training, he would have passed anywhere as a highly respectable retired tradesman.

"Sir Everard Dominey?" he enquired.

Dominey nodded assent. "That is my name. Have I seen you before?"

The man shook his head. "I am a cousin of Doctor Schmidt. I arrived in the Colony from Rhodesia, after your Excellency had left."

"And how is the doctor?"

"My cousin is, as always, busy but in excellent health," was the reply. "He sends his respectful compliments and his good wishes. Also this letter."

With a little flourish the man produced an envelope inscribed:

> *To Sir Everard Dominey, Baronet,*
> *Dominey Hall,*
> *In the County of Norfolk,*
> *England.*

Dominey broke the seal just as Seaman entered.

"A messenger here from Doctor Schmidt, an acquaintance of mine in East Africa," he announced. "Mr. Seaman came home from South Africa with me," he explained to his visitor.

The two men looked steadily into each other's eyes. Dominey watched them, fascinated. Neither betrayed himself by even the fall of an eyelid. Yet Dominey, his perceptive powers at their very keenest in this moment which instinct told him was one of crisis, felt the unspoken, unbetokened recognition which passed between them. Some commonplace remark was uttered and responded to. Dominey read the few lines which seemed to take him back for a moment to another world:

"Honoured and Honourable Sir,

"I send you my heartiest and most respectful greeting. Of the progress of all matters here you will learn from another source.

"I recommend to your notice and kindness my cousin, the bearer of this letter—Mr. Ludwig Miller. He will lay before you certain circumstances of which it is advisable for you to have knowledge. You may speak freely with him. He is in all respects to be trusted."

(Signed) "KARL SCHMIDT."

"Your cousin is a little mysterious," Dominey remarked, as he passed the letter to Seaman. "Come, what about these circumstances?"

Ludwig Miller looked around the little room and then at Seaman. Dominey affected to misunderstand his hesitation.

"Our friend here knows everything," he declared. "You can speak to him as to myself."

The man began as one who has a story to tell.

"My errand here is to warn you," he said, "that the Englishman whom you left for dead at Big Bend, on the banks of the Blue River, has been heard of in another part of Africa."

Dominey shook his head incredulously. "I hope you have not come all this way to tell me that! The man was dead."

"My cousin himself," Miller continued, "was hard to convince. The man left his encampment with whisky enough to kill him, thirst enough to drink it all, and no food."

"So I found him," Dominey assented, "deserted by his boys and raving. To silence him forever was a child's task."

"The task, however, was unperformed," the other persisted. "From three places in the Colony he has been heard of, struggling to make his way to the coast."

"Does he call himself by his own name?" Dominey asked.

"He does not," Miller admitted. "My cousin, however, desired me to point out to you the fact that in any case he would probably be shy of doing so. He is behaving in an absurd manner; he is in a very weakly state; and without a doubt he is to some degree insane. Nevertheless, the fact remains that he is in the Colony, or was three months ago, and that if he succeeds in reaching the coast you may at any time be surprised by a visit from him here. I am sent to warn you in order that you may take what steps may be necessary and not be placed at a disadvantage if he should appear."

"This is queer news you have brought us, Miller," Seaman said thoughtfully.

"It is news which greatly disturbed Doctor Schmidt," the man replied. "He has had the natives up one after the other for cross-examination. Nothing can shake their story."

"If we believed it," Seaman continued, "this other European, if he had business in this direction, might walk in here at any moment."

"It was to warn you of that possibility that I am here."

"How much do you know personally," Seaman asked, "of the existent circumstances?"

The man shook his head vaguely.

"I know nothing," he admitted. "I went out to East Africa some years ago, and I have been a trader in Mozambique in a small way. I supplied outfits for officers and hospitals and sportsmen. Now and then I have to return to Europe to buy fresh stock. Doctor Schmidt knew that, and he came to see me just before I sailed. He first thought of writing a very long letter. Afterwards he changed his mind. He wrote only those few lines I brought, but he told me those other things."

"You have remembered all that he told you?" Dominey asked.

"I can think of nothing else," was the reply, after a moment's pause. "The whole affair has been a great worry to Doctor Schmidt. There are things connected with it which he has never understood, things connected with it which he has always found mysterious."

"Hence your presence here, Johann Wolff, eh?" Seaman asked, in an altered tone.

The visitor's expression remained unchanged except for the faint surprise which shone out of his blue eyes.

"Johann Wolff," he repeated. "That is not my name. I am Ludwig Miller, and I know nothing of this matter beyond what I have told you. I am just a messenger."

"Once in Vienna and twice in Cracow, my friend, we have met," Seaman reminded him softly but very insistently.

The other shook his head gently. "A mistake. I have been in Vienna once, many years ago, but Cracow never."

"You have no idea with whom you are talking?"

"Herr Seaman was the name, I understood."

"It is a very good name," Seaman scoffed. "Look here and think."

He undid his coat and waistcoat and displayed a plain vest of chamois leather. Attached to the left-hand side of it was a bronze decoration, with lettering and a number. Miller stared at it blankly and shook his head.

"Information Department, Bureau Twelve, password—'The Day is coming,'" Seaman continued, dropping his voice.

His listener shook his head and smiled with the puzzled ignorance of a child.

"The gentleman mistakes me for some one else," he replied. "I know nothing of these things."

Seaman sat and studied this obstinate visitor for several minutes without speaking, his finger tips pressed together, his eyebrows gently contracted. His vis-à-vis endured this scrutiny without flinching, calm, phlegmatic, the very prototype of the bourgeois German of the tradesman class.

"Do you propose," Dominey enquired, "to stay in these parts long?"

"One or two days—a week, perhaps," was the indifferent answer. "I have a cousin in Norwich who makes toys. I love the English country. I spend my holiday here, perhaps."

"Just so," Seaman muttered grimly. "The English country under a foot of snow! So you have nothing more to say to me, Johann Wolff?"

"I have executed my mission to his Excellency," was the apologetic reply. "I am sorry to have caused displeasure to you, Herr Seaman."

The latter rose to his feet. Dominey had already turned towards the door.

"You will spend the night here, of course, Mr. Miller?" he invited. "I dare say Mr. Seaman would like to have another talk with you in the morning."

"I shall gladly spend the night here, your Excellency," was the polite reply. "I do not think that I have anything to say, however, which would interest your friend."

"You are making a great mistake, Wolff," Seaman declared angrily. "I am your superior in the Service, and your attitude towards me is indefensible."

"If the gentleman would only believe," the culprit begged, "that he is mistaking me for some one else!"

There was trouble in Seaman's face as the two men made their way to the front of the house and trouble in his tone as he answered his companion's query.

"What do you think of that fellow and his visit?"

"I do not know yet what to think, but there is a great deal that I know," Seaman replied gravely. "The man is a spy, a favourite in the Wilhelmstrasse and only made use of on important occasions. His name is Wolff—Johann Wolff."

"And this story of his?"

"You ought to be the best judge of that."

"I am," Dominey assented confidently. "Without the shadow of a doubt I threw the body of the man I killed into the Blue River and watched it sink."

"Then the story is a fake," Seaman decided. "For some reason or other we have come under the suspicion of our own secret service."

Seaman, as they emerged into the hall, was summoned imperiously to her side by the Princess Eiderstrom. Dominey disappeared for a moment and returned presently, having discarded some of his soaked shooting garments. He was followed by his valet, bearing a note upon a silver tray.

"From the person in Mr. Parkins' room—to Mr. Seaman, sir," the man announced, in a low tone.

Dominey took it from the salver with a little nod. Then he turned to where the youngest and most frivolous of his guests was in the act of rising from the tea table.

"A game of pills, Eddy," he proposed. "They tell me that pool is one of your great accomplishments."

"I'm pretty useful," the young man confessed, with a satisfied chuckle. "Give you a black at snooker, what?"

Dominey took his arm and led him into the billiard-room.

"You will give me nothing, young fellow," he replied. "Set them up, and I will show you how I made a living for two months at Johannesburg!"

# CHAPTER XXII

THE EVENING at Dominey Hall was practically a repetition of the previous one, with a different set of guests from the outer world. After dinner, Dominey was absent for a few minutes and returned with Rosamund upon his arm. She received the congratulations of her neighbours charmingly, and a little court soon gathered around her. Doctor Harrison, who had been dining, remained upon its outskirts, listening to her light-hearted and at times almost brilliant chatter with grave and watchful interest. Dominey, satisfied that she was being entertained, obeyed Terniloff's gestured behest and strolled with him to a distant corner of the hall.

"Let me now, my dear host," the Prince began, with some eagerness in his tone, "continue and, I trust, conclude the conversation to which all that I said this morning was merely the prelude."

"I am entirely at your service," murmured his host.

"I have tried to make you understand that from my own point of view—and I am in a position to know something— the fear of war between this country and our own has passed. England is willing to make all reasonable sacrifices to ensure peace. She wants peace, she intends peace, therefore there will be peace. Therefore, I maintain, my young friend, it is better for you to disappear at once from this false position."

"I am scarcely my own master," Dominey replied. "You yourself must know that. I am here as a servant under orders."

"Join your protest with mine," the Prince suggested. "I will make a report directly I get back to London. To my mind, the matter is urgent. If anything should lead to the discovery of your false position in this country, the friendship between us which has become a real pleasure to me must seriously undermine my own position."

Dominey had risen to his feet and was standing on the hearthrug, in front of a fire of blazing logs. The Ambassador was sitting with crossed legs in a comfortable easy-chair, smoking one of the long, thin cigars which were his particular fancy.

"Your Excellency," Dominey said, "there is just one fallacy in all that you have said."

"A fallacy?"

"You have come to the absolute conclusion," Dominey continued, "that because England wants peace there will be peace. I am of Seaman's mind. I believe in the ultimate power of the military party of Germany. I believe that in time they will thrust their will upon the Kaiser, if he is not at the present moment secretly in league with them. Therefore, I believe that there will be war."

"If I shared that belief with you, my friend," the Ambassador said quietly, "I should consider my position here one of dishonour. My mandate is for peace, and my charge is from the Kaiser's lips."

Stephanie, with the air of one a little weary of the conversation, broke away from a distant group and came towards them. Her beautiful eyes seemed tired, she moved listlessly, and she even spoke with less than her usual assurance.

"Am I disturbing a serious conversation?" she asked. "Send me away if I am."

"His Excellency and I," Dominey observed, "have reached a cul-de-sac in our argument,—the blank wall of good-natured but fundamental disagreement."

"Then I shall claim you for a while," Stephanie declared, taking Dominey's arm. "Lady Dominey has attracted all the men to her circle, and I am lonely."

The Prince bowed.

"I deny the cul-de-sac," he said, "but I yield our host! I shall seek my opponent at billiards."

He turned away and Stephanie sank into his vacant place.

"So you and my cousin," she remarked, as she made room for Dominey to sit by her side, "have come to a disagreement."

"Not an unfriendly one," her host assured her.

"That I am sure of. Maurice seems, indeed, to have taken a wonderful liking to you. I cannot remember that you ever met before, except for that day or two in Saxony?"

"That is so. The first time I exchanged any intimate conversation with the Prince was in London. I have the utmost respect and regard for him, but I cannot help feeling that the pleasant intimacy to which he has admitted me is to a large extent owing to the desire of our friends in Berlin. So far as I am concerned, I have never met any one, of any nation, whose character I admire more."

"Maurice lives his life loftily. He is one of the few great aristocrats I have met who carries his nobility of birth into his simplest thought and action. There is just one thing," she added, "which would break his heart."

"And that?"

"The subject upon which you two disagree—a war between Germany and this country."

"The Prince is an idealist," Dominey said. "Sometimes I wonder why he was sent here, why they did not send some one of a more intriguing character."

She shrugged her shoulders.

"You agree with that great Frenchman," she observed, "that no ambassador can remain a gentleman—politically."

"Well, I have never been a diplomat, so I cannot say," Dominey replied.

"You have many qualifications, I should think," she observed cuttingly.

"Such as?"

"You are absolutely callous, absolutely without heart or sympathy where your work is concerned."

"I do not admit it," he protested.

"I go back to London tomorrow," she continued, "a very miserable and unhappy woman. I take with me the letter which should have brought me happiness. The love for which I have sacrificed my life has failed me. Not even the whip of a royal command, not even all that I have to offer, can give me even five seconds of happiness."

"All that I have pleaded for," Dominey reminded her earnestly, "is delay."

"And what delay do you think," she asked, with a sudden note of passion in her tone, "would the Leopold von Ragastein of six years ago have pleaded for? Delay! He found words then which would have melted an iceberg. He found words the memory of which comes to me sometimes in the night and which mock me. He had no country then save the paradise where lovers walk, no ruler but a queen, and I was she. And now—"

Dominey felt a strange pang of distress. She saw the unusual softening in his face, and her eyes lit up.

"Just for a moment," she broke off, "you were like Leopold. As a rule, you know, you are not like him. I think that you left him somewhere in Africa and came home in his likeness."

"Believe that for a little time," Dominey begged earnestly.

"What if it were true?" she asked abruptly. "There are times when I do not recognise you. There are words Leopold used to use which I have never heard from your lips. Is not West Africa the sorcerer's paradise? Perhaps you are an impostor, and the man I love is there still, in trouble—perhaps ill. You play the part of Everard Dominey like a very king of actors. Perhaps before you came here you played the part of Leopold. You are not my Leopold. Love cannot die as you would have me believe."

"Now," he said coolly, "you are coming round to my way of thinking. I have been assuring you, from the very first moment we met at the Carlton, that I was not your Leopold—that I was Everard Dominey."

"I shall put you to the test," she exclaimed suddenly, rising to her feet. "Your arm, if you please."

She led him across the hall to where little groups of people were gossiping, playing bridge, and Seaman, the centre of a little group of gullible amateur speculators, was lecturing on mines. They stopped to say a word or two here and there, but Stephanie's fingers never left her companion's arm. They passed down a corridor hung with a collection of wonderful sporting prints in which she affected some interest, into a small gallery which led into the ballroom. Here they were alone. She laid her hands upon his shoulders and looked up into his eyes. Her lips drew nearer to his.

"Kiss me—upon the lips, Leopold," she ordered.

"There is no Leopold here," he replied; "you yourself have said it."

She came a little nearer. "Upon the lips," she whispered.

He held her, stooped down, and their lips met. Then she stood apart from him. Her eyes were for a moment closed, her hands were extended as though to prevent any chance of his approaching her again.

"Now I know the truth," she muttered.


Dominey found an opportunity to draw Seaman away from his little group of investment-seeking friends.

"My friend," he said, "trouble grows."

"Anything more from Schmidt's supposed emissary?" Seaman asked quickly.

"No. I am going to keep away from him this evening, and I advise you to do the same. The trouble is with the Princess."

"With the Princess," declared Seaman. "I think you have blundered. I quite appreciate your general principles of behaving internally and externally as though you were the person whom you pretend to be. It is the very essence of all successful espionage. But you should know when to make exceptions. I see grave objections myself to your obeying the Kaiser's behest. On the other hand, I see no objection whatever to your treating the Princess in a more human manner, to your visiting her in London, and giving her more ardent proofs of your continued affection."

"If I once begin—"

"Look here," Seaman interrupted, "the Princess is a woman of the world. She knows what she is doing, and there is a definite tie between you. I tell you frankly that I could not bear to see you playing the idiot for a moment with Lady Dominey, but with the Princess, scruples don't enter into the question at all. You should by no means make an enemy of her."

"Well, I have done it," Dominey acknowledged. "She has gone off to bed now, and she is leaving early tomorrow morning. She thinks I have borrowed some West African magic, that I have left her lover's soul out there and come home in his body."

"Well, if she does," Seaman declared, "you are out of your troubles."

"Am I!" Dominey replied gloomily. "First of all, she may do a lot of mischief before she goes. And then, supposing by any thousand-to-one chance the story of this cousin of Schmidt's should be true, and she should find Dominey out there, still alive? The Princess is not of German birth, you know. She cares nothing for Germany's future. As a matter of fact, I think, like a great many Hungarians, she prefers England. They say that an Englishman has as many lives as a cat. Supposing that chap Dominey did come to life again and she brings him home? You say yourself that you do not mean to make much use of me until after the war has started. In the parlance of this country of idioms, that will rather upset the apple cart, will it not?"

"Has the Princess a suite of rooms here?" Seaman enquired.

"Over in the west wing. Good idea! You go and see what you can do with her. She will not think of going to bed at this time of night."

Seaman nodded.

"Leave it to me," he directed. "You go out and play the host."

Dominey played the host first and then the husband. Rosamund welcomed him with a little cry of pleasure.

"I have been enjoying myself so much, Everard!" she exclaimed. "Everybody has been so kind, and Mr. Mangan has taught me a new Patience."

"And now, I think," Doctor Harrison intervened a little gruffly, "it's time to knock off for the evening."

She turned very sweetly to Everard.

"Will you take me upstairs?" she begged. "I have been hoping so much that you would come before Doctor Harrison sent me off."

"I should have been very disappointed if I had been too late," Dominey assured her. "Now say good night to everybody."

"Why, you talk to me as though I were a child," she laughed. "Well, good-bye, everybody, then. You see, my stern husband is taking me off. When are you coming to see me, Doctor Harrison?"

"Nothing to see you for," was the gruff reply. "You are as well as any woman here."

"Just a little unsympathetic, isn't he?" she complained to Dominey. "Please take me through the hall, so that I can say good-bye to every one else. Is the Princess Eiderstrom there?"

"I am afraid that she has gone to bed," Dominey answered, as they passed out of the room. "She said something about a headache."

"She is very beautiful," Rosamund said wistfully. "I wish she looked as though she liked me a little more. Is she very fond of you, Everard?"

"I think that I am rather in her bad books just at present," Dominey confessed.

"I wonder! I am very observant, and I have seen her looking at you sometimes—Of course," Rosamund went on, "as I am not really your wife and you are not really my husband, it is very stupid of me to feel jealous, isn't it, Everard?"

"Not a bit," he answered. "If I am not your husband, I will not be anybody else's."

"I love you to say that," she admitted, with a little sigh, "but it seems wrong somewhere. Look how cross the Duchess looks! Some one must have played the wrong card."

Rosamund's farewells were not easily made; Terniloff especially seemed reluctant to let her go. She excused herself gracefully, however, promising to sit up a little later the next evening. Dominey led the way upstairs, curiously gratified at her lingering progress. He took her to the door of her room and looked in. The nurse was sitting in an easy-chair, reading, and the maid was sewing in the background.

"Well, you look very comfortable here," he declared cheerfully. "Pray do not move, nurse."

Rosamund held his hands, as though reluctant to let him go. Then she drew his face down and kissed him.

"Yes," she said a little plaintively, "it's very comfortable.— Everard?"

"Yes, dear?"

She drew his head down and whispered in his ear.

"May I come in and say good night for two minutes?"

He smiled—a wonderfully kind smile—but shook his head.

"Not tonight, dear," he replied. "The Prince loves to sit up late, and I shall be downstairs with him. Besides, that bully of a doctor of yours insists upon ten hours' sleep."

She sighed like a disappointed child.

"Very well." She paused for a moment to listen. "Wasn't that a car?" she asked.

"Some of our guests going early, I dare say," he replied, as he turned away.

# CHAPTER XXIII

SEAMAN did not at once start on his mission to the Princess. He made his way instead to the servants' quarters and knocked at the door of the butler's sitting-room. There was no reply. He tried the handle in vain. The door was locked. A tall, grave-faced man in sombre black came out from an adjoining apartment.

"You are looking for the person who arrived this evening from abroad, sir?" he enquired.

"I am," Seaman replied. "Has he locked himself in?"

"He has left the Hall, sir!"

"Left!" Seaman repeated. "Do you mean gone away for good?"

"Apparently, sir. I do not understand his language myself, but I believe he considered his reception here, for some reason or other, unfavourable. He took advantage of the car which went down to the station for the evening papers and caught the last train."

Seaman was silent for a moment. The news was a shock to him.

"What is your position here?" he asked his informant.

"My name is Reynolds, sir," was the respectful reply. "I am Mr. Pelham's servant."

"Can you tell me why, if this man has left, the door here is locked?"

"Mr. Parkins locked it before he went out, sir. He accompanied—Mr. Miller, I think his name was—to the station."

Seaman had the air of a man not wholly satisfied.

"Is it usual to lock up a sitting-room in this fashion?" he asked.

"Mr. Parkins always does it, sir. The cabinets of cigars are kept there, also the wine-cellar key and the key of the plate chest.

None of the other servants use the room except at Mr. Parkins' invitation."

"I understand," Seaman said, as he turned away. "Much obliged for your information, Reynolds. I will speak to Mr. Parkins later."

"I will let him know that you desire to see him, sir."

"Good night, Reynolds!"

"Good night, sir!"

Seaman passed back again to the crowded hall and billiard-room, exchanged a few remarks here and there, and made his way up the southern flight of stairs towards the west wing. Stephanie consented without hesitation to receive him. She was seated in front of the fire, reading a novel, in a boudoir opening out of her bedroom.

"Princess," Seaman declared, with a low bow, "we are in despair at your desertion."

She put down her book.

"I have been insulted in this house," she said. "Tomorrow I leave it."

Seaman shook his head reproachfully.

"Your Highness," he continued, "believe me, I do not wish to presume upon my position. I am only a German tradesman, admitted to circles like these for reasons connected solely with the welfare of my country. Yet I know much, as it happens, of the truth of this matter, the matter which is causing you distress. I beg you to reconsider your decision. Our friend here is, I think, needlessly hard upon himself. So much the greater will be his reward when the end comes. So much the greater will be the rapture with which he will throw himself on his knees before you."

"Has he sent you to reason with me?"

"Not directly. I am to a certain extent, however, his major-domo in this enterprise. I brought him from Africa. I have watched over him from the start. Two brains are better than one. I try to show him where to avoid mistakes, I try to point out the paths of danger and of safety."

"I should imagine Sir Everard finds you useful," she remarked calmly.

"I hope he does."

"It has doubtless occurred to you," she continued, "that our friend has accommodated himself wonderfully to English life and customs?"

"You must remember that he was educated here. Nevertheless, his aptitude has been marvellous."

"One might almost call it supernatural," she agreed. "Tell me, Mr. Seaman, you seem to have been completely successful in the installation of our friend here as Sir Everard. What is going to be his real value to you? What work will he do?"

"We are keeping him for the big things. You have seen our gracious master lately?" he added hesitatingly.

"I know what is at the back of your mind," she replied. "Yes! Before the summer is over I am to pack up my trunks and fly. I understand."

"It is when that time comes," Seaman said impressively, "that we expect Sir Everard Dominey, the typical English country gentleman, of whose loyalty there has never been a word of doubt, to be of use to us. Most of our present helpers will be under suspicion. The authorised staff of our secret service can only work underneath. You can see for yourself the advantage we gain in having a confidential correspondent who can day by day reflect the changing psychology of the British mind in all its phases. We have quite enough of the other sort of help arranged for. Plans of ships, aerodromes and harbours, sailings of convoys, calling up of soldiers—all these are the A. B. C. of the secret service profession. We shall never ask our friend here for a single fact, but, from his town house in Berkeley Square, the host of Cabinet Ministers, of soldiers, of the best brains of the country, our fingers will never leave the pulse of Britain's day-by-day life."

Stephanie threw herself back in her easy-chair and clasped her hands behind her head.

"These things you are expecting from our present host?"

"We are, and we expect to get them. I have watched him day by day. My confidence in him has grown."

Stephanie was silent. She sat looking into the fire. Seaman, keenly observant as always, realised the change in her, yet found something of mystery in her new detachment of manner.

"Your Highness," he urged, "I am not here to speak on behalf of the man who at heart is, I know, your lover. He will plead his own cause when the time comes. But I am here to plead for patience, I am here to implore you to take no rash step, to do nothing which might imperil in any way his position here. I stand outside the gates of the world which your sex can make a paradise. I am no judge of the things that happen here. But in your heart I feel there is bitterness, because the man for whom you care has chosen to place his country first. I implore your patience, Princess. I implore you to believe what I know so well,—that it is the sternest sense of duty only which is the foundation of Leopold von Ragastein's obdurate attitude."

"What are you afraid that I shall do?" she asked curiously.

"I am afraid of nothing—directly."

"Indirectly, then? Answer me, please."

"I am afraid," he admitted frankly, "that in some corner of the world, if not in this country, you might whisper a word, a scoffing or an angry sentence, which would make people wonder what grudge you had against a simple Norfolk baronet. I would not like that word spoken in the presence of any one who knew your history and realised the rather amazing likeness between Sir Everard Dominey and Baron Leopold von Ragastein."

"I see," Stephanie murmured, a faint smile parting her lips. "Well, Mr. Seaman, I do not think that you need have many fears. What I shall carry away with me in my heart is not for you or any man to know. In a few days I shall leave this country."

"You are going back to Berlin—to Hungary?"

She shook her head, beckoned her maid to open the door, and held out her hand in token of dismissal.

"I am going to take a sea voyage," she announced. "I shall go to Africa."


The morrow was a day of mild surprises. Eddy Pelham's empty place was the first to attract notice, towards the end of breakfast time.

"Where's the pink and white immaculate?" the Right Honourable gentleman asked. "I miss my morning wonder as to how he tied his tie."

"Gone," Dominey replied, looking round from the sideboard.

"Gone?" every one repeated.

"I should think such a thing has never happened to him before," Dominey observed. "He was wanted in town."

"Fancy any one wanting Eddy for any serious purpose!" Caroline murmured.

"Fancy any one wanting him badly enough to drag him out of bed in the middle of the night with a telephone call and send him up to town by the breakfast train from Norwich!" their host continued. "I thought we had started a new ghost when he came into my room in a purple dressing-gown and broke the news."

"Who wanted him?" the Duke enquired. "His tailor?"

"Business of importance was his pretext," Dominey replied.

There was a little ripple of good-humoured laughter.

"Does Eddy do anything for a living?" Caroline asked, yawning.

"Mr. Pelham is a director of the Chelsea Motor Works," Mangan told them. "He received a small legacy last year, and his favourite taxicab man was the first to know about it."

"You're not suggesting," she exclaimed, "that it is business of that sort which has taken Eddy away!"

"I should think it most improbable," Mangan confessed. "As a matter of fact, he asked me the other day if I knew where their premises were."

"We shall miss him," she acknowledged. "It was quite one of the events of the day to see his costume after shooting."

"His bridge was reasonably good," the Duke commented.

"He shot rather well the last two days," Mangan remarked.

"And he had told me confidentially," Caroline concluded, "that he was going to wear brown today. Now I think Eddy would have looked nice in brown."

The missing young man's requiem was finished by the arrival of the local morning papers. A few moments later Dominey rose and left the room. Seaman, who had been unusually silent, followed him.

"My friend," he confided, "I do not know whether you have heard, but there was another curious disappearance from the Hall last night."

"Whose?" Dominey asked, pausing in the act of selecting a cigarette.

"Our friend Miller, or Wolff—Doctor Schmidt's emissary," Seaman announced, "has disappeared."

"Disappeared?" Dominey repeated. "I suppose he is having a prowl round somewhere."

"I have left it to you to make more careful enquiries," Seaman replied. "All I can tell you is that I made up my mind last night to interview him once more and try to fathom his very mysterious behaviour. I found the door of your butler's sitting-room locked, and a very civil fellow—Mr. Pelham's valet he turned out to be—told me that he had left in the car which went for the evening papers."

"I will go and make some enquiries," Dominey decided, after a moment's puzzled consideration.

"If you please," Seaman acquiesced. "The affair disconcerts me because I do not understand it. When there is a thing which I do not understand, I am uncomfortable."

Dominey vanished into the nether regions, spent half an hour with Rosamund, and saw nothing of his disturbed guest again until they were walking to the first wood. They had a moment together after Dominey had pointed out the stands.

"Well?" Seaman enquired.

"Our friend," Dominey announced, "apparently made up his mind to go quite suddenly. A bed was arranged for him—or rather it is always there—in a small apartment opening out of the butler's room, on the ground floor. He said nothing about leaving until he saw Parkins preparing to go down to the station with the chauffeur. Then he insisted upon accompanying him, and when he found there was a train to Norwich he simply bade them both good night. He left no message whatever for either you or me."

Seaman was thoughtful.

"There is no doubt," he said, "that his departure was indicative of a certain distrust in us. He came to find out something, and

I suppose he found it out. I envy you your composure, my friend. We live on the brink of a volcano, and you shoot pheasants."

"We will try a partridge for a change," Dominey observed, swinging round as a single Frenchman with a dull whiz crossed the hedge behind them and fell a little distance away, a crumpled heap of feathers. "Neat, I think?" he added, turning to his companion.

"Marvellous!" Seaman replied, with faint sarcasm. "I envy your nerve."

"I cannot take this matter very seriously," Dominey acknowledged. "The fellow seemed to me quite harmless."

"My anxieties have also been aroused in another direction," Seaman confided.

"Any other trouble looming?" Dominey asked.

"You will find yourself minus another guest when you return this afternoon."

"The Princess?"

"The Princess," Seaman assented. "I did my best with her last night, but I found her in a most peculiar frame of mind. We are to be relieved of any anxiety concerning her for some time, however. She has decided to take a sea voyage."

"Where to?"

"Africa!"

Dominey paused in the act of inserting a cartridge into his gun. He turned slowly around and looked into his companion's expressionless face.

"Why the mischief is she going out there?" he asked.

"I can no more tell you that," Seaman replied, "than why Johann Wolff was sent over here to spy upon our perfect work. I am most unhappy, my friend. The things which I understand, however threatening they are, I do not fear. Things which I do not understand oppress me."

Dominey laughed quietly.

"Come," he said, "there is nothing here which seriously threatens our position. The Princess is angry, but she is not likely to give us away. This man Wolff could make no adverse report about either of us. We are doing our job and doing it well. Let our clear consciences console us."

"That is well," Seaman replied, "but I feel uneasy. I must not stay here any longer. Too intimate an association between you and me is unwise."

"Well, I think I can be trusted," Dominey observed, "even if I am to be left alone."

"In every respect except as regards the Princess," Seaman admitted, "your deportment has been most discreet."

"Except as regards the Princess," Dominey repeated irritably. "Really, my friend, I cannot understand your point of view in this matter. You could not expect me to mix up a secret honeymoon with my present commitments!"

"There might surely have been some middle way?" Seaman persisted. "You show so much tact in other matters."

"You do not know the Princess," Dominey muttered.

Rosamund joined them for luncheon, bringing news of Stephanie's sudden departure, with notes and messages for everybody. Caroline made a little grimace at her host.

"You're in trouble!" she whispered in his ear. "All the same, I approve. I like Stephanie, but she is an exceedingly dangerous person."

"I wonder whether she is," Dominey mused.

"I think men have generally found her so," Caroline replied. "She had one wonderful love affair, which ended, as you know, in her husband being killed in a duel and her lover being banished from the country. Still, she's not quite the sort of woman to be content with a banished lover. I fancied I noticed distinct signs of her being willing to replace him whilst she has been down here!"

"I feel as though a blight had settled upon my house party," Dominey remarked with bland irrelevancy. "First Eddy, then Mr. Ludwig Miller, and now Stephanie."

"And who on earth was Mr. Ludwig Miller, after all?" Caroline enquired.

"He was a fat, flaxen-haired German who brought me messages from old friends in Africa. He had no luggage but a walking stick, and he seems to have upset the male part of my domestics last night by accepting a bed and then disappearing!"

"With the plate?"

"Not a thing missing. Parkins spent an agonised half hour, counting everything. Mr. Ludwig appears to be one of those unsolved mysteries which go to make up an imperfect world."

"Well, we've had a jolly time," Caroline said reminiscently. "Tomorrow Henry and I are off, and I suppose the others. I must say on the whole I am delighted with our visit."

"You are very gracious," Dominey murmured.

"I came, perhaps, expecting to see a little more of you," she went on deliberately, "but there is a very great compensation for my disappointment. I think your wife, Everard, is worth taking trouble about. She is perfectly sweet, and her manners are most attractive."

"I am very glad you think that," he said warmly.

She looked away from him.

"Everard," she sighed, "I believe you are in love with your wife."

There was a strange, almost a terrible mixture of expressions in his face as he answered,—a certain fear, a certain fondness, a certain almost desperate resignation. Even his voice, as a rule so slow and measured, shook with an emotion which amazed his companion.

"I believe I am," he muttered. "I am afraid of my feelings for her. It may bring even another tragedy down upon us."

"Don't talk rubbish!" Caroline exclaimed. "What tragedy could come between you now? You've recovered your balance. You are a strong, steadfast person, just fitted to be the protector of anything so sweet and charming as Rosamund. Tragedy, indeed! Why don't you take her down to the South of France, Everard, and have your honeymoon all over again?"

"I can't do that just yet."

She studied him curiously. There were times when he seemed wholly incomprehensible to her.

"Are you still worried about that Unthank affair?" she asked.

He hesitated for a moment.

"There is still an aftermath to our troubles," he told her, "one cloud which leans over us. I shall clear it up in time,—but other things may happen first."

"You take yourself very seriously, Everard," she observed, looking at him with a puzzled expression. "One would think that there was a side of your life, and a very important one, which you kept entirely to yourself. Why do you have that funny little man Seaman always round with you? You're not being blackmailed or anything, are you?"

"On the contrary," he told her, "Seaman was the first founder of my fortunes."

She shrugged her shoulders.

"I have made a little money once or twice on the Stock Exchange," she remarked, "but I didn't have to carry my broker about in my pocket afterwards."

"Seaman is a good-hearted little fellow, and he loves companionship. He will drift away presently, and one won't see anything of him for ages."

"Henry began to wonder," she concluded drily, "whether you were going to stand for Parliament on the Anglo-German alliance ticket."

Dominey laughed as he caught Middleton's reproachful eye in the doorway of the farmer's kitchen in which they were lunching. He gave the signal to rise.

"I have had some thoughts of Parliament," he admitted, "but—well, Henry need not worry."

# CHAPTER XXIV

THE NEXT MORNING saw the breaking-up of Dominey's carefully arranged shooting party. The Prince took his host's arm and led him to one side for a few moments, as the cars were being loaded up. His first few words were of formal thanks. He spoke then more intimately.

"Von Ragastein," he said, "I desire to refer back for a moment to our conversation the other day."

Dominey shook his head and glanced behind.

"I know only one name here, Prince."

"Dominey, then. I will confess that you play and carry the part through perfectly. I have known English gentlemen all my life, and you have the trick of the thing. But listen. I have already told you of my disapproval of this scheme in which you are the central figure."

"It is understood," Dominey assented.

"That," the Prince continued, "is a personal matter. What I am now going to say to you is official. I had despatches from Berlin last night. They concern you."

Dominey seemed to stiffen a little.

"Well?"

"I am given to understand," the Ambassador continued, "that you practically exist only in the event of that catastrophe which I, for one, cannot foresee. I am assured that if your exposure should take place at any time, your personation will be regarded as a private enterprise, and there is nothing whatever to connect you with any political work."

"Up to the present that is absolutely so," Dominey agreed.

"I am further advised to look upon you as my unnamed and unsuspected successor here, in the event of war. For that reason I am begged to inaugurate terms of intimacy with you, to treat you with the utmost confidence, and, if the black end should come, to leave in your hands all such unfulfilled work as can be continued in secrecy and silence. I perhaps express myself in a somewhat confused manner."

"I understand perfectly," Dominey replied. "The authorities have changed their first ideas as to my presence here. They want to keep every shadow of suspicion away from me, so that in the event of war I shall have an absolutely unique position, an unsuspected yet fervently patriotic German, living hand in glove with the upper classes of English Society. One can well imagine that there would be work for me."

"Our understanding is mutual," Terniloff declared. "What I have to say to you, therefore, is that I hope you will soon follow us to London and give me the opportunity of offering you the constant hospitality of Carlton House Gardens."

"You are very kind, Prince," Dominey said. "My instructions are, as soon as I have consolidated my position here—an event which I fancy I may consider attained—to establish myself in London and to wait orders. I trust that amongst other things you will then permit me to examine the memoirs you spoke of the other day."

"Naturally, and with the utmost pleasure," the Ambassador assented. "They are a faithful record of my interviews and negotiations with certain Ministers here, and they reflect a desire and intention for peace which will, I think, amaze you.—I venture now upon a somewhat delicate question," he continued, changing the subject of their conversation abruptly, as they turned back along the terrace. "Lady Dominey will accompany you?"

"Of that I am not sure," Dominey replied thoughtfully. "I have noticed, Prince, if I may be allowed to say so, your chivalrous regard for that lady. You will permit me to assure you that in the peculiar position in which I am placed I shall never forget that she is the wife of Everard Dominey."

Terniloff shook hands heartily.

"I wanted to hear that from you," he admitted. "You I felt instinctively were different, but there are many men of our race who are willing enough to sacrifice a woman without the slightest scruple, either for their passions or their policy. I find Lady Dominey charming."

"She will never lack a protector in me," Dominey declared.

There were more farewells and, soon after, the little procession of cars drove off. Rosamund herself was on the terrace, bidding all her guests farewell. She clung to Dominey's arm when at last they turned back into the empty hall.

"What dear people they were, Everard!" she exclaimed. "I only wish that I had seen more of them. The Duchess was perfectly charming to me, and I never knew any one with such delightful manners as Prince Terniloff. Are you going to miss them very much, dear?"

"Not a bit," he answered. "I think I shall take a gun now and stroll down the meadows and across the rough ground. Will you come with me, or will you put on one of your pretty gowns and entertain me downstairs at luncheon? It is a very long time since we had a meal alone together."

She shook her head a little sadly.

"We never have had," she answered. "You know that, Everard, and, alas! I know it. But we are going on pretending, aren't we?"

He raised her fingers to his lips and kissed them.

"You shall pretend all that you like, dear Rosamund," he promised, "and I will be the shadow of your desires. No!—No tears!" he added quickly, as she turned away. "Remember there is nothing but happiness for you now. Whoever I am or am not, that is my one aim in life."

She clutched at his hand passionately, and suddenly, as though finding it insufficient, twined her arms around his neck and kissed him.

"Let me come with you," she begged. "I can't bear to let you go. I'll be very quiet. Will you wait ten minutes for me?"

"Of course," he answered.

He strolled down towards the gun room, stood by the fire for a moment, and then wandered out into the courtyard, where Middleton and a couple of beaters were waiting for him with the dogs. He had scarcely taken a step towards them, however, when he stopped short. To his amazement Seaman was there, standing a little on one side, with his eyes fixed upon the windows of the servants' quarters.

"Hullo, my friend!" he exclaimed. "Why, I thought you went by the early train from Thursford Station?"

"Missed it by two minutes," Seaman replied with a glance towards the beaters. "I knew all the cars were full for the eleven o'clock, so I thought I'd wait till the afternoon."

"And where have you been to for the last few hours, then?"

Seaman had reached his side now and was out of earshot of the others.

"Trying to solve the mystery of Johann Wolff's sudden departure last night. Come and walk down the avenue with me a little way."

"A very short distance, then. I am expecting Lady Dominey."

They passed through the thin iron gates and paced along one of the back entrances to the Hall.

"Do not think me indiscreet," Seaman began. "I returned without the knowledge of any one, and I kept out of the way until they had all gone. It is what I told you before. Things which I do not understand depress me, and behold! I have found proof this morning of a further significance in Wolff's sudden departure."

"Proceed," Dominey begged.

"I learned this morning, entirely by accident, that Mr. Pelham's servant was either mistaken or wilfully deceived me. Wolff did not accompany your butler to the station."

"And how did you find that out?" Dominey demanded.

"It is immaterial! What is material is that there is a sort of conspiracy amongst the servants here to conceal the manner of his leaving. Do not interrupt me, I beg! Early this morning there was a fresh fall of snow which has now disappeared. Outside the window of the room which I found locked were the marks of footsteps and the tracks of a small car."

"And what do you gather from all this?" Dominey asked.

"I gather that Wolff must have had friends in the neighbourhood," Seaman replied, "or else—"

"Well?"

"My last supposition sounds absurd," Seaman confessed, "but the whole matter is so incomprehensible that I was going to say—or else he was forcibly removed."

Dominey laughed softly.

"Wolff would scarcely have been an easy man to abduct, would he," he remarked, "even if we could hit upon any plausible reason for such a thing! As a matter of fact, Seaman," he concluded, turning on his heel a little abruptly as he saw Rosamund standing in the avenue, "I cannot bring myself to treat this Johann Wolff business seriously. Granted that the man was a spy, well, let him get on with it. We are doing our job here in the most perfect and praiseworthy fashion. We neither of us have the ghost of a secret to hide from his employers."

"In a sense that is true," Seaman admitted.

"Well, then, cheer up," Dominey enjoined. "Take a little walk with us, and we will see whether Parkins cannot find us a bottle of that old Burgundy for lunch. How does that sound, eh?"

"If you will excuse me from taking the walk," Seaman begged, "I would like to remain here until your return."

"You are more likely to do harm," Dominey reminded him, "and set the servants talking, if you show too much interest in this man's disappearance."

"I shall be careful," Seaman promised, "but there are certain things which I cannot help. I work always from instinct, and my instinct is never wrong. I will ask no more questions of your servants, but I know that there is something mysterious about the sudden departure of Johann Wolff."

Dominey and Rosamund returned about one o'clock to find only a note from Seaman, which the former tore open as his companion stood warming her feet in front of the fire. There were only a few lines:

"I am following an idea. It takes me to London. Let us meet there within a few days."

"S."

"Has he really gone?" Rosamund asked.

"Back to London."

She laughed happily. "Then we shall lunch *à deux* after all! Delightful! I have my wish!"

There was a sudden glow in Dominey's face, a glow which was instantly suppressed.

"Shall I ever have mine?" he asked, with a queer little break in his voice.

# CHAPTER XXV

TERNILOFF and Dominey, one morning about six months later, lounged underneath a great elm tree at Ranelagh, having iced drinks after a round of golf. Several millions of perspiring Englishmen were at the same moment studying with dazed wonder the headlines in the midday papers.

"I suppose," the Ambassador remarked, as he leaned back in his chair with an air of lazy content, "that I am being accused of fiddling while Rome burns."

"Every one has certainly not your confidence in the situation," Dominey rejoined calmly.

"There is no one else who knows quite so much," Terniloff reminded him.

Dominey sipped his drink for a moment or two in silence.

"Have you the latest news of the Russian mobilisation?" he asked. "They had some startling figures in the city this morning."

The Prince waved his hand.

"My faith is not founded on these extraneous incidents," he replied. "If Russia mobilises, it is for defence. No nation in the world would dream of attacking Germany, nor has Germany the slightest intention of imperilling her coming supremacy amongst the nations by such crude methods as military enterprise. Servia must be punished, naturally, but to that, in principle, every nation in Europe is agreed. We shall not permit Austria to overstep the mark."

"You are at least consistent, Prince," Dominey remarked.

Terniloff smiled.

"That is because I have been taken behind the scenes," he said. "I have been shown, as is the privilege of ambassadors, the mind of our rulers. You, my friend," he went on, "spent your youth amongst the military faction. You think that you are the most important people in Germany. Well, you are not. The Kaiser has willed it otherwise.—By-the-by, I had yesterday a most extraordinary cable from Stephanie."

Dominey ceased swinging his putter carelessly over the head of a daisy and turned his head to listen.

"Is she on the way home?"

"She is due in Southampton at any moment now. She wants to know where she can see me immediately upon her arrival, as she has information of the utmost importance to give me."

"Did she ever tell you the reason for her journey to Africa?"

"She was most mysterious about it. If such an idea had had any logical outcome, I should have surmised that she was going there to seek information as to your past."

"She gave Seaman the same idea," Dominey observed. "I scarcely see what she has to gain. In Africa, as a matter of fact," he went on, "my life would bear the strictest investigation."

"The whole affair is singularly foolish," the Prince declared. "Still, I am not sure that you have been altogether wise. Even accepting your position, I see no reason why you should not have obeyed the Kaiser's behest. My experience of your Society here is that love affairs between men and women moving in the same circles are not uncommon."

"That," Dominey urged, "is when they are all tarred with the same brush. My behaviour towards Lady Dominey has been culpable enough as it is. To have placed her in the position of a neglected wife would have been indefensible. Further, it might have affected the position which it is in the interests of my work that I should maintain here."

"An old subject," the Ambassador sighed, "best not rediscussed. Behold, our womenkind!"

Rosamund and the Princess had issued from the house, and the two men hastened to meet them. The latter looked charming, exquisitely gowned, and stately in appearance. By her side Rosamund, dressed with the same success but in younger fashion, seemed almost like a child. They passed into the luncheon room, crowded with many little parties of distinguished and interesting people, brilliant with the red livery of the waiters, the profusion of flowers—all that nameless elegance which had made the place Society's most popular rendezvous. The women, as they settled into their places, asked a question which was on the lips of a great many English people that day.

"Is there any news?"

Terniloff perhaps felt that he was the cynosure of many eager and anxious eyes. He smiled light-heartedly as he answered:

"None. If there were, I am convinced that it would be good. I have been allowed to play out my titanic struggle against Sir Everard without interruption."

"I suppose the next important question to whether it is to be peace or war is, how did you play?" the Princess asked.

"I surpassed myself," her husband replied, "but of course no ordinary human golfer is of any account against Dominey. He plays far too well for any self-respecting Ger—"

The Ambassador broke off and paused while he helped himself to mayonnaise.

"For any self-respecting German to play against," he concluded.

Luncheon was a very pleasant meal, and a good many people noticed the vivacity of the beautiful Lady Dominey whose picture was beginning to appear in the illustrated papers. Afterwards they drank coffee and sipped liqueurs under a great elm tree on the lawn, listening to the music and congratulating themselves upon having made their escape from London. In the ever-shifting panorama of gaily-dressed women and flannel-clad men, the monotony of which was varied here and

there by the passing of a diplomatist or a Frenchman, scrupu-
lously attired in morning clothes, were many familiar faces.
Caroline and a little group of friends waved to them from the
terrace. Eddy Pelham, in immaculate white, and a long tennis
coat with dark blue edgings, paused to speak to them on his
way to the courts.

"How is the motor business, Eddy?" Dominey asked, with a
twinkle in his eyes.

"So, so! I'm not quite so keen as I was. To tell you the
truth," the young man confided, glancing around and lowering his voice so that no one should share the momentous
information, "I was lucky enough to pick up a small share in
Jere Moore's racing stable at Newmarket, the other day. I fancy
I know a little more about gee-gees than I do about the inside
of motors, what?"

"I should think very possibly that you are right," Dominey
assented, as the young man passed on with a farewell salute.

Terniloff looked after him curiously.

"It is the type of young man, that," he declared, "which we
cannot understand. What would happen to him, in the event
of a war?—In the event of his being called upon, say, either
to fight or do some work of national importance for his
country?"

"I expect he would do it," Dominey replied. "He would
do it pluckily, whole-heartedly and badly. He is a type of the
upper-class young Englishman, over-sanguine and entirely
undisciplined. They expect, and their country expects for
them, that in the case of emergency pluck would take the
place of training."

The Right Honourable Gerald Watson stood upon the steps
talking to the wife of the Italian Ambassador. She left him
presently, and he came strolling down the lawn with his hands

behind his back and his eyes seeming to see out past the golf links.

"There goes a man," Terniloff murmured, "whom lately I have found changed. When I first came here he met me quite openly. I believe, even now, he is sincerely desirous of peace and amicable relations between our two countries, and yet something has fallen between us. I cannot tell what it is. I cannot tell even of what nature it is, but I have an instinct for people's attitude towards me, and the English are the worst race in the world at hiding their feelings. Has Mr. Watson, I wonder, come under the spell of your connection, the Duke of Worcester? He seemed so friendly with both of us down in Norfolk."

Their womenkind left them at that moment to talk to some acquaintances seated a short distance away. Mr. Watson, passing within a few yards of them, was brought to a standstill by Dominey's greeting. They talked for a moment or two upon idle subjects.

"Your news, I trust, continues favourable?" the Ambassador remarked, observing the etiquette which required him to be the first to leave the realms of ordinary conversation.

"It is a little negative in quality," the other answered, after a moment's hesitation. "I am summoned to Downing Street again at six o'clock."

"I have already confided the result of my morning despatches to the Prime Minister," Terniloff observed.

"I went through them before I came down here," was the somewhat doubtful reply.

"You will have appreciated, I hope, their genuinely pacific tone?" Terniloff asked anxiously.

His interlocutor bowed and then drew himself up. It was obvious that the strain of the last few days was telling upon him.

There were lines about his mouth, and his eyes spoke of sleepless nights.

"Words are idle things to deal with at a time like this," he said. "One thing, however, I will venture to say to you, Prince, here and under these circumstances. There will be no war unless it be the will of your country."

Terniloff was for a moment unusually pale. It was an episode of unrecorded history. He rose to his feet and raised his hat.

"There will be no war," he said solemnly.

The Cabinet Minister passed on with a lighter step. Dominey, more clearly than ever before, understood the subtle policy which had chosen for his great position a man as chivalrous and faithful and yet as simple-minded as Terniloff. He looked after the retreating figure of the Cabinet Minister with a slight smile at the corner of his lips.

"In a time like this," he remarked significantly, "one begins to understand why one of our great writers—was it Bernhardi, I wonder?—has written that no island could ever breed a race of diplomatists."

"The seas which engirdle this island," the Ambassador said thoughtfully, "have brought to England great weal, as they may bring to her much woe. The too-nimble brain of the diplomat has its parallel of insincerity in the people whose interests he seems to guard. I believe in the honesty of the English politicians. I have placed that belief on record in the small volume of memoirs which I shall presently entrust to you. But we talk too seriously for a summer afternoon. Let us illustrate to the world our opinion of the political situation and play another nine holes at golf."

Dominey rose willingly to his feet, and the two men strolled away towards the first tee.

"By the by," Terniloff asked, "what of our cheerful little friend Seaman? He ought to be busy just now."

"Curiously enough, he is returning from Germany tonight," Dominey announced. "I expect him at Berkeley Square. He is coming direct to me."

# CHAPTER XXVI

THESE WERE days, to all dwellers in London, of vivid impressions, of poignant memories, reasserting themselves afterwards with a curious sense of unreality, as though belonging to another set of days and another world. Dominey long remembered his dinner that evening in the sombre, handsomely furnished dining-room of his town house in Berkeley Square. Although it lacked the splendid proportions of the banqueting hall at Dominey, it was still a fine apartment, furnished in the Georgian period, with some notable pictures upon the walls, and with a wonderful ceiling and fireplace. Dominey and Rosamund dined alone, and though the table had been reduced to its smallest proportions, the space between them was yet considerable. As soon as Parkins had gravely put the port upon the table, Rosamund rose to her feet and, instead of leaving the room, pointed for the servant to place a chair for her by Dominey's side.

"I shall be like your men friends, Everard," she declared, "when the ladies have left, and draw up to your side. Now what do we do? Tell stories? I promise you that I will be a wonderful listener."

"First of all you drink half a glass of this port," he declared, filling her glass, "then you peel me one of those peaches, and we divide it. After which we listen for a ring at the bell. Tonight I expect a visitor."

"A visitor?"

"Not a social one," he assured her. "A matter of business which I fear will take me from you for the rest of the evening. So let us make the most of the time until he comes."

She commenced her task with the peach, talking to him all the time a little gravely, a sweet and picturesque picture of a graceful and very desirable woman, her delicate shape and artistic fragility more than ever accentuated by the sombreness of the background.

"Do you know, Everard," she said, "I am so happy in London here with you, and I feel all the time so strong and well. I can read and understand the books which were a maze of print to me before. I can see the things in the pictures, and feel the thrill of the music, which seemed to come to me, somehow, before, all dislocated and discordant. You understand, dear?"

"Of course," he answered gravely.

"I do not wonder," she went on, "that Doctor Harrison is proud of me for a patient, but there are many times when I feel a dull pain in my heart, because I know that, whatever he or anybody else might say, I am not quite cured."

"Rosamund dear," he protested.

"Ah, but don't interrupt," she insisted, depositing his share of the peach upon his plate. "How can I be cured when all the time there is the problem of you, the problem which I am just as far off solving as ever I was? Often I find myself comparing you with the Everard whom I married."

"Do I fail so often to come up to his standard?" he asked.

"You never fail," she answered, looking at him with brimming eyes. "Of course, he was very much more affectionate," she went on, after a moment's pause. "His kisses were not like yours. And he was far fonder of having me with him. Then, on the other hand, often when I wanted him he was not there, he did wild things, mad things; he seemed to forget me altogether. It was that," she went on, "that was so terrible. It was that which made me so nervous. I think that I should even have been able to stand those awful moments when he came back to me, covered with blood and reeling, if it had not been that I was already almost a wreck. You know, he killed Roger Unthank that night. That is why he was never able to come back."

"Why do you talk of these things tonight, Rosamund," Dominey begged.

"I must, dear," she insisted, laying her fingers upon his hand and looking at him curiously. "I must, even though I see how they distress you. It is wonderful that you should mind so much, Everard, but you do, and I love you for it."

"Mind?" he groaned. "Mind!"

"You are so like him and yet so different," she went on meditatively. "You drink so little wine, you are always so self-controlled, so serious. You live as though you had a life around you of which others knew nothing. The Everard I remember would never have cared about being a magistrate or going into Parliament. He would never have had ambassadors for his friends. He would have spent his time racing or yachting, hunting or shooting, as the fancy took him. And yet—"

"And yet what?" Dominey asked, a little hoarsely.

"I think he loved me better than you," she said very sadly.

"Why?" he demanded.

"I cannot tell you," she answered, with her eyes upon her plate, "but I think that he did."

Dominey walked suddenly to the window and leaned out. There were drops of moisture upon his forehead, he felt the fierce need of air. When he came back she was still sitting there, still looking down.

"I have spoken to Doctor Harrison about it," she went on, her voice scarcely audible. "He told me that you probably loved more than you dared to show, because some day the real Everard might come back."

"That is quite true," he reminded her softly. "He may come back at any moment."

She gripped his hand, her voice shook with passion. She leaned towards him, her other arm stole around his neck.

"But I don't want him to come back!" she cried. "I want you!"

Dominey sat for a moment motionless, like a figure of stone. Through the wide-flung, blind-shielded windows came the raucous cry of a newsboy, breaking the stillness of the summer evening. And then another and sharper interruption,—the stopping of a taxicab outside, the firm, insistent ringing of the front doorbell. Recollection came to Dominey, and a great strength. The fire which had leaped up within him was thrust back. His response to her wave of passion was infinitely tender.

"Dear Rosamund," he said, "that front doorbell summons me to rather an important interview. Will you please trust in me a little while longer? Believe me, I am not in any way cold. I am not indifferent. There is something which you will have to be told,—something with which I never reckoned, something which is beginning to weigh upon me night and day. Trust me, Rosamund, and wait!"

She sank back into her chair with a piquant and yet pathetic little grimace.

"You tell me always to wait," she complained. "I will be patient, but you shall tell me this. You are so kind to me. You make or mar my life. You must care a little? Please?"

He was standing up now. He kissed her hands fondly. His voice had all the old ring in it.

"More than for any woman on earth, dear Rosamund!"

Seaman, in a light grey suit, a panama, and a white beflowered tie, had lost something of the placid urbanity of a few months ago. He was hot and tired with travel. There were new lines in his face and a queer expression of anxiety about his eyes, at the corners of which little wrinkles had begun to appear. He responded to Dominey's welcome with a fervour which was almost feverish, scrutinised him closely, as though expecting to find some change, and finally sank into an easy-chair with a little gesture of relief. He had been carrying a small, brown despatch case, which he laid on the carpet by his side.

"You have news?" Dominey asked.

"Yes," was the momentous reply, "I have news."

Dominey rang the bell. He had already surmised, from the dressing-case and coats in the hall, that his visitor had come direct from the station.

"What will you have?" he enquired.

"A bottle of hock with seltzer water, and ice if you have it," Seaman replied. "Also a plate of cold meat, but it must be served here. And afterwards the biggest cigar you have. I have indeed news, news disturbing, news magnificent, news astounding."

Dominey gave some orders to the servant who answered his summons. For a few moments they spoke trivialities of the journey. When everything was served, however, and the door closed, Seaman could wait no longer. His appetite, his thirst, his speech, seemed all stimulated to swift action.

"We are of the same temperament," he said. "That I know. We will speak first of what is more than disturbing—a little terrifying. The mystery of Johann Wolff has been solved."

"The man who came to us with messages from Schmidt in South Africa?" Dominey asked. "I had almost forgotten about him."

"The same. What was at the back of his visit to us that night I cannot even now imagine. Neither is it clear why he held aloof from me, who am his superior in practically the same service. There we are, from the commencement, confronted with a very singular happening, but scarcely so singular as the dénouement. Wolff vanished from your house that night into an English fortress."

"It seems incredible," Dominey declared bluntly.

"It is nevertheless true," Seaman insisted. "No member of our service is allowed to remain more than one month without communicating his existence and whereabouts to headquarters. No word has been received from Wolff since that night in January. On the other hand, indirect information has reached us that he is in durance over here."

"But such a thing is against the law, unheard of," Dominey protested. "No country can keep the citizen of another country in prison without formulating a definite charge or bringing him up for trial."

Seaman smiled grimly.

"That's all very well in any ordinary case," he said. "Wolff has been a marked man for years, though. Wilhelmstrasse would soon make fuss enough, if it were of any use, but it would not be. There are one or two Englishmen in German prisons at the present moment, concerning whose welfare the English Foreign Office has not even thought it worth while to enquire. What troubles me more than the actual fact of Wolff's disappearance is the mystery of his visit to you and his apprehension practically on the spot."

"They must have tracked him down there," Dominey remarked.

"Yes, but they couldn't thrust a pair of tongs into your butler's sitting-room, extract Johann Wolff, and set him down inside Norwich Castle or whatever prison he may be in," Seaman objected. "However, the most disquieting feature about Wolff is that it introduces something we don't understand. For the rest, we have many men as good, and better, and the time for their utility is past. You are our great hope now, Dominey."

"It is to be, then?"

Seaman took a long and ecstatic draught of his hock and seltzer.

"It is to be," he declared solemnly. "There was never any doubt about it. If Russia ceases to mobilise tomorrow, if every statesman in Servia crawls to Vienna with a rope around his neck, the result would still be the same. The word has gone out. The whole of Germany is like a vast military camp. It comes exactly twelve months before the final day fixed by our great authorities, but the opportunity is too great, too wonderful for hesitation. By the end of August we shall be in Paris."

"You bring news indeed!" Dominey murmured, standing for a moment by the opened window.

"I have been received with favour in the very loftiest circles," Seaman continued. "You and I both stand high in the list of those to whom great rewards shall come. His Majesty approves altogether of your reluctance to avail yourself of his permission to wed the Princess Eiderstrom. 'Von Ragastein has decided well,' he declared. 'These are not the days for marriage or giving in marriage, these, the most momentous days the world has ever known, the days when an empire shall spring into being, the mightiest since the Continents fell into shape and the stars looked down upon this present world.' Those are the words of the All Highest. In his eyes the greatest of all attributes is singleness of purpose. You followed your own purpose, contrary to my advice, contrary to Terniloff's. You will gain by it."

Seaman finished his meal in due course, and the tray was removed. Soon the two men were alone again, Seaman puffing out dense volumes of smoke, gripping his cigar between his teeth, brandishing it sometimes in his hand to give effect to his words. A little of his marvellous caution seemed to have deserted him. For the first time he spoke directly to his companion.

"Von Ragastein," he said, "it is a great country, ours. It is a wonderful empire we shall build. Tonight I am on fire with the mighty things. I have a list of instructions for you, many details. They can wait. We will talk of our future, our great and glorious destiny as the mightiest nation who has ever earned for herself the right to govern the world. You would think that in Germany there was excitement. There is none. The task of every one is allotted, their work made clear to them. Like a mighty piece of gigantic machinery, we move towards war. Every regiment knows its station, every battery commander knows his positions, every general knows his exact line of attack. Rations, clothing, hospitals, every unit of which you can think, has its movements calculated out for it to the last nicety."

"And the final result?" Dominey asked. "Is that also calculated?"

Seaman, with trembling fingers, unlocked the little despatch box which stood by his side and took from it jealously a sheet of linen-backed parchment.

"You, my friend," he said, "are one of the first to gaze upon this. This will show you the dream of our Kaiser. This will show you the framework of the empire that is to be."

He laid out a map upon the table. The two men bent over it. It was a map of Europe, in which England, a diminished France, Spain, Portugal and Italy, were painted in dark blue. For the rest, the whole of the space included between two lines, one from Hamburg to Athens, the other from Finland to the Black Sea, was painted a deep scarlet, with here and there portions of it in slightly lighter colouring. Seaman laid his palm upon the map.

"There lies our future Empire," he said solemnly and impressively.

"Explain it to me," Dominey begged.

"Broadly speaking, everything between those two lines belongs to the new German Empire. Poland, Courland, Lithuania and the

Ukraine will possess a certain degree of autonomous government, which will practically amount to nothing. Asia is there at our feet. No longer will Great Britain control the supplies of the world. Raw materials of every description will be ours. Leather, tallow, wheat, oil, fats, timber—they are all there for us to draw upon. And for wealth—India and China! What more would you have, my friend?"

"You take my breath away. But what about Austria?"

Seaman's grin was almost sardonic.

"Austria," he said, "must already feel her doom creeping upon her. There is no room in middle Europe for two empires, and the House of Hapsburg must fall before the House of Hohenzollern. Austria, body and soul, must become part of the German Empire. Then further down, mark you. Roumania must become a vassal state or be conquered. Bulgaria is already ours. Turkey, with Constantinople, is pledged. Greece will either join us or be wiped out. Servia will be blotted from the map; probably also Montenegro. Those countries which are painted in fainter red, like Turkey, Bulgaria and Greece, become vassal states, to be absorbed one by one as opportunity presents itself."

Dominey's finger strayed northward.

"Belgium," he observed, "has disappeared."

"Belgium we shall occupy and enslave," Seaman replied. "Our line of advance into France lies that way, and we need her ports to dominate the Thames. Holland and the Scandinavian countries, as you observe, are left in the lighter shade of red. If an opportunity occurs, Holland and Denmark may be incited to take the field against us. If they do so, it means absorption. If they remain, as they probably will, scared neutrals, they will none the less be our vassal states when the last gun has been fired."

"And Norway and Sweden?"

Seaman looked down at the map and smiled.

"Look at them," he said. "They lie at our mercy. Norway has her western seaboard, and there might always be the question of British aid, so far as she is concerned. But Sweden is ours, body and soul. More than any other of these vassal states, it is our master's plan to bring her into complete subjection. We need her lusty manhood, the finest cannon food in the world, for later wars, if indeed such a thing should be. She has timber and minerals which we also need.—But there—it is enough. First of all men in this country, my friend, you, Von Ragastein, have gazed upon this picture of the future."

"This is marvellously conceived," Dominey muttered, "but what of Russia with her millions? How is it that we propose, notwithstanding her countless millions of men, to help ourselves to her richest provinces, to drive a way through the heart of her empire?"

"This," Seaman replied, "is where genius steps in. Russia has been ripe for a revolution any time for the last fifteen years. We have secret agents now in every city and country place and throughout the army. We shall teach Russia how to make herself a free country."

Dominey shivered a little with an almost involuntary repulsion. For the second time that almost satyr-like grin on Seaman's face revolted him.

"And what of my own work?"

Seaman helped himself to a liqueur. He was, as a rule, a moderate man, but this was the third time he had replenished his glass since his hasty meal.

"My brain is weary, friend," he admitted, passing his hand over his forehead. "I have a great fatigue. The thoughts jump about. This last week has been one of fierce excitements. Everything, almost your daily life, has been planned. We shall go over it within a day or so. Meanwhile, remember this. It is our great aim to keep England out of the war."

"Terniloff is right, then, after all!" Dominey exclaimed.

Seaman laughed scornfully.

"If we want England out of the war," he pointed out, "it is not that we desire her friendship. It is that we may crush her the more easily when Calais, Boulogne and Havre are in our hands. That will be in three months' time. Then perhaps our attitude towards England may change a little! Now I go."

Dominey folded up the map with reluctance. His companion shook his head. It was curious that he, too, for the first time in his life upon the same day, addressed his host differently.

"Baron von Ragastein," he said, "there are six of those maps in existence. That one is for you. Lock it away and guard it as though it were your greatest treasure on earth, but when you are alone, bring it out and study it. It shall be your inspiration, it shall lighten your moments of depression, give you courage when you are in danger; it shall fill your mind with pride and wonder. It is yours."

Dominey folded it carefully up, crossed the room, unlocked a little safe and deposited it therein.

"I shall guard it, according to your behest, as my greatest treasure," he assured his departing guest, with a fervour which surprised even himself.

# CHAPTER XXVII

THERE WAS something dramatic, in the most lurid sense of the word, about the brief telephone message which Dominey received, not so many hours later, from Carlton House Terrace. In a few minutes he was moving through the streets, still familiar yet already curiously changed. Men and women were going about their business as usual, but an air of stupefaction was everywhere apparent. Practically every loiterer was studying a newspaper, every chance acquaintance had stopped to confer with his fellows. War, alternately the joke and bogey of the conversationalist, stretched her grey hands over the sunlit city. Even the lightest-hearted felt a thrill of apprehension at the thought of the horrors that were to come. In a day or two all this was to be changed. People went about then counting the Russian millions; the steamroller fetish was to be evolved. The most peaceful stockbroker or shopkeeper, who had never even been to a review in his life, could make calculations of man power with a stump of pencil on the back of an old envelope, which would convince the greatest pessimist that Germany and Austria were outnumbered by at least three to one. But on this particular morning, people were too stunned for calculations. The incredible had happened. The long-discussed war—the nightmare of the nervous, the derision of the optimist—had actually materialised. The happy-go-lucky years of peace and plenty had suddenly come to an end. Black tragedy leaned over the land.

Dominey, avoiding acquaintances as far as possible, his own mind in a curious turmoil, passed down St. James's Street and along Pall Mall and presented himself at Carlton House Terrace. Externally, the great white building, with its rows of flower boxes, showed no signs of undue perturbation. Inside, however, the anteroom was crowded with callers, and it was only by the intervention of Terniloff's private secretary, who was awaiting him, that Dominey was able to reach the inner sanctum where the Ambassador was busy dictating letters. He broke off immediately his visitor was announced and dismissed every one, including his secretaries. Then he locked the door.

"Von Ragastein," he groaned, "I am a broken man!"

Dominey grasped his hand sympathetically. Terniloff seemed to have aged years even in the last few hours.

"I sent for you," he continued, "to say farewell, to say farewell and to make a confession. You were right, and I was wrong. It would have been better if I had remained and played the country farmer on my estates. I was never shrewd enough to see until now that I have been made the cat's-paw of the very men whose policy I always condemned."

His visitor still remained silent. There was so little that he could say.

"I have worked for peace," Terniloff went on, "believing that my country wanted peace. I have worked for peace with honourable men who were just as anxious as I was to secure it. But all the time those for whom I laboured were making faces behind my back. I was nothing more nor less than their tool. I know now that nothing in this world could have hindered what is coming."

"Every one will at least realise," Dominey reminded him, "that you did your best for peace."

"That is one reason why I sent for you," was the agitated reply. "Not long ago I spoke of a little volume, a diary which I have been keeping of my work in this country. I promised to show it to you. You have asked me for it several times lately. I am going to show it to you now. It is written up to yesterday. It will tell you of all my efforts and how they were foiled. It is an absolutely faithful narrative of my work here and the English response to it."

The Prince crossed the room, unlocked one of the smaller safes, which stood against the side of the wall, withdrew a morocco-bound volume the size of a small portfolio, and returned to Dominey.

"I beg you," he said earnestly, "to read this with the utmost care and to await my instructions with regard to it. You can judge, no doubt," he went on a little bitterly, "why I give it into your keeping. Even the Embassy here is not free from our own spies, and the existence of these memoirs is known. The moment I reach Germany, their fate is assured. I am a German and a patriot, although my heart is bitter against those who are bringing this blot upon our country. For that reason, these memoirs must be kept in a safe place until I see a good use for them."

"You mean if the governing party in Germany should change?"

"Precisely! They would then form at once my justification, and place English diplomacy in such a light before the saner portion of my fellow countrymen that an honourable peace might be rendered possible. Study them carefully, Von Ragastein. Perhaps even your own allegiance to the Party you serve may waver for a moment as you read."

"I serve no Party," Dominey said quietly, "only my Country."

Terniloff sighed.

"Alas! there is no time for us to enter into one of our old arguments on the ethics of government. I must send you away, Von Ragastein. You have a terrible task before you. I am bound to wish you Godspeed. For myself I shall not raise my head again until I have left England."

"There is no other commission?" Dominey asked. "No other way in which I can serve you?"

"None," Terniloff answered sadly. "I am permitted to suffer no inconveniences. My departure is arranged for as though

I were royalty. Yet believe me, my friend, every act of courtesy and generosity which I receive in these moments bites into my heart. Farewell!"

Dominey found a taxicab in Pall Mall and drove back to Berkeley Square. He found Rosamund with a little troop of dogs, just entering the gardens, and crossed to her side.

"Dear," he asked, taking her arm, "would you mind very much coming down to Norfolk for a few days?"

"With you?" she asked quickly.

"Yes! I want to be in retreat for a short time. There are one or two things I must settle before I take up some fresh work."

"I should love it," she declared enthusiastically. "London is getting so hot, and every one is so excited."

"I shall order the touring car at three o'clock," Dominey told her. "We shall get home about nine. Parkins and your maid can go down by train. Does that suit you?"

"Delightfully!"

He took her arm and they paced slowly along the hot walk.

"Rosamund dear," he said, "the time has come which many people have been dreading. We are at war."

"I know," she murmured.

"You and I have had quite a happy time together, these last few months," he went on, "even though there is still that black cloud between us. I have tried to treat you as kindly and tenderly as though I were really your husband and you were indeed my wife."

"You're not going away?" she cried, startled. "I couldn't bear that! No one could ever be so sweet as you have been to me."

"Dear," he said, "I want you to think—of your husband—of Everard. He was a soldier once for a short time, was he not? What do you think he would have done now that this terrible war has come?"

"He would have done what you will do," she answered, with the slightest possible tremor in her tone. "He would have become a soldier again, he would have fought for his country."

"And so must I—fight for my country," he declared. "That is why I must leave you for an hour now while I make some calls. I shall be back to luncheon. Directly afterwards we must start. I have many things to arrange first, though. Life is not going to be very easy for the next few days."

She held on to his arm. She seemed curiously reluctant to let him go.

"Everard," she said, "when we are at Dominey shall I be able to see Doctor Harrison?"

"Of course," he assured her.

"There is something I want to say to him," she confided, "something I want to ask you, too. Are you the same person, Everard, when you are in town as when you are in the country?"

He was a little taken aback at her question—asked, too, with such almost plaintive seriousness. The very aberration it suggested seemed altogether denied by her appearance. She was wearing a dress of black and white muslin, a large black hat, Paris shoes. Her stockings, her gloves, all the trifling details of her toilette, were carefully chosen, and her clothes themselves gracefully and naturally worn. Socially, too, she had been amazingly successful. Only the week before, Caroline had come to him with a little shrug of the shoulders.

"I have been trying to be kind to Rosamund," she said, "and finding out instead how unnecessary it is. She is quite the most popular of the younger married women in our set. You don't deserve such luck, Everard."

"You know the proverb about the old roué," he had replied.

His mind had wandered for a moment. He realised Rosamund's question with a little start.

"The same person, dear?" he repeated. "I think so. Don't I seem so to you?"

She shook her head.

"I am not sure," she answered, a little mysteriously. "You see, in the country I still remember sometimes that awful night when I so nearly lost my reason. I have never seen you look as you looked that night."

"You would rather not go back, perhaps?"

"That is the strange part of it," she replied. "There is nothing in the world I want so much to do. There's an empty taxi, dear," she added, as they reached the gate. "I shall go in and tell Justine about the packing."

# CHAPTER XXVIII

WITHIN the course of the next few days, a strange rumour spread through Dominey and the district,—from the farm labourer to the farmer, from the school children to their homes, from the village post-office to the neighbouring hamlets. A gang of woodmen from a neighbouring county, with an engine and all the machinery of their craft, had started to work razing to the ground everything in the shape of tree or shrub at the north end of the Black Wood. The matter of the war was promptly forgotten. Before the second day, every man, woman and child in the place had paid an awed visit to the outskirts of the wood, had listened to the whirr of machinery, had gazed upon the great bridge of planks leading into the wood, had peered, in the hope of some strange discovery, into the tents of the men who were camping out. The men themselves were not communicative, and the first time the foreman had been known to open his mouth was when Dominey walked down to discuss progress, on the morning after his arrival.

"It's a dirty bit of work, sir," he confided. "I don't know as I ever came across a bit of woodland as was so utterly, hopelessly rotten. Why, the wood crumbles when you touch it, and the men have to be within reach of one another the whole of the time, though we've a matter of five hundred planks down there."

"Come across anything unusual yet?"

"We ain't come across anything that isn't unusual so far, sir. My men are all wearing extra leggings to keep them from being bitten by them adders—as long as my arm, some on 'em. And there's fungus there which, when you touch it, sends out a smell enough to make a strong man faint. We killed a cat the first day, as big and as fierce as a young tigress. It's a queer job, sir."

"How long will it take?"

"Matter of three weeks, sir, and when we've got the timber out you'll be well advised to burn it. It's not worth a snap of the fingers.—Begging your pardon, sir," the man went on, "the old lady in the distance there hangs about the whole of the time. Some of my men are half scared of her."

Dominey swung around. On a mound a little distance away in the park, Rachael Unthank was standing. In her rusty black clothes, unrelieved by any trace of colour, with white cheeks and strange eyes, even in the morning light she was a repellent figure. Dominey strolled across to her.

"You see, Mrs. Unthank," he began—

She interrupted him. Her skinny hand was stretched out towards the wood.

"What are those men doing, Sir Everard Dominey?" she demanded. "What is your will with the wood?"

"I am carrying out a determination I came to in the winter," Dominey replied. "Those men are going to cut and hew their way from one end of the Black Wood to the other, until not a tree or a bush remains upright. As they cut, they burn. Afterwards, I shall have it drained. We may live to see a field of corn there, Mrs. Unthank."

"You will dare to do this?" she asked hoarsely.

"Will you dare to tell me why I should not, Mrs. Unthank?"

She relapsed into silence, and Dominey passed on. But that night, as Rosamund and he were lingering over their dessert, enjoying the strange quiet and the wonderful breeze which crept in at the open window, Parkins announced a visitor.

"Mrs. Unthank is in the library, sir," he announced. "She would be glad if you could spare her five minutes."

Rosamund shivered slightly but nodded as Dominey glanced towards her enquiringly.

"Don't let me see her, please," she begged. "You must go, of course.—Everard!"

"Yes, dear?"

"I know what you are doing out there, although you have never said a word to me about it," she continued, with an odd little note of passion in her tone. "Don't let her persuade you to stop. Let them cut and burn and hew till there isn't room for a mouse to hide. You promise?"

"I promise," he answered.

Mrs. Unthank was making every effort to keep under control her fierce discomposure. She rose as Dominey entered the room and dropped an old-fashioned curtsey.

"Well, Mrs. Unthank," he enquired, "what can I do for you?"

"It's about the wood again, sir," she confessed. "I can't bear it. All night long I seem to hear those axes, and the calling of the men."

"What is your objection, Mrs. Unthank, to the destruction of the Black Wood?" Dominey asked bluntly. "It is nothing more nor less than a noisome pest-hole. Its very presence there, after all that she has suffered, is a menace to Lady Dominey's nerves. I am determined to sweep it from the face of the earth."

The forced respect was already beginning to disappear from her manner.

"There's evil will come to you if you do, Sir Everard," she declared doggedly.

"Plenty of evil has come to me from that wood as it is," he reminded her.

"You mean to disturb the spirit of him whose body you threw there?" she persisted.

Dominey looked at her calmly. Some sort of evil seemed to have lit in her face. Her lips had shrunk apart, showing her yellow teeth. The fire in her narrowed eyes was the fire of hatred.

"I am no murderer, Mrs. Unthank," he said. "Your son stole out from the shadow of that wood, attacked me in a cowardly manner, and we fought. He was mad when he attacked me, he fought like a madman, and, notwithstanding my superior strength, I was glad to get away alive. I never touched his body. It lay where he fell. If he crept into the wood and died there, then his death was not at my door. He sought for my life as I never sought for his."

"You'd done him wrong," the woman muttered.

"That again is false. His passion for Lady Dominey was uninvited and unreciprocated. Her only feeling concerning him was one of fear; that the whole countryside knows. Your son was a lonely, a morose and an ill-living man, Mrs. Unthank. If either of us had murder in our hearts, it was he, not I. And as for you," Dominey went on, after a moment's pause, "I think that you have had your revenge, Mrs. Unthank. It was you who nursed my wife into insanity. It was you who fed her with the horror of your son's so-called spirit. I think that if I had stayed away another two years, Lady Dominey would have been in a madhouse today."

"I would to Heaven," the woman cried, "that you'd rotted to death in Africa!"

"You carry your evil feelings far, Mrs. Unthank," he replied. "Take my advice. Give up this foolish idea that the Black Wood is still the home of your son's spirit. Go and live on your annuity in another part of the country and forget."

He moved across the room to throw open a window. Her eyes followed him wonderingly.

"I have heard a rumour," she said slowly; "there has been a word spoken here and there about you. I've had my doubts sometimes. I have them again every time you speak. Are you really Everard Dominey?"

He swung around and faced her.

"Who else?"

"There's one," she went on, "has never believed it, and that's her ladyship. I've heard strange talk from the people who've come under your masterful ways. You're a harder man than the Everard Dominey I remember. What if you should be an impostor?"

"You have only to prove that, Mrs. Unthank," Dominey replied, "and a portion, at any rate, of the Black Wood may remain standing. You will find it a little difficult, though.—You must excuse my ringing the bell. I see no object in asking you to remain longer."

She rose unwillingly to her feet. Her manner was sullen and unyielding.

"You are asking for the evil things," she warned him.

"Be assured," Dominey answered, "that if they come I shall know how to deal with them."

Dominey found Rosamund and Doctor Harrison, who had walked over from the village, lingering on the terrace. He welcomed the latter warmly.

"You are a godsend, Doctor," he declared. "I have been obliged to leave my port untasted for want of a companion. You will excuse us for a moment, Rosamund?"

She nodded pleasantly, and the doctor followed his host into the dining-room and took his seat at the table where the dessert still remained.

"Old woman threatening mischief, eh?" the latter asked, with a keen glance from under his shaggy grey eyebrows.

"I think she means it," Dominey replied, as he filled his guest's glass. "Personally," he went on, after a moment's pause, "the present situation is beginning to confirm an old suspicion of mine. I am a hard and fast materialist, you know, Doctor, in certain matters, and I have not the slightest faith in the vindictive mother, terrified to death lest the razing of a wood of unwholesome character should turn out into the cold world the spirit of her angel son."

"What do you believe?" the doctor asked bluntly.

"I would rather not tell you at the present moment," Dominey answered. "It would sound too fantastic."

"Your note this afternoon spoke of urgency," the doctor observed.

"The matter is urgent. I want you to do me a great favour—to remain here all night."

"You are expecting something to happen?"

"I wish, at any rate, to be prepared."

"I'll stay, with pleasure," the doctor promised. "You can lend me some paraphernalia, I suppose? And give me a shake-down somewhere near Lady Dominey's. By-the-by," he began, and hesitated.

"I have followed your advice, or rather your orders," Dominey interrupted, a little harshly. "It has not always been easy, especially in London, where Rosamund is away from these associations.—I am hoping great things from what may happen tonight, or very soon."

The doctor nodded sympathetically.

"I shouldn't wonder if you weren't on the right track," he declared.

Rosamund came in through the window to them and seated herself by Dominey's side.

"Why are you two whispering like conspirators?" she demanded.

"Because we are conspirators," he replied lightly. "I have persuaded Doctor Harrison to stay the night. He would like a room in our wing. Will you let the maids know, dear?"

She nodded thoughtfully.

"Of course! There are several rooms quite ready. Mrs. Midgeley thought that we might be bringing down some guests. I am quite sure that we can make Doctor Harrison comfortable."

"No doubt about that, Lady Dominey," the doctor declared. "Let me be as near to your apartments as possible."

There was a shade of anxiety in her face.

"You think that tonight something will happen?" she asked.

"Tonight, or one night very soon," Dominey assented. "It is just as well for you to be prepared. You will not be afraid, dear? You will have the doctor on one side of you and me on the other."

"I am only afraid of one thing," she answered a little enigmatically. "I have been so happy lately."

Dominey, changed into ordinary morning clothes, with a thick cord tied round his body, a revolver in his pocket, and a loaded stick in his hand, spent the remainder of that night and part of the early morning concealed behind a great clump of rhododendrons, his eyes fixed upon the shadowy stretch of park which lay between the house and the Black Wood. The night was moonless but clear, and when his eyes were once accustomed to the pale but sombre twilight, the whole landscape and the moving objects upon it were dimly visible. The habits of his years of bush life seemed instinctively, in those few hours of waiting, to have re-established themselves. Every sense was strained and active; every night sound—of which the hooting of some owls, disturbed from their lurking place in the Black Wood, was predominant—heard and accounted for. And then, just as he had glanced at his watch and found that it was close upon two o'clock, came the first real intimation that something was likely to happen. Moving across the park towards him he heard the sound of a faint patter, curious and irregular in rhythm, which came from behind a range of low hillocks. He raised himself on his hands and knees to watch. His eyes were fastened upon a certain spot,—a stretch of the open park between himself and the hillocks. The patter ceased and began again. Into the open there came a dark shape, the irregularity of its movements swiftly explained. It moved at first upon all fours, then on two legs, then on all fours again. It crept nearer and nearer, and Dominey, as he watched, laid aside his stick. It reached the terrace, paused underneath Rosamund's window, now barely half a dozen yards from where he was crouching. Deliberately he waited, waited for what he knew must soon come. Then the deep silence of the breathless night was broken by that familiar, unearthly scream. Dominey waited till even its echoes had died away. Then he ran a few steps, bent double, and stretched out his hands. Once more, for the last time, that devil's cry broke the deep stillness of the August morning, throbbing a little as though with a new fear, dying away as though the fingers which crushed it back down the straining throat had indeed crushed with it the last flicker of some unholy life.

When Doctor Harrison made his hurried appearance, a few moments later, he found Dominey seated upon the terrace, furiously smoking a cigarette. On the ground, a few yards away, lay something black and motionless.

"What is it?" the doctor gasped.

For the first time Dominey showed some signs of a lack of self-control. His voice was choked and uneven.

"Go and look at it, Doctor," he said. "It's tied up, hand and foot. You can see where the spirit of Roger Unthank has hidden itself."

"Bosh!" the doctor answered, with grim contempt. "It's Roger Unthank himself. The beast!"

A little stream of servants came running out. Dominey gave a few orders quickly.

"Ring up the garage," he directed, "and I shall want one of the men to go into Norwich to the hospital. Doctor, will you go up and see Lady Dominey?"

The habits of a lifetime broke down: Parkins, the immaculate, the silent, the perfect automaton, asked an eager question.

"What is it, sir?"

There was the sound of a window opening overhead. At that moment Parkins would not have asked in vain for an annuity. Dominey glanced at the little semicircle of servants and raised his voice.

"It is the end, I trust, of these foolish superstitions about Roger Unthank's ghost. There lies Roger Unthank, half beast, half man. For some reason or other—some lunatic's reason, of course—he has chosen to hide himself in the Black Wood all these years. His mother, I presume, has been his accomplice and taken him food. He is still alive but in a disgusting state."

There was a little awed murmur. Dominey's voice had become quite matter of fact.

"I suppose," he continued, "his first idea was to revenge himself upon us and this household, by whom he imagined himself badly treated. The man, however, was half a madman when he came to the neighbourhood and has behaved like one ever since.—Johnson," Dominey continued, singling out a sturdy footman with sound common sense, "get ready to take this creature into Norwich Hospital. Say that if I do not come in during the day, a letter of explanation will follow from me. The rest of you, with the exception of Parkins, please go to bed."

With little exclamations of wonder they began to disperse. Then one of them paused and pointed across the park.

Moving with incredible swiftness came the gaunt, black figure of Rachael Unthank, swaying sometimes on her feet, yet in their midst before they could realise it. She staggered to the prostrate body and threw herself upon her knees. Her hands rested upon the unseen face, her eyes glared across at Dominey.

"So you've got him at last!" she gasped.

"Mrs. Unthank," Dominey said sternly, "you are in time to accompany your son to the hospital at Norwich. The car will be here in two minutes. I have nothing to say to you. Your own conscience should be sufficient punishment for keeping that poor creature alive in such a fashion and ministering during my absence to his accursed desires for vengeance."

"He would have died if I hadn't brought him food," she muttered. "I have wept all the tears a woman's broken heart could wring out, beseeching him to come back to me."

"Yet," Dominey insisted, "you shared his foul plot for vengeance against a harmless woman. You let him come and make his ghoulish noises, night by night, under these windows, without a word of remonstrance. You knew very well what their accursed object was—you, with a delicate woman in your charge who trusted you. You are an evil pair, but of the two you are worse than your half-witted son."

The woman made no reply. She was still on her knees, bending over the prostrate figure, from whose lips now came a faint moaning. Then the lights of the car flashed out as it left the garage, passed through the iron gates and drew up a few yards away.

"Help him in," Dominey ordered. "You can loosen his cords, Johnson, as soon as you have started. He has very little strength. Tell them at the hospital I shall probably be there during the day, or tomorrow."

With a little shiver the two men stooped to their task. Their prisoner muttered to himself all the time, but made no resistance. Rachael Unthank, as she stepped in to take her place by his side, turned once more to Dominey. She was a broken woman.

"You're rid of us," she sobbed, "perhaps forever.—You've said harsh things of both of us. Roger isn't always—so bad. Sometimes he's more gentle than at others. You'd have thought then that he was just a baby, living there for love of the wind and the trees and the birds. If he comes to—"

Her voice broke. Dominey's reply was swift and not unkind. He pointed to the window above.

"If Lady Dominey recovers, you and your son are forgiven. If she never recovers, I wish you both the blackest corner of hell."

The car drove off. Doctor Harrison met Dominey on the threshold as he turned towards the house.

"Her ladyship is unconscious now," he announced. "Perhaps that is a good sign. I never liked that unnatural calm. She'll be unconscious, I think, for a great many hours. For God's sake, come and get a whisky and soda and give me one!"

The early morning sunshine lay upon the park when the two men at last separated. They stood for a moment looking out. From the Black Wood came the whirr of a saw. The little troop of men had left their tents. The crash of a fallen tree heralded their morning's work.

"You are still going on with that?" the doctor asked.

"To the very last stump of a tree, to the last bush, to the last cluster of weeds," Dominey replied, with a sudden passion in his tone. "I will have that place razed to the bare level of the earth, and I will have its poisonous swamps sucked dry. I have hated that foul spot," he went on, "ever since I realised what suffering it meant to her. My reign here may not be long, Doctor—I have my own tragedy to deal with—but those who come after me will never feel the blight of that accursed place."

The doctor grunted. His inner thoughts he kept to himself.

"Maybe you're right," he conceded.

# CHAPTER XXIX

THE HEAT of a sulphurous afternoon—a curious parallel in its presage of a coming storm to the fast-approaching crisis in Dominey's own affairs—had driven Dominey from his study out onto the terrace. In a chair by his side lounged Eddy Pelham, immaculate in a suit of white flannels. It was the fifth day since the mystery of the Black Wood had been solved.

"Ripping, old chap, of you to have me down here," the young man remarked amiably, his hand stretching out to a tumbler which stood by his side. "The country, when you can get ice, is a paradise this weather, especially when London's so full of ghastly rumours and all that sort of thing, eh? What's the latest news of her ladyship?"

"Still unconscious," Dominey replied. "The doctors, however, seem perfectly satisfied. Everything depends on her waking moments."

The young man abandoned the subject with a murmur of hopeful sympathy. His eyes were fixed upon a little cloud of dust in the distance.

"Expecting visitors today?" he asked.

"Should not be surprised," was the somewhat laconic answer.

The young man stood up, yawned and stretched himself.

"I'll make myself scarce," he said. "Jove!" he added approvingly, lingering for a moment. "Jolly well cut, the tunic of your uniform, Dominey! If a country in peril ever decides to waive the matter of my indifferent physique and send me out to the rescue, I shall go to your man."

Dominey smiled.

"Mine is only the local Yeomanry rig-out," he replied. "They will nab you for the Guards!"

Dominey stepped back through the open windows into his study as Pelham strolled off. He was seated at his desk, poring over some letters, when a few minutes later Seaman was ushered into the room. For a single moment his muscles tightened, his frame became tense. Then he realised his visitor's outstretched hands of welcome and he relaxed. Seaman was perspiring, vociferous and excited.

"At last!" he exclaimed. "Donner und!—My God, Dominey, what is this?"

"Thirteen years ago," Dominey explained, "I resigned a commission in the Norfolk Yeomanry. That little matter, however, has been adjusted. At a crisis like this—"

"My friend, you are wonderful!" Seaman interrupted solemnly. "You are a man after my own heart, you are thorough, you leave nothing undone. That is why," he added, lowering his voice a little, "we are the greatest race in the world. Drink before everything, my friend," he went on, "drink I must have. What a day! The very clouds that hide the sun are full of sulphurous heat."

Dominey rang the bell, ordered hock and seltzer and ice. Seaman drank and threw himself into an easy-chair.

"There is no fear of your being called out of the country because of that, I hope?" he asked a little anxiously, nodding his head towards his companion's uniform.

"Not at present," Dominey answered. "I am a trifle over age to go with the first batch or two. Where have you been?"

Seaman hitched his chair a little nearer.

"In Ireland," he confided. "Sorry to desert you as I did, but you do not begin to count for us just yet. There was just a faint doubt as to what they were going to do about internment. That is why I had to get the Irish trip off my mind."

"What has been decided?"

"The Government has the matter under consideration," Seaman replied, with a chuckle. "I can certainly give myself six months before I need to slip off. Now tell me, why do I find you down here?"

"After Terniloff left," Dominey explained, "I felt I wanted to get away. I have been asked to start some recruiting work down here."

"Terniloff—left his little volume with you?"

"Yes!"

"Where is it?"

"Safe," Dominey replied.

Seaman mopped his forehead.

"It needs to be," he muttered. "I have orders to see it destroyed. We can talk of that presently. Sometimes, when I am away from you, I tremble. It may sound foolish, but you have in your possession just the two things—that map and Von Terniloff's memoirs—which would wreck our propaganda in every country of the world."

"Both are safe," Dominey assured him. "By the by, my friend," he went on, "do you know that you yourself are forgetting your usual caution?"

"In what respect?" Seaman demanded quickly.

"As you stooped to sit down just now, I distinctly saw the shape of your revolver in your hip pocket. You know as well as I do that with your name and the fact that you are only a naturalised Englishman, it is inexcusably foolish to be carrying firearms about just now."

Seaman thrust his hand into his pocket and threw the revolver upon the table.

"You are quite right," he acknowledged. "Take care of it for me. I took it with me to Ireland, because one never knows what may happen in that amazing country."

Dominey swept it carelessly into the drawer of the desk at which he was sitting.

"Our weapons, from now on," Seaman continued, "must be weapons of guile and craft. You and I will have, alas! to see less of one another, Dominey. In many ways it is unfortunate that we have not been able to keep England out of this for a few more months. However, the situation must be dealt with as it exists. So far as you are concerned, you have practically secured yourself against suspicion. You will hold a brilliant and isolated place amongst those who are serving the great War Lord. When I do approach you, it will be for sympathy and assistance against the suspicions of these far-seeing Englishmen!"

Dominey nodded.

"You will stay the night?" he asked.

"If I may," Seaman assented. "It is the last time for many months when it will be wise for us to meet on such intimate terms. Perhaps our dear friend Parkins will take vinous note of the occasion."

"In other words," Dominey said, "you propose that we shall drink the Dominey cabinet hock and the Dominey port to the glory of our country."

"To the glory of our country," Seaman echoed. "So be it, my friend.—Listen."

A car had passed along the avenue in front of the house. There was the sound of voices in the hall, a knock at the door, the rustle of a woman's clothes. Parkins, a little disturbed, announced the arrivals.

"The Princess of Eiderstrom and—a gentleman. The Princess said that her errand with you was urgent, sir," he added, turning apologetically towards his master.

The Princess was already in the room, and following her a short man in a suit of sombre black, wearing a white tie, and carrying a black bowler hat. He blinked across the room through his thick glasses, and Dominey knew that the end had come. The door was closed behind them. The Princess came a little further into the room. Her hand was extended towards Dominey, but not in greeting. Her white finger pointed straight at him. She turned to her companion.

"Which is that, Doctor Schmidt?" she demanded.

"The Englishman, by God!" Schmidt answered.

The silence which reigned for several seconds was intense and profound. The coolest of all four was perhaps Dominey. The Princess was pale with a passion which seemed to sob behind her words.

"Everard Dominey," she cried, "what have you done with my lover? What have you done with Leopold von Ragastein?"

"He met with the fate," Dominey replied, "which he had prepared for me. We fought and I conquered."

"You killed him?"

"I killed him," Dominey echoed. "It was a matter of necessity. His body sleeps on the bed of the Blue River."

"And your life here has been a lie!"

"On the contrary, it has been the truth," Dominey objected. "I assured you at the Carlton, when you first spoke to me, and I have assured you a dozen times since, that I was Everard Dominey. That is my name. That is who I am."

Seaman's voice seemed to come from a long way off. For the moment the man had neither courage nor initiative. He seemed as though he had received some sort of stroke. His mind was travelling backwards.

"You came to me at Cape Town," he muttered; "you had all Von Ragastein's letters, you knew his history, you had the Imperial mandate."

"Von Ragastein and I exchanged the most intimate confidences in his camp," Dominey said, "as Doctor Schmidt there knows. I told him my history, and he told me his. The letters and papers I took from him."

Schmidt had covered his face with his hands for a moment. His shoulders were heaving.

"My beloved chief!" he sobbed. "My dear devoted master! Killed by that drunken Englishman!"

"Not so drunk as you fancied him," Dominey said coolly, "not so far gone in his course of dissipation but that he was able to pull himself up when the great incentive came."

The Princess looked from one to the other of the two men. Seaman had still the appearance of a man struggling to extricate himself from some sort of nightmare.

"My first and only suspicion," he faltered, "was that night when Wolff disappeared!"

"Wolff's coming was rather a tragedy," Dominey admitted. "Fortunately, I had a secret service man in the house who was able to dispose of him."

"It was you who planned his disappearance?" Seaman gasped.

"Naturally," Dominey replied. "He knew the truth and was trying all the time to communicate with you."

"And the money?" Seaman continued, blinking rapidly. "One hundred thousand pounds, and more?"

"I understood that was a gift," Dominey replied. "If the German Secret Service, however, cares to formulate a claim and sue me—"

The Princess suddenly interrupted. Her eyes seemed on fire.

"What are you, you two?" she cried, stretching out her hands towards Schmidt and Seaman. "Are you lumps of earth—clods—creatures without courage and intelligence? You can let him stand there—the Englishman who has murdered my lover, who has befooled you? You let him stand there and mock you, and you do and say nothing! Is his life a sacred thing? Has he none of your secrets in his charge?"

"The great God above us!" Seaman groaned, with a sudden white horror in his face. "He has the Prince's memoirs! He has the Kaiser's map!"

"On the contrary," Dominey replied, "both are deposited at the Foreign Office. We hope to find them very useful a little later on."

Seaman sprang forward like a tiger and went down in a heap as he almost threw himself upon Dominey's out-flung fist. Schmidt came stealing across the room, and from underneath his cuff something gleamed.

"You are two to one!" the Princess cried passionately, as both assailants hesitated. "I would to God that I had a weapon, or that I were a man!"

"My dear Princess," a good-humoured voice remarked from the window, "four to two the other way, I think, what?"

Eddy Pelham, his hands in his pockets, but a very alert gleam in his usually vacuous face, stood in the windowed doorway. From behind him, two exceedingly formidable-looking men slipped into the room. There was no fight, not even a struggle. Seaman, who had never recovered from the shock of his surprise, and was now completely unnerved, was handcuffed in a moment, and Schmidt disarmed. The latter was the first to break the curious silence.

"What have I done?" he demanded. "Why am I treated like this?"

"Doctor Schmidt?" Eddy asked pleasantly.

"That is my name, sir," was the fierce reply. "I have just landed from East Africa. We knew nothing of the war when we started. I came to expose that man. He is an impostor—a murderer! He has killed a German nobleman."

"He has committed *lèse majesté*!" Seaman gasped. "He has deceived the Kaiser! He has dared to sit in his presence as the Baron von Ragastein!"

The young man in flannels glanced across at Dominey and smiled.

"I say, you two don't mean to be funny but you are," he declared. "First of all, there's Doctor Schmidt accuses Sir Everard here of being an impostor because he assumed his own name; accuses him of murdering a man who had planned in cold blood—you were in that, by the by, Schmidt—to kill him; and then there's our friend here, the secretary of the society for propagating better relations between the business men of England and Germany, complaining because Sir Everard carried through in Germany, for England, exactly what he believed the Baron von Ragastein was carrying out here—for Germany. You're a curious, thick-headed race, you Germans."

"I demand again," Schmidt shouted, "to know by what right I am treated as a criminal?"

"Because you are one," Eddy answered coolly. "You and Von Ragastein together planned the murder of Sir Everard Dominey in East Africa, and I caught you creeping across the floor just now with a knife in your hand. That'll do for you. Any questions to ask, Seaman?"

"None," was the surly reply.

"You are well-advised," the young man remarked coolly. "Within the last two days, your house in Forest Hill and your offices in London Wall have been searched."

"You have said enough," Seaman declared. "Fate has gone against me. I thank God that our master has abler servants than I and the strength to crush this island of popinjays and fools!"

"Popinjays seems severe," Eddy murmured, in a hurt tone. "However, to get on with this little matter," he added, turning to one of his two subordinates. "You will find a military car outside. Take these men over to the guardroom at the Norwich Barracks. I have arranged for an escort to see them to town. Tell the colonel I'll be over later in the day."

The Princess rose from the chair into which she had subsided a few moments before. Dominey turned towards her.

"Princess," he said, "there can be little conversation between us. Yet I shall ask you to remember this. Von Ragastein planned my death in cold blood. I could have slain him as an assassin, without the slightest risk, but I preferred to meet him face to face with the truth upon my lips. It was his life or mine. I fought for my country's sake, as he did for his."

The Princess looked at him with glittering eyes.

"I shall hate you to the end of my days," she declared, "because you have killed the thing I love, but although I am a woman, I know justice. You were chivalrous towards me. You treated Leopold perhaps better than he would have treated you. I pray that I shall never see your face again. Be so good as to suffer me to leave this house at once, and unattended."

Dominey threw open the windows which led on to the terrace and stood on one side. She passed by without a glance at him and disappeared. Eddy came strolling along the terrace a few moments later.

"Nice old ducks, those two, dear heart," he confided. "Seaman has just offered Forsyth, my burly ruffian in the blue serge suit, a hundred pounds to shoot him on the pretence that he was escaping."

"And what about Schmidt?"

"Insisted on his rights as an officer and demanded the front seat and a cigar before the car started! A pretty job, Dominey, and neatly cleaned up."

Dominey was watching the dust from the two cars which were disappearing down the avenue.

"Tell me, Eddy," he asked, "there's one thing I have always been curious about. How did you manage to keep that fellow Wolff when there wasn't a war on, and he wasn't breaking the law?"

The young man grinned.

"We had to stretch a point there, old dear," he admitted. "Plans of a fortress, eh?"

"Do you mean to say that he had plans of a fortress upon him?" Dominey asked.

"Picture post-card of Norwich Castle," the young man confided, "but keep it dark. Can I have a drink before I get the little car going?"

The turmoil of the day was over, and Dominey, after one silent but passionate outburst of thankfulness at the passing from his life of this unnatural restraint, found all his thoughts absorbed by the struggle which was being fought out in the bedchamber above. The old doctor came down and joined him at dinner time. He met Dominey's eager glance with a little nod.

"She's doing all right," he declared.

"No fever or anything?"

"Bless you, no! She's as near as possible in perfect health physically. A different woman from what she was this time last year, I can tell you. When she wakes up, she'll either be herself again, without a single illusion of any sort, or—"

The doctor paused, sipped his wine, emptied his glass and set it down approvingly.

"Or?" Dominey persisted.

"Or that part of her brain will be more or less permanently affected. However, I am hoping for the best. Thank heavens you're on the spot!"

They finished their dinner almost in silence. Afterwards, they smoked for a few minutes upon the terrace. Then they made their way softly upstairs. The doctor parted with Dominey at the door of the latter's room.

"I shall remain with her for an hour or so," he said. "After that I shall leave her entirely to herself. You'll be here in case there's a change?"

"I shall be here," Dominey promised.

The minutes passed into hours, uncounted, unnoticed. Dominey sat in his easy-chair, stirred by a tumultuous wave of passionate emotion. The memory of those earlier days of his return came back to him with all their poignant longings. He felt again the same tearing at his heart-strings, the same strange, unnerving tenderness. The great world's drama, in which he knew that he, too, would surely continue to play his part, seemed like a thing far off, the concern of another race of men. Every fibre of his being seemed attuned to the magic and the music of one wild hope. Yet when there came what he had listened for so long, the hope seemed frozen into fear. He sat a little forward in his easy-chair, his hands gripping its sides, his eyes fixed upon the slowly widening crack in the panel. It was as it had been before. She stooped low, stood up again and came towards him. From behind an unseen hand closed the panel. She came to him with her arms outstretched and all the wonderful things of life and love in her shining eyes. That faint touch of the somnambulist had passed. She came to him as she had never come before. She was a very real and a very live woman.

"Everard!" she cried.

He took her into his arms. At their first kiss she thrilled from head to foot. For a moment she laid her head upon his shoulder.

"Oh, I have been so silly!" she confessed. "There were times when I couldn't believe that you were my Everard—mine! And now I know."

Her lips sought his again, his parched with the desire of years. Along the corridor, the old doctor tiptoed his way to his room, with a pleased smile upon his face.

**THE END**